SOMETHING WICKED DRAWS NEAR

TED TAYLER

BOOKS

Vinci Books

vinci-books.com

Published by Vinci Books Ltd in 2026

1

Copyright © Ted Tayler 2017

The author has asserted their moral right to be identified as the author of this work in accordance with the Copyright, Designs and Patents Act 1988. This work is a work of fiction. Names, characters, places and incidents are the product of the author's imagination or are used fictitiously. Any resemblance to actual persons, living or dead, places and incidents is entirely coincidental.

All rights reserved. No part of this publication may be copied, reproduced, distributed, stored in any retrieval system, or transmitted in any form or by any means, including photocopying, recording, or other electronic or mechanical methods, nor used as a source for any form of machine learning including AI datasets, without the prior written permission of the publisher.

The publisher and the author have made every effort to obtain permissions for any third party material used in this book and to comply with copyright law. Any queries in this respect should be brought to the attention of the publisher and any omissions will be corrected in future editions.

A CIP catalogue record for this book is available from the British Library.

Paperback ISBN: 9781036700553

The EU GPSR authorised representative is Logos Europe, 9 rue Nicolas Poussion, 17000 La Rochelle, France

contact@logoseurope.eu

By Ted Tayler

The Phoenix

The Olympus Project
Gold, Silver and Bombs
Nothing Is Ever Forever
In the Lap of the Gods
The Price of Treachery
A New Dawn
Something Wicked Draws Near
Evil Always Finds A Way
Revenge Comes in Many Colours
Three Weeks in September
A Frequent Peal of Bells
Larcombe Manor

The Freeman Files

Fatal Decision
Last Orders
Pressure Point
Deadly Formula
Final Deal
Barking Mad
Creature Discomforts

Silent Terror

Night Train

All Things Bright

Buried Secrets

A Genuine Mistake

Strange Beginnings

Dead Reckoning

A Normal November

Into the Sunlight

Tame the Storm

One True Friend

Whispered Truths

A Morning Murder

Quick to Anger

Red Herring Season

Gathering Clouds

Still Standing

Chapter One

It had been a typical Bank Holiday Monday following the wedding, with strong winds, thunderstorms and conditions better suited to staying indoors. Phoenix and Athena ventured outside for a walk with Hope to clear the cobwebs when a brief break appeared in the foul weather.

"Do you think someone is trying to tell us something?" asked Phoenix.

"We're happy," replied Athena, "that's what matters."

Hope was wrapped up warm in her buggy without a care in the world. She kicked her feet out and gave her parents a gummy grin.

The excitement of the celebrations was fading; the old manor house felt quiet and empty once her parents and Sarah Gough returned to their respective homes. That was why Athena insisted on getting outside. Phoenix would have lounged around in their rooms, feeling sorry for himself.

"I'm getting too old for a series of late nights in a row," he grumbled when Hope woke them up before seven that morning.

Athena had brought her from the nursery, plopped her next to her father, and headed for the shower.

"Talk sense into your father, Hope. Daddy's back to work in the morning. There's no rest from the wicked."

Phoenix smiled at that quip. He cuddled his daughter and wondered what he had done to be so lucky. He had a new wife, a beautiful daughter and a job he enjoyed, working with friends and colleagues he trusted and admired. Many never even had one of those things. He should be grateful.

A few hours later, he wheeled Hope's buggy into the house. He kicked off his muddy boots as he and Athena returned upstairs. Phoenix reminded himself that if he wanted to hold on to the things he cherished, they needed protection to his last breath.

Once they got dry and warm, Athena gazed over the lawns in front of the house. The subsequent passing storm battered the windows. Dark menacing clouds appeared to touch the rooftops of the stable block and the buildings on the edge of the estate. The tiny church where they had married on Saturday was just a shimmering haze in the distance.

"What a horrid day," she sighed.

"Erebus always thought of Larcombe Manor as his sanctuary," said Phoenix, as he joined her by the window, with Hope half-asleep on his shoulder.

"Those long years in the Royal Navy buffeted by mountainous seas, wondering whether he'd ever see dry land again. Larcombe offered a guaranteed haven; built to last by his ancestors."

The last days of April were due to deliver a mixture of sunshine and showers to the West Country. Larcombe Manor had seen it over the centuries, and its current guardians had plenty to occupy their minds. Everything would survive the battering of the winds and the heavy rainfall. It always did.

As May prepared to begin, the old manor house would shake itself dry and carry on as it had in the past. Phoenix and Athena needed to do the same.

Hayden Vincent had informed Athena of the telephone conversation he received from Orion on Easter Sunday morning. The tip-off suggested a possible cryptic connection between a series of gangland deaths around the country.

At the first meeting of the new week following the Bank Holiday, Athena gave Giles and Artemis the task of discovering any truth behind it.

Minos and Alastor had their vital research to carry out. They identified four potential candidates for the Olympus Project at the last Olympus meeting in London. Their backgrounds needed vetting with extreme care to ensure no possible rotten eggs slipped through the process. Zeus was cautious in the extreme, and with good reason, after the trials and tribulations caused by the Titans.

Athena decided she would leave her senior colleagues to do the groundwork alone. She felt confident she could trust them to leave no stone unturned. Phoenix could work with her on the finer details later. To be one hundred per cent sure that Zeus selected the right candidates.

The next item on the list concerned the training of the new agent intake. Finally, Kelly Dexter and Hayden Vincent were ready to start. The training manuals had been reviewed and revised. Rusty Scott checked them over, and when Athena asked if he was satisfied with the results, he nodded his approval.

"The sooner the first group of recruits arrive, the

better," he grunted, "I fear we'll need every pair of hands we can get this summer."

"We have enough to cope with," said Phoenix, "at home and abroad. We may have to prioritise our activities and channel our resources to areas with the most benefit. The one-off targets Zeus sends our way will have to wait. We need to concentrate on the bigger picture."

"I agree," said Athena, "perhaps our salvation lies on our doorstep? I suggest we check this data from Orion to see if it proves valuable. As well as a financial reward, it might be possible to offer Hounsell Security Services a role more aligned with that of Olympus. They could carry out the investigations on those singular names supplied to us by Zeus. A rogue policeman, a suspect politician; that type of thing. We wouldn't expect them to take direct action themselves. They report their findings, and an agent will do whatever we decide is necessary."

Henry Case's mind drifted while these matters were under discussion. The Reverend Sarah Gough left for home last evening. The transport team had patched together her battered VW camper van 'Maggie'. Despite a weary shake of the head from the mechanic that told a different tale to the words he uttered, "Maggie," he pronounced, "is good to go."

"I'll be in touch," Henry had said as the odd couple said their goodbyes.

"You'd better, Henry," Sarah had shouted. Her van spluttered and coughed along the winding drive towards the stone pillars marking the estate's boundary.

Henry glanced across the table at his colleague, Giles Burke. He looked weary this morning. Maria Elena must have worn him out, he thought. Lucky devil! Perhaps if he and the padre saw one another more often, their relationship might become more physical.

Henry had been content with their progress in their short time together, but it was unfamiliar territory. He hadn't wanted to force the pace and make a fool of himself, Sarah being an ordained minister. They probably had an unwritten set of rules somewhere. If Sarah had been a real padre, it would come under Queen's Regulations, and he would have known where he stood.

Civvy Street proved a minefield for Henry Case. The Army and the Security Services had surrounded him throughout his adult life. His lack of experience with the opposite sex had never been an issue. Henry always thought marriage was not an option for him, given his line of work.

Until happy couples popped up everywhere, he looked at Larcombe; he never wondered what he might have been missing. Even when Maria Elena arrived, although he had been as interested as Giles Burke, he knew the younger, more attractive man stood far more chance. But, with his looks and occupation, his options were limited.

"A penny for them, Henry?" Athena asked, sensing her security chief's distraction this morning.

"Beggars can't be choosers," blurted out Henry, startled by the question.

"My thoughts too, Henry," said Rusty. He assumed Henry commented on the HSS relationship. "Orion and his workforce can offer useful intelligence now and then, but Olympus mustn't form too close a partnership. It might lead to weaker security here at Larcombe."

Phoenix could see Henry was floundering. Their enforcer wondered whether he could extricate himself from the hole he dug with his outburst. Or to keep quiet in case he made matters worse and convinced everyone he hadn't been listening.

Athena's facial expression contained a mixture of amusement and confusion, which didn't help the poor devil much. Phoenix intervened to allow the security chief a breathing space to gather his wits and get himself back on track.

"With the tasks allocated so far this morning," he said, "we have reached a suitable point to finish matters for the day. We enjoyed a busy and exciting weekend. That might have caught up with us; we need a break. I suggest we take the rest of the day off and recharge our batteries. Then, we can pick up where we left off in the morning."

Nobody was in the mood to argue. Henry was grateful, and as the room emptied, the friendly atmosphere suggested Phoenix gauged things to perfection. Everyone present needed to catch up on a few hours of sleep.

Phoenix and Athena watched as the weary line of colleagues left. Then they headed upstairs to their apartment. Maria Elena returned with Hope from a quick turn around the grounds. But, unfortunately, the English weather didn't agree with the young nanny from Estepona. She missed her home country's three hundred days of sunshine each year.

"You are returning early?" she asked, "shall I take Hope to the nursery for the rest of the morning?"

"That won't be necessary," said Athena, "we'll look after her. You can put your feet up for an hour."

Phoenix spotted the puzzled expression on the young girl's face.

"Athena means for you to relax and have time to yourself. We'll look after Hope until after lunch. We'll see you again at two o'clock."

"Okay." With that, Maria Elena headed for the door. As she turned the handle, Phoenix called out to her.

"Giles has time off now, too," he said, "perhaps you can relax together?"

Maria Elena turned her head, and her smile said everything. It was as if the sun had come out. Then she blushed and scurried outside onto the corridor.

"You're terrible," said Athena, "you embarrassed the poor girl."

"It's not as if it's a big secret anymore. Those two spent less than a second apart at the wedding reception."

"Somehow, I don't think Giles will get the rest he hoped for," said Athena. "Neither will we. A few extra hours with our daughter is no hardship."

"When we said our goodbyes before your parents travelled home, what did you and Grace discuss in your deep conversation?" asked Phoenix.

"Mummy's keen that Hope gets christened as soon as possible. However, I want to wait until she's older. Hope often sleeps through the night now at four months. She'll be more of a person towards the end of the summer. I want her to be more aware of what's happening around her. So we might get her christened here in late August. What do you think?"

Phoenix tried to remember how it had been for him, but he couldn't recall the occasion. He knew he went to church once or twice when growing up, but it never left a lasting impression on him, except that it was never warm.

"Sharron screamed right through the service when we had her christened," he recalled. "She was in good company. Three or four others lined up on the production line with her that Sunday. None of them seemed keen on the old bloke hanging on to them, nor on the icy water in the font. I was glad to get out. My ears rang for hours. Karen and her mother were happy enough. Her Dad and her brothers used it as an excuse to get drunk, as usual. My mother left as soon as she could. It's not a day that lived long in the memory."

"You poor thing," teased Athena. "What an impoverished upbringing you suffered.

They both fell silent. Hope played with one of her favourite toys and looked at her parents. She wondered why everything had gone so quiet.

Athena wished she hadn't made that last remark. She and Phoenix met four years ago, and their lives had altered dramatically ever since that day. Erebus made the Larcombe family aware of the new agent's history. But, as far as Olympus was concerned, the past stayed at the gates when he arrived that night.

Although specific incidents prompted the occasional remark directly linked to something he had done or resembled an occasion he attended, nothing that happened before his arrival was described in any detail. It was strange the mention of a christening prompted the revelation of a personal event from over a quarter of a century ago.

He hadn't talked much about his weddings either. Except that last Saturday was the first to involve a church service. Phoenix now possessed a registry office, a beach in The Gambia, and the Larcombe Manor church on his CV. Few men matched that, nor would they welcome it.

"I'm sorry, darling," she said at last, "that was unnecessary. The past is the past. You don't have to tell me more."

"There's nothing to apologise for, darling," he replied. "My childhood was impoverished in other ways. We weren't poor in financial terms. My parents clothed and fed me well enough. It was their love they denied me. I was a loner.

Even after I married and had a young daughter, I never felt the strength most people experience of having family surrounding them. I loved my daughter without reservation, but I had so many things I needed to deal with."

Athena picked up Hope and sat her on her lap, facing the two of them on the settee.

"How did life in The Gambia affect your feelings?"

"Sharron's murder devastated me. I lashed out and took revenge on as many of my tormentors as possible. Sue Owens got me out of harm's way, and our life in the sun was idyllic, but I couldn't let things rest. Every month I lived abroad. I spent hours checking the internet for news on what happened back in the UK. When doctors diagnosed Sue with breast cancer, she fought hard, but to no avail. One of the last conversations we shared was about what I would do when she died. I told her I would find a way to get home. I needed to complete that unfinished business."

"Sharron's killer?" Athena whispered.

"He was number one on my list. I didn't realise the others I identified as needing to be dealt with brought me to the attention of Erebus and the Olympus Project."

"You kept busy in those few months, I understand?" asked Athena.

"I prepared well, as usual. However, I didn't account for the tenacity of our neighbourhood copper and his fresh-faced companion. By June, I was no longer the hunter but the hunted. Strange how things work out. Orion is still on our doorstep, with no idea how close he lives to his nemesis, and as for Artemis, that fresh-faced young detective is now a valued colleague who lives with my best friend."

"So much has changed here in four years, haven't they?"

"The biggest change was that I found somewhere I wasn't alone. Erebus became the father I never had, Rusty became my first real friend, and even you and the Three Stooges made me feel as if I belonged. Finally, I found the family I had been seeking. Things have just grown from there."

"And now our family of three can look forward to the future,"

"With caution," sighed Phoenix, "this business that Giles and Artemis are investigating worries me somewhat. It could pose a significant threat. Evil is only just around the corner; you mark my words. As for this little one, let's plan the christening for the Late Summer Bank Holiday. Sarah Gough should have plenty of time to free herself up to officiate."

"That should bring a smile to Henry's face at least," said Athena. "I'm sure he's smitten by her, although where his head was at this morning, who knows?"

Silence fell in the room again. Phoenix was drifting off to sleep. He felt dog-tired and shook his head and stood.

"Let's take Hope for a walk. First, we'll need to get wrapped up against this wind and rain. Then, if we do it in stages, we can make it to the orangery and wait for the next shower to blow through. Then we can dart over to the swimming pool via the ice-house entrance. An hour playing with her in the shallow end, taking turns to swim lengths on our own, will serve us better than lazing around here."

"Translated, that means Daddy wants time alone to think, Hope," said Athena to their daughter, who knew when a smile was required and obliged.

"You know me so well, darling," said Phoenix.

"I'm learning," replied Athena. "Let's face whatever the weather or the future throws at us. Together we're a match for anything."

Chapter Two

Wednesday, 23rd April 2014

Hugo Hanigan breakfasted alone in his penthouse in London. A panoramic view of the capital's financial heart greeted him through his window every morning.

London replaced Amsterdam as the world's leading financial centre by the early nineteenth century. It had been a significant centre of lending and investment for two centuries. During the second half of the twentieth century, it played an essential role in developing new financial products such as Eurobonds in the Sixties.

English contract law was adopted in many markets for international finance, with legal services provided in London and financial institutions located there providing global services. Names such as Lloyd's of London for insurance and the Baltic Exchange for shipping were world-famous.

London held a leading position as a financial centre and maintained the largest trade surplus in financial services worldwide. Like New York, it faced new competitors, including fast-rising eastern financial centres like Hong Kong and Shanghai.

When Hugo arrived from Dublin in 2005, as Ardal James Hannon, changes were already underway. New products, such as derivatives launched in the Nineties, were ripe for exploitation. His first-class honours degree in Finance opened many doors. His innate instinct for choosing the right path served him well for a decade.

London continued to be the largest centre for derivatives markets, a minefield covering futures, contracts, or options. But, whether exchange-traded or over-the-counter derivatives he set his mind to, the Irishman excelled in turning a profit.

He had amassed a considerable fortune in the last four years since leaving his old haunts in Cricklewood to become Hugo Hanigan. He found success in foreign exchange markets and trading gold, silver and base metals.

London benefited from its position in Asian and American time zones and within the European Union. If an angle could turn an extra pound, Hugo found it and worked it until the well ran dry. He had few friends in the City; they thought him arrogant; he couldn't have agreed more. They believed him to be lucky, but they were wrong. Hugo Hanigan never relied on luck.

If others got their fingers burned by picking the wrong options to back or staying too long in a specialised market, that was their problem. Hugo never overstayed his welcome, nor did he support any worthless schemes. That wasn't luck. Hugo called it prudent management. He never mentioned the assistance he gained from the occasional well-placed bribe.

Hugo always identified the right person to contact and

paid well for his insider information. He never took the chance he might lose money on a product. Hugo had to cover every angle to ensure continued growth. The fortune he amassed was vital to support The Grid and his ambitions for what it might achieve.

Hugo never worried about anybody reporting him to the authorities with suspicions over how he conducted his business. But, of course, there might be a handful of fellow bankers who believed Hanigan's private bank was a cover for laundering proceeds from organised crime; none of them would ever be brave enough to express those opinions in public.

Everyone who ever met him told you the same thing. Hugo Hanigan - a thug in a Savile Row suit.

Hugo looked over the top of his copy of the day's Financial Times at the square mile of the capital that held his domain. He knew what others thought of him. He couldn't give a toss. They would be sensible to fear him. He would crush a few under the heel of his handmade shoes before long.

Hugo still read nothing in the media concerning the well-orchestrated campaign he ordered just before Easter. Just how thick were these people? He thought of advertising on national television; nothing pretentious, not what incomprehensible rubbish the marketing teams dreamed up these days that defied the viewer to realise which product the advert related to until the last few frames.

What they required was a basic map of Britain. A red bloodstain shows where a gang member's death had occurred over the previous weeks—a big arrow points out the connection.

Hugo buttered another slice of toast and poured a fresh cup of coffee. His watch told him it was ten-thirty. Hugo never visited his bank until noon. He could sit and seethe for a while longer.

One of his mobile phones rang. The 'Whisky in the Jar' ringtone told him which one to answer. A fellow countryman and one of his gangland colleagues.

"This had better not be bad news, Sean Walsh," he growled.

Hugo listened. Sean couldn't soften the blow. The jury reached a verdict at the Old Bailey in the case against Tommy O'Riordan.

"They found him guilty, boss," said Sean, "sentencing will take place next Monday."

"Right," screamed Hugo. "I want the names of every single fucking juror, get me the address of where that prosecution witness is hiding, and Sean, find out where that Judge and his family live. We need to send a message. One they can't ignore or sweep off the front page by a no-account celebrity with a sob story to sell. Tommy is one of our own."

Tommy O'Riordan was the head of a London crime family. In his mid-fifties with six brothers and three sisters, Tommy was the eldest son of Irish-Catholic parents who moved to Kilburn in North-West London after the Derry riots in August 1969.

Tommy's mother hoped the move to London would keep her children safe from the troubles. But, unfortunately, things went south soon after they moved onto the South Kilburn estate. Her feckless husband, Tommy Senior, soon found low-level criminals with whom to associate. He got caught every time he stepped out of line and spent most of the next two decades in prison.

The children finished school as soon as legal and found work helping keep the family together. Tommy took on his father's role as head of the family. However, life on the large council estate held too many temptations for him to follow an honest career for long.

The well-established Irish street gangs were eager for fresh blood to join them. So Tommy became the first in his family to join. As the years passed, his younger brothers followed his lead.

The female chicks didn't fall far from the nest either. One by one, as they entered their teens, his three sisters soon found themselves on the arm of one of the other gang members. The three girls married before they reached twenty years old. They now formed part of the Kelly, Walsh and O'Regan tribes that comprised a large part of the criminal fraternity lording it over the borough.

Tommy rose through the ranks until he made 'top dog'. He had his mother's stubborn streak, a reasonable degree of intelligence and determined nature. If only he hadn't inherited his father's weakness for petty theft, Tommy might have made something of his life. By sixteen, he was bigger and more robust than most of his peers. But, despite his mother scolding him for setting a bad example to his younger siblings, he started on the slippery slope towards a life of crime.

Tommy Senior made brief appearances at the family home. In between terms of imprisonment of various lengths. He did little more than drink when out of prison. Tommy wrote him off as a waste of space and kept asking his mother why she didn't throw him out. His mother shook her head.

"We married for life, Tommy. It may have always been a struggle for better or worse, but we had ten children to look after. If I threw him out, Social Services would soon be around here. They'd look to take the kids away from us. That was even more likely when the young ones still went to school. Only you and Colleen Walsh are in the house with me these days. They won't be bothering us anymore. Anyway, where else will he go when he comes out next time? Do you want to turn your father out onto the streets? Imagine what our neighbours would think then."

Ten years ago, his father died in prison. Nothing dramatic, aged sixty-six, he suffered a massive heart attack. Tommy's mother stood at her husband's graveside, surrounded by her family. Sons and daughters gathered with their various wives, husbands and partners. Dozens of grandchildren darted among the headstones to swell the congregation.

Members of other Irish families present, ingrained in the crime culture on the estates, stood shoulder to shoulder to see Tommy's father laid to rest. They didn't attend out of respect for the older man. They stood there because Tommy told them to be there for his mother's sake. Only people with a death wish refused a request from Tommy O'Riordan.

In the months that followed that bitter December morning, at St. Mary's Cemetery, in Kensal Green, Orla O'Riordan shrank in stature. Her daughters pleaded with her to eat, see a doctor, and ask for help, but Orla told them not to fuss over her and continued to decline.

Orla's old priest persuaded her she should look after her health for once.

"You've put your family first since I've known you, Mrs O'Riordan. It's your time now. I've made an appointment; you make sure you get along and see the doctor on Monday morning."

Orla did just that. It was pancreatic cancer.

Tommy came back with his family to St. Mary's a year after his father's burial to watch his mother lowered into the ground beside him.

At the wake in the biggest Irish social club in the borough, Tommy drowned his sorrows. Sean Walsh and his other lieutenants came to the top table to pay their respects. Others drifted around the hall, drinking, chatting in hushed tones, and polishing off the free food.

Sean Walsh returned from the bar with a bottle of Irish whiskey. The two men sat together and started on the hard stuff.

"Where's Devlin?" asked Tommy.

"Not seen him for a day or two, Tommy," replied Sean.

"I think it's time I had a word with Michael Devlin," muttered Tommy.

"Say the word. I'll have Devlin found and brought to you," said Sean.

Tommy nodded. Sean sent a text message.

The two colleagues continued to drink in silence. Tommy thought of Michael Devlin. He was a gang member he grew up with on the estate and only six months younger than himself. They had known one another for over forty years.

When Tommy joined the street gang in the early Seventies, he started with a series of petty thefts. As he matured, his talents graduated to extortion from market traders and armed robbery. The proceeds from his criminal enterprises were significant, and Tommy never drank his profits away or wasted them on fast cars and women.

He invested his cash wisely; the banks he used didn't ask too many questions. He married Sean's raven-haired sister, and their two children went to private schools and now lived and worked in Spain.

The O'Riordan gang were thought by the police to have committed over a dozen murders. Tommy reckoned they should think of a higher number. Drug dealing on a massive scale provided the most substantial contribution to the gang's war chest. The murders were necessary; but incidental. Although the police arrested dozens of soldiers that scuttled around the streets and alleyways across the South Kilburn estate like ants, they never found enough evidence to lay specific charges against the gang leaders. Eyewitnesses were thin on the ground.

Michael Devlin displayed many valuable talents within the gang's structure over the decades. Whenever they needed muscle on a job, he was one of the first two names they called. He was a follower, not a leader. Tommy needed men such as Devlin. Above all, though, he demanded their loyalty.

Rumours filtered through in recent weeks that Michael Devlin had done something unforgivable. So when the police swooped on the house in Kensal Rise, arresting five gang members in their early twenties, something didn't feel right. They seized a large amount of cash and several kilos of drugs.

The police declared it to be a significant event in the war against crime on the estates. A DCI with whom Tommy O'Riordan clashed dozens of times over the years appeared on TV. He declared the wall of silence destroyed, and it was only a matter of time before the police cleaned up the borough's estates.

Somebody had talked.

The wake continued until Tommy O'Riordan was ready to call it a day. Few men left the hall. They knew Tommy had an eye on them, even though he was well on the way to being drunk. Their wives and girlfriends drifted away, along with the children, and it was midnight before Tommy stumbled to the toilets. A few minutes later, Sean followed him. He helped him back off the floor and called for a hand to get their leader into a car.

It was early afternoon before Tommy surfaced. Colleen knew better than to disturb him. So when she heard him get up and head into the shower, she checked his coffee was available just as he liked it; black and hot.

Tommy was a man of few words when hungover. He flopped onto the settee and nodded when Colleen brought him his first cup. He picked up the daily paper, skimmed through it, and cast it aside. She left him alone, with the coffee jug on the side table, and made herself scarce. Tommy found a Racing channel on TV and waited for the coffee to ease the pain.

Colleen stuck her head around the door thirty minutes later.

"Do you want something to eat, Tommy?"

He shook his head.

Another hour passed, and Colleen heard him go back upstairs. Five minutes later, he came back. He had dressed in old clothes and was on his way out the door before she could ask where he was going.

Tommy decided to walk. The fresh air might benefit him, and he didn't want to risk getting pulled over by a snotty-nosed young copper. Tommy would still bust the breathalyser, even now. He called Sean Walsh.

"Have you found him yet, Sean?" he asked

"He's at the car recycling yard," replied his trusted lieutenant.

"I'll be there in ten minutes," said Tommy.

As he cut through the familiar side streets and alleyways, he recalled many occasions when he, Sean and Michael Devlin chased their rivals before beating the living daylights out of them. He remembered times, too, when these byways had seen them chased by the law. But, because they always held the upper hand with their local knowledge, they rarely got caught.

You thought you knew people, Tommy thought, as he turned the corner and saw the scrapyard on the far side of the street. When you grew up together and fought shoulder to shoulder, it was only natural that you believed it was for life. There was no excuse for what Devlin had done.

Tommy walked with his hands stuffed into his coat pockets. As he crossed the street, he withdrew his gloved right hand to feel the weight of the gun he carried under his old overcoat and inside his leather jacket. He hadn't brought the Smith and Wesson 45 Compact that had been his weapon of choice for a while. This one was a throwaway. A Glock with any identifying marks filed smooth. It would disappear as soon as this was over.

Tommy waited for a few seconds as he neared the gates, looking both ways along the street. Then, finally, he darted inside the yard, convinced nobody saw him. Tommy noticed Sean's car parked near the site office. That needed to move sharpish; links to him or his colleagues must be many miles away from what occurred here today.

He walked straight into the office without knocking. Maurice Kelly, the owner, sat behind the wooden desk. Sean Walsh stood beside him, facing the door. Kelly sat with the chair, rocking back on its legs, his back against the wall. When Tommy burst in, he almost fell off the chair.

"Tommy," he pleaded. "I want nothing to do with this, you understand?"

"I know, Maurice," Tommy growled, "where is the bastard?"

"In the workshop, Tommy," replied Sean. "I'll take you to him."

"I'll find him," said Tommy, turning on his heel and heading back out the door. "You keep an eye on this one and make sure he keeps his mouth shut. When he's got the message, we need to get rid of your motor. Get Maurice to drive it as far away from here on what's left in the tank. He can get a train back. You get off home and report it stolen in the morning."

"Maurice gave his men the afternoon off, Tommy, as we asked. It's empty. What are you going to do?" asked Sean, following Tommy as far as the office doorway.

"Deal with the problem; what else?" said Tommy in a whisper.

Michael Devlin sat on a metal chair in the middle of the workshop floor, his hands tied behind his back. His legs were strapped together. The chair stood in the middle of a large sheet of orange plastic sheeting. The smell suggested Devlin had messed himself. When he saw the big workshop doors slide open and Tommy O'Riordan entered, closing them behind him, he started to sob.

Tommy didn't speak. He didn't even turn his head towards Devlin. Instead, he skirted the plastic sheeting and headed for the tools lying on the long table at the side of the room. Tommy picked up a heavy spanner and felt the weight of it in his hand. He dropped it back on the table and sensed Devlin jump at the sound. He smiled to himself.

He continued walking around the floor covered by the sheeting. Devlin still sobbed quietly. Tommy had seen what he wanted as soon as he entered. The walk was just a charade. He wanted Devlin to sweat.

The four-foot-long metal bar would be perfect. Tommy picked it up by one end and trailed it along the floor behind him as he continued to circle his former friend. When he drew level with him, he stopped.

"Do you know the lowest form of a human being, Michael Devlin?" he whispered.

He crossed to the long table and turned the radio up full blast. Radio One music echoed around the workshop. Tommy took hold of the bar in both hands and, swinging from the hip, smashed it into Devlin's right knee.

The sounds from the tannoy muffled Devlin's screams. Tommy strolled around to the other side. Devlin's head dropped to his chest; Tommy aimed once more. The metal bar found its target. Devlin's left knee shattered, the same as the right.

Tommy dropped the bar and strolled back over to the table. He lowered the volume. For the first time, Tommy walked onto the plastic sheeting. He gagged at the smell coming from Devlin, but he needed to tell him the answer to his question.

"A grass, Michael. A grass."

He didn't know if Devlin heard him, but no matter.

Tommy made a final trip to the table to turn the music to the maximum. Then he walked around behind Devlin. Tommy removed the Glock from his jacket pocket. He placed the muzzle against the back of Devlin's head.

"I had so much more pain in mind for you, Michael. Because we were friends for so long, I've decided to be merciful."

Tommy fired once.

The loud music was superfluous; Tommy turned off the tannoy. It had been getting on his nerves. He removed the ties that bound Devlin and kicked away the metal chair so the lifeless body slithered onto the floor. Tommy wrapped the body in the sheeting, sealing it with tape. He winced at the crunching sounds from Devlin's knees when he tried to straighten his legs. He had a few tidying-up jobs, and then he could head home.

Tommy looked at the old clock on the workshop wall. It was four-thirty, and Kelly finished working on the cars at five. A nosy neighbour would comment upon any activity in the yard after that. So he needed to move fast. Tommy knew how the crushing process worked. When he walked back outside, Sean's car had disappeared. Maurice Kelly should be miles away, and his second-in-command tucked up at home.

The next car off the rank for the crusher was a two-litre Audi. Tommy saw that the rear seats were as far forward as possible. He made a mental note to add a fifty-pound note to the hush money he handed over to Maurice Kelly. The boot space could have been a problem, but not now. He returned inside, dragged Michael Devlin's body outside, and hoisted him up and into the boot. He closed the door shut.

"Bags of room," he muttered.

Tommy moved the mobile crane into position, attached the chains, and transferred the Audi into the car crusher. It took half as long again as Maurice Kelly or one of his regular staff because Tommy was out of practice. It had been one of a hundred legitimate skills he had acquired since he arrived here from Ireland. The problem was that grafting for a living didn't pay as much as the other skills he'd learned.

Finding the 'Start' button on the control panel proved simple enough. The old compactor started work, and the car and contents were pancaked. Tommy transferred the

Audi to the stack Maurice suggested at the far end of the site.

It could rust, and its contents rot away against the back fence. There was no rush.

Tommy searched the office and found cleaning materials for what passed for the toilets in the corner of the building. Then he took a hose to the car crusher, pouring a bottle of bleach around the interior in case blood seeped through the plastic sheeting.

When he was ready to leave, Tommy checked the street was empty. Then, he slipped out onto the street, closing the gates of the yard behind him. It was a pleasant summer evening, ideal weather for a stroll. He paid a visit to Little Venice for a walk by the canal. The effects of the hangover were long gone. His head had cleared; he needed somewhere quiet, away from the scrapyard, to dispose of the Glock. He passed dog walkers, joggers and cyclists with the same idea as himself; to find a quiet spot.

"It's Piccadilly Circus out here," he groaned, "who knew?"

Tommy found himself on a stretch of the pathway leading up to a bridge. He bent over as if to tie a loose shoelace and, looking left and right, satisfied himself that he was alone. Tommy removed the Glock from his jacket and dropped it into the canal. He climbed up the steep embankment and scrambled over the wall onto the walkway that led to the bridge.

Tommy knew this part of the borough. It had been one of several adventure playgrounds he and his brothers used as children. Unfortunately, the nearby streets got gentrified in the past twenty years. House prices had skyrocketed since the O'Riordan's spent their holidays playing around here. Tommy soon found his way back to the more familiar surroundings of the South Kilburn estate. That was his patch.

He entered his home through the back door. Colleen heard him come in but kept her distance. Tommy would speak to her when ready and not a minute before. She carried on watching her favourite soap on the TV.

Tommy removed his old coat, trousers, gloves and shoes. He bundled them in a bag and took them to the bottom of the garden. None of the neighbours hung any washing out on the line this late in the evening, but nobody would complain if Tommy O'Riordan lit a bonfire. Thirty minutes later, any trace of his clothes had gone for good. Tommy stood and watched, thinking back over the past few hours. Nothing he could think of would cause him to lose sleep. Nobody dared talk. Not unless they wanted to suffer the same fate as Michael Devlin.

Tommy kicked the glowing embers across the rough patch of grass and scattered several handfuls of topsoil and compost over the surface. He was no gardener but had learned to be a dab hand at covering his tracks. He strolled up the path to the back door and entered the house.

"I'm home, darling," he called, "do we have any food to eat?"

Colleen sighed, turned off the TV and headed for the kitchen. Life didn't change much in the O'Riordan household.

Chapter Three

Life continued much as ever for other families on the South Kilburn estate for a few weeks.

Sean Walsh called to report his stolen car first thing the following morning. Unfortunately, the police weren't that concerned. Instead, they added it to a high number of things towards the bottom of their list of priorities.

Maurice Kelly arrived home from Nantwich at lunchtime the next day. He had reached the outskirts of the Cheshire town with a flashing light on the petrol gauge warning him he had been driving on fumes. The quiet lay-by was screened from the main road by trees and bushes.

The conversation with Sean Walsh yesterday afternoon was brief. When he abandoned the car, it had to be in no condition for the police to know who drove it. Maurice removed the one-gallon plastic container of petrol he had brought with him from the boot. He poured the contents over the driver's seat and dashboard, then dropped a lighted rag through the open window.

Maurice Kelly set off across the fields behind the lay-by.

He skirted the main road until he scaled a gate and got onto a pavement beside a minor road that took him into town. He treated himself to a meal and five pints of Guinness at a pub just off the centre, then climbed the stairs on unsteady legs to his room.

Despite the hassle of driving so far away from Kilburn, today had been a nice little earner for Maurice Kelly. He slept well, his conscience clear. Michael Devlin had grassed on his colleagues. The Kelly family knew better than to rat out their mates. He took a train to Euston after breakfast. The tube to Kilburn delivered him back to familiar ground.

The scrapyard staff arrived at eight-thirty to open the business for the day. It wasn't uncommon for the boss to start later than they did. Kelly was getting on in years, he liked a drink, and he was the boss.

Maurice waved to his lads when he arrived later and disappeared into the office. His desk phone flashed. Someone left a message shortly after he went in Sean Walsh's car yesterday. Maurice played it back.

"Mr Kelly? It's John here; John Kelly, no relation. Ha-ha. My wife's Audi A3 is there to scrap, I believe? She's getting herself into a state. She left her Rick Springfield CDs in the glove compartment. Several of them are irreplaceable. Can you rescue them for her, please? We're going back to Oz to see family. Back in six weeks. You've got my number. I look forward to hearing from you."

Maurice closed his eyes for a second. It was too late; what could he do? He deleted the message, not bothering to highlight the incoming number.

On the other side of the estate, Colleen had cooked a meal for Tommy last evening, and then they sat together in silence, watching the TV. He never mentioned where he had been nor what he had been doing. Colleen never asked. The only thing she noticed the following morning was Tommy's better mood. She had to be thankful for small mercies.

Mairead Devlin, on the other hand, was a worried wife and mother. Her husband, Michael, didn't return home last night. She knew better than to jump to conclusions. He had been in and out of trouble with the law ever since she met him at St Mary's primary school.

It wasn't inconceivable he had been with another woman; he always had a roving eye. She had her suspicions over the years, but if he stayed out at night, it often turned out he was with his thieving friends. Mairead talked to her eldest daughter, Faith, on the phone.

"Give him the benefit of the doubt, mum," suggested Faith, "he'll creep in before the day's out. I haven't heard of any trouble or robberies on the estate."

Mairead remained worried. She spent a restless night, then still with no sign of Michael returning, she phoned her family for their support. When the Devlins arrived at the police station, they came in force. Her eight children accompanied her. The many grandchildren stayed at school, at a nursery, or with a childminder.

Mairead didn't want the police to dismiss the possibility of her husband being missing as something of little consequence. Michael's history might suggest he would turn up in his own good time. But, on the other hand, she wanted to ensure they took the matter seriously. The father of a large and loving family had disappeared without a trace.

The desk sergeant took the details; he promised it would be a priority. Mairead's children had heard the rumours about their father; nothing had been allowed to reach Mairead's ears.

The sergeant knew those rumours to be true. He gave

little away to the Devlins while they stood in front of him inside the station. When they left, he phoned the detectives that dealt with Devlin when he gave his evidence.

"There may be a problem," he reported, "Michael Devlin has gone missing."

The information was received and noted by the Metropolitan CID. Investigations followed. Everyone on the estate they talked to remained tight-lipped.

Michael Devlin was nowhere around; neither alive and well, seriously injured, nor dead.

The O'Riordan's, Walsh's, and Kelly's came under scrutiny over the following weeks. Questions arose about Sean Walsh. He reported a car stolen the day that Michael Devlin disappeared. Was that a coincidence? Or could these events be connected?

Had the stolen vehicle been sighted anywhere? The answers were either of little use or took a long time to arrive. Finally, local crime scene investigations officers checked the burnt-out car near Nantwich. They gathered nothing useful from the car's blackened interior. It was never involved in any criminal activity, according to their records.

They identified Sean Walsh as the legal owner from the rear number plate that remained legible after the fire burnt itself out. He received notification of his car's whereabouts, informing him he was responsible for its removal. Sean arranged for a local scrapyard to collect it and had it destroyed a week later. Tommy settled the bill. One more possible loose end had gone away.

There was confusion at the police station in Kilburn when they heard from their Cheshire colleagues. Had Michael Devlin done a runner? What should they tell his wife when she asks for an update? Mrs Devlin came to the station every other day.

The police tried to confirm where Tommy and the rest of his gang had been that afternoon. Nobody knew. A few brave souls criticized the cops for annoying the family.

"What do you think they did? Tommy buried his mother the previous day. The wake carried on until the early hours. They would have been in bed for most of the next day."

Despite the Devlin family's attempts to sustain the police's interest in discovering what happened to Michael Devlin, the trail had gone cold. Any possible leads were exhausted. Tommy started to relax. Sean bought himself a new motor. Maurice Kelly carried on with the car and metal recycling business, always sailing close to the wind.

A phrase that's been around for centuries, the luck of the Irish, suggests they profit from extreme good fortune. Many consider it derisory, implying they hadn't the brains to have pulled something off, so it must have happened by pure luck.

A combination of events followed around six weeks after Michael Devlin's death. Things suggest dumb luck caused Tommy O'Riordan to find himself in the dock at the Old Bailey. His being Irish had nothing to do with it.

An Environment Agency official paid a visit to the Kelly scrapyard. He was there to investigate a report of illegal waste tipping. He went to the office and asked Maurice to show him his licences to check they were in order.

The scrapyard owner was frantic as he tried to think if anything outside might raise suspicions. Maurice couldn't recall any problem items. He needed to have a word with his staff to make sure they took more care over where they dumped stuff in the future. He tried to think who reported him to the Council in the first place.

A sudden thought occurred to Maurice. He would have to steer this bloke away from the far end of the yard. That stack of compacted cars remained on site. He hadn't gotten around to clearing it yet.

"I'll inspect the site now, if I may," the official said, "your paperwork appears to be in order."

"I'll come with you," said Maurice, more in hope than expectation.

"I'd prefer to do it alone," said the officer, "it will only take five minutes. So please don't trouble yourself."

Maurice watched him as far as he could from the office window. Five minutes was a long time. He could walk to the far fence and back in that time. With luck, he wouldn't be standing and staring too long at any one place, though.

A sudden movement caught his eye as he watched to see if he could work out where the official was headed. A cherry picker appeared above the fence in the distance. A man in a hi-viz jacket and a white hard hat inspected the street light. That gave Maurice as good an excuse as any to wander out into the yard. He would chat with the bloke and keep an eye on the Environment Agency fellow at the same time.

Maurice trotted over towards the fence.

"What's happening here then?" he asked.

"The Council has subcontracted us," the man replied. "I'm removing half of the light bulbs in these streets altogether and then replacing the others with energy-saving, long-life bulbs. It's part of the budget cuts, mate. The Council reckon they'll save money, but the streets won't be safe to walk at night."

Maurice could see where this was heading. He relied on

the nearby street lighting to deter opportunist thieves from risking the spiked fences and climbing into the yard. Maurice didn't want them salvaging items from cars before he got around to them. He might have to invest in security lighting. Terrific.

The official returned, and there didn't appear to be anything troubling him.

"I'm off for now," he said, shaking Maurice by the hand. "Keep an eye on that stack of crushed cars by the back fence, won't you?"

"Oh, I will," replied Maurice, relief spreading through his body. He needed a drink. As soon as this bloke disappeared, he would get the bottle of vodka out of the desk drawer.

Maurice watched the hi-viz jacketed subcontractor as he bobbed up above the fence at different points around the site. However, his thirst got the better of him, and he went inside the office to take a few well-deserved swigs.

In Perth, Western Australia, John Kelly and his wife Carol had been visiting relatives. Carol was a native, born and bred; she emigrated to the UK in the Seventies and met John in Nottingham. Rick Springfield had been her favourite performer since the Sixties. When a job change for John meant a move to Maida Vale, his workmates dubbed him 'Ned' as they already had two Johns in their factory department.

John was a hen-pecked husband. Throughout their trip, he put up with Carol's moaning over her CDs. In the end, she persuaded him to call the police in Kilburn.

"OK, don't keep on, Carol. Though what good it will do, I don't know," he said, picking up the phone.

As 'dumb luck' had it, he got through to the same desk sergeant that dealt with Mairead Devlin. John Kelly told him they called Maurice Kelly, begging him to retrieve precious items from a scrapped car before leaving for Australia. They left a contact number but hadn't heard a thing.

"What date was this, sir?" the sergeant asked. Kelly told him; the sergeant snapped his pencil. That date rang a loud bell.

Heaven knows what this bloke thought they could do about these CDs at this late stage, but that lined three ducks up in a row. Devlin's disappearance, The report of the theft of Walsh's car, and now a car in a scrapyard. A yard slap bang in the middle of the square mile controlled by the Irish gang run by Tommy O'Riordan. The man suffered financial pain following Devlin's cooperation with the police. What were the odds against three things happening on the same day in a confined space, such as that not being connected?

After assuring John Kelly they would have a word with the scrapyard owner in due course, the sergeant ended the conversation. The desk phone rang again at once.

The officer made the obligatory introductions and asked the caller how he could be of service. The sentence that followed changed everything. Instead of a bored copper dealing with yet another annoying member of the public, his day got a lot brighter.

"Hello, there; look, it might be nothing," the voice began, "but I did a job for the council today."

And so, the reliance on breaking the walls of silence became less relevant. First thing in the morning, WPC Lizzie Burchell and newly promoted Sergeant Paul Gattiker left Kilburn police station for Kelly's scrapyard. Their presence was unwelcome, but Maurice Kelly was wary of unsettling the police or the Environment Agency any more than necessary. No way would he refuse to cooperate. It was likely to be a report of kids seen climbing over the fence to nick hubcaps. Items they used later as a Frisbee in the park.

"How can I help you, officers?" he asked, giving them a broad smile.

"Someone working for the Council spotted something suspicious by your back fence," replied young Gattiker.

"Kids?" asked Maurice.

"Not this time, sir," replied the sergeant.

Maurice took an instant dislike to the little scrote. He looked twelve years old, and he talked posh. The sweat breaking out on Maurice Kelly's brow suggested to Lizzie Burchell that the informant might be on to something.

"The vantage point afforded by the cherry-picker enabled him to look into the cars piled up by the fence at the rear of your property," the baby-faced sergeant continued. "You accept that the vehicles in the yard have been prepared for recycling by your operatives?"

"It's difficult to squash a car as flat as that under the heel of your boot, lad?" snapped Maurice. This conversation was not going well. He needed that bottle of vodka.

"Our informant compared one vehicle, near the top, with the rest of the pile and wondered why it showed far higher amounts of rust compared to the rest." Lizzie Burchell added. The three now stood directly in front of the offending stack of cars.

"He couldn't swear to the make and model," said Paul Gattiker, "but he had never seen a white car with what resembled an orange stripe. It felt wrong, if you understand me?"

"Then he saw a loose piece of fabric flapping in the breeze," said Lizzie, "initially, he thought the width of the material fitted with it being a seatbelt."

"The longer he looked, the more it felt something didn't belong. It was an adhesive tape."

Paul Gattiker turned to Maurice Kelly.

"How do you explain that, Mr Kelly?"

Maurice shrugged.

"You'd have to ask my lads. I wasn't here that day."

"I think we need to investigate further, don't you?" asked Paul. "Maybe we can go to your office and wait for our forensic people to arrive. We may need one of your staff to remove the cars above it and the white Audi A3 in question. We could be here for a while."

"How can you tell it's an Audi," snorted Maurice. "It's a white pancake twenty feet off the ground."

"Just a hunch, sir," said Paul Gattiker, "the previous owner contacted the station. He said he asked you to salvage treasured souvenirs within hours of dropping off the vehicle. His messages got ignored, so he complained."

The three of them stepped inside the office building. Maurice Kelly felt the walls closing in on him.

"I'm not saying another word," he muttered and slumped into his chair.

The forensic team arrived within the hour. Kelly's staff removed the crushed vehicles from the pile, and the CSI team went to work on the Audi A3 once it reached the ground. In the days that followed, the excessive rust proved to be blood. Blood that used to course through the veins of Michael Devlin. They had little trouble making the match; his frequent brushes with the law meant the police possessed a lot of knowledge of the unfortunate victim.

Mairead Devlin received notification of the discovery of her husband's body. Family liaison officers who delivered the news dissuaded her from viewing the collection of shattered bones, flesh and clothing the forensic team retrieved at the scene. Her children gathered around the matriarch, and the family grieved the loss of the murdered father, grandfather, and former villain.

The South Kilburn estate overflowed with speculation on who had been responsible for his death. Rumours that Devlin had been responsible for the arrests earlier in the year were confirmed true. However, the person most affected by those arrests, apart from the low-level criminals in prison, was Tommy O'Riordan.

Tommy heard the news concerning Devlin; he was disappointed with Maurice Kelly. He had paid him well; why didn't he get rid of the car? Tommy called Sean Walsh and ordered a punishment beating when the dust settled on affairs at the scrapyard.

Tommy still believed he had nothing to fear. He covered his tracks. Nothing could trace back to his door. The police and the people on the estate could point the finger as much as they wished, proving his involvement would be a different kettle of fish. Colleen got fed up with the dirty looks she got from neighbours and shop staff. She asked Tommy whether they could have a holiday.

"Why can't we go over to Marbella to see the kids? They're always asking when we will go over to spend time with them."

Tommy thought about it. What was stopping them? Sean could keep things running while they went away. This fuss would be over in days.

Tommy and Colleen flew to Malaga from Stansted the following afternoon.

The forensic examination of the Audi continued. The sad news had to be relayed to John and Carol Kelly that Rick Springfield was beyond help. Carol felt tearful for a few days, but John bought her a retro record player and fetched her vinyl collection from the attic. She soon reacquainted herself with Affair of the Heart, Jessie's Girl, and the rest of her heartthrob's greatest hits. John disappeared to his shed at the bottom of the garden more often than in the past, but journeys in their new Honda Jazz became more enjoyable. At least the radio had more variety.

Meanwhile, they grasped at the last few straws left to examine in the forensic department. They needed a lucky break.

Dumb luck did for Tommy O'Riordan in the end.

It came in the shape of that flapping piece of tape that caught the eye of the subcontractor working on the streetlights. As the CSI team teased more and more parts of the mangled Audi apart, they determined that Michael Devlin was inside the orange plastic sheeting. Sheeting that was visible as a thin stripe after the compactor had done its work.

Part of the tape securing the sheeting wrapped around the dead body had come loose. It was a painstaking job, but they recovered several sections of tape-covered sheeting in the end. In the laboratory, they tested them for fingerprints. The results drew a blank. It was another blank alongside others from the Audi wreckage and the scrapyard.

Teresa Green, a twenty-three-year-old trainee, who cursed her parents every day for her first name, stared at a section of orange sheeting and its attached grey tape. What was she seeing? Had the killer joined these two pieces of tape?

Whoever wrapped the body, it proved impossible to use one continuous length. The killer had to break a strip off, seal it, and then tear another piece from the roll to continue wrapping.

No fingerprints were found anywhere in or on the car,

so the killer or killers must have worn gloves. How did they break the tape? Did they cut it with a knife or scissors? Evidently, they hadn't removed their gloves to tear it across the width. It was uneven, so it wasn't a clean cut.

Teresa knew what she always did when faced with a similar problem at Christmas; when wrapping an odd-shaped present. She nicked it with her teeth, and then it was easier to tear. Even if it didn't always stay dead straight,

It might be worth testing for DNA. Teresa swabbed the area around the joint. They had to wait ten days to a fortnight to get the results. It was a long shot, but all they had.

Tommy O'Riordan lay on a sun lounger on the balcony, basking in the sun. Colleen had gone shopping. The children were both at work. The four of them planned to go out for a meal together this evening. It had been their routine over the past couple of weeks. The children had wondered if and when their parents were leaving.

Tommy had made himself at home. He had bumped into a few old colleagues living out their retirement years in Marbella. Who says crime doesn't pay? Maybe he was thinking of quitting the game and moving here permanently.

Colleen trotted back into the apartment, loaded with designer label bags. She looked forward to showing Tommy what she had bought and then joining him on a lounger with a glass of wine for the rest of the afternoon.

"Alright, sweetheart?" she purred.

"Mustn't grumble," Tommy replied, "fetch us a bottle of lager from the fridge, darling."

Colleen dumped her bags on one of the large leather sofas and trotted off to the kitchen.

The doorbell rang.

"Who's that now, I wonder," she groaned. The colour drained from her tanned face when she opened the door. Five armed men burst into the flat. Two plain-clothes police officers followed them inside, waving warrant cards.

Tommy heard the noise and was still getting his bulky frame up from the lounger when the armed men arrived on the balcony. He wore a pair of swim shorts, flip-flops, and sunglasses. Tommy saw the guns pointed at him and grinned.

"First day in the sun, lads? You're looking red-faced. Get my brief on the phone, Colleen. I can't imagine what you're doing here."

The two detectives pushed their way through onto the balcony.

"Thomas Henry O'Riordan, you're under arrest for the murder of Michael Devlin..."

"Bollocks," shouted Tommy, "you've got nothing on me, copper, and you know it. You're on a fishing expedition. But, yeah, red-faced is right. I reckon."

DI Jonathan Barclay smiled.

"We have your DNA on the tape you used to wrap his body. If you used a knife or scissors, you might have gotten away with it. But instead, you used your teeth to cut the tape between the strips. The saliva you left behind has done for you. Schoolboy error."

Tommy re-ran the scene in the workshop from that afternoon in his head. The sick feeling in his stomach spread. How stupid had he been? He had left there as fast as possible. The stench was terrible. He couldn't be bothered to walk to the work table to hunt for something with which to cut the bloody tape. What dumb luck!

Six months later, Tommy O'Riordan would stand in the

dock at the Central Criminal Court. The police never found the murder weapon. For weeks, DI Barclay and his squad only had the DNA on the tape as evidence.

O'Riordan had plenty of motive; nobody could dispute that. Despite his being at his mother's wake the night before, he still had the opportunity. Unfortunately, the only people who could give him an alibi for the afternoon in question were unreliable witnesses. His brothers and sisters were economical with the truth by nature. Colleen, his beloved wife, said he never left the house.

"Well, she would, wouldn't she?" Barclay when he met with the prosecution's brief.

"We could do with more," the lawyer said. "Is there nobody on the estate prepared to talk?"

"They're not lining up around the corner, no," admitted Jonathan Barclay. "Still, there's time yet for us to get a break in the case."

A week later, it arrived in the shape of Maurice Kelly. In truth, Maurice wasn't in good health at the time. He had recently left the hospital. Sean Walsh had sent his heavies to the scrapyard late one Friday afternoon.

They said they had a message from Tommy O'Riordan. Leaving the Audi on site for six weeks with Michael Devlin's body inside had been a mistake. They left him with fractures in more places than he could count on his fingers.

An eye socket, his nose, and half a dozen ribs required treatment. His ten fingers got broken too, which hindered his counting. Maurice Kelly still hurt, but with O'Riordan on remand, having been judged a flight risk, he decided a word with the authorities might help his cause.

The police questioned him over his involvement in Devlin's murder. He told them he had travelled to Nantwich that night. They checked and confirmed he couldn't have been in the yard later than two in the afternoon. Kelly agreed to give the police a statement, provided they looked after him.

"Do you have a big family, Maurice?" asked DI Barclay.

"Not around here," he replied, "they're either back home in Ireland or dead. So it's just the wife and me."

"We'll consider getting you into witness protection if what you tell us is of any value."

DI Barclay didn't want to take any chances. If Maurice helped clinch the case against O'Riordan, he would offer him personal protection twenty-four-seven. Arrests and convictions of criminals such as Tommy O'Riordan made people's careers.

"Tommy was in my office that afternoon. I'll swear to that. I had to drive to Nantwich; he was still here when I left. He went to the workshop."

"Was he alone?" asked Jonathan Barclay.

Maurice knew Sean Walsh was still at large in the neighbourhood. Tommy hadn't talked throughout his time in custody. The police had found nothing to link Walsh to the murder.

"There was nobody else here," Maurice replied.

"Who brought Devlin here in the first place?" asked the inspector.

"No idea," shrugged Maurice, "I sent the lads home at one o'clock because we weren't that busy, and I had to drive north. Tommy arrived in the afternoon and said he would pay me for using the workshop for an hour or two. I wanted nothing to do with whatever he planned. He told me to keep my mouth shut about him being there and make myself scarce. So that's what I did."

"How did you receive the injuries that put you in the hospital?" Barclay asked.

"In my line of business, people always reckon they've had a raw deal. It's a hard game in which to make a living. I won't deny that I'm no saint. Half a dozen customers could have thought I'd ripped them off. I never saw the faces of the two thugs that hurt me. They wore masks."

DI Barclay didn't believe a word of it, but once Kelly's statement was tidied up and signed, it would be the clincher they needed.

After the trial that ended on the twenty-third of April found Tommy O'Riordan guilty, Maurice Kelly's scrapyard closed for business. His staff got laid off. Finally, the site cleared, and a For Sale notice was posted on the fence outside the gates. After that, he and his wife Dierdre never surfaced again in North London, nor anywhere in Britain.

Hugo Hanigan seethed with frustration in his penthouse suite in the nation's capital. In the beautiful Somerset countryside at Larcombe Manor, the hunt was on to confirm the connection between the series of murders before Easter. Hugo planned more atrocities to signal the degree of control The Grid had over the country's criminal affairs. Olympus was several steps behind him.

Phoenix had been correct. Evil was just around the corner. Olympus had to play 'catch-up', and any delay in identifying the megalomaniac banker could prove fatal.

Chapter Four

Thursday, 24th April 2014

In the ice-house, Giles Burke and Artemis were hard at work. Their official shift started at eight, but Giles had called last night to suggest a six o'clock start. Artemis didn't need asking twice. They had an important task, and Phoenix had insisted they take time yesterday to catch up on their sleep. No point in wasting any more time.

"We need to get as much information on these murders as possible, Giles," she said. "Try to discover what lay behind them before the morning meeting. One hour of investigating will only scratch the surface, but an earlier start might help us bring something useful to the table for nine o'clock. I'll be there at six."

Artemis had slipped from under the duvet at half-past five; Rusty snored in peace beside her. She saw no point in disturbing her partner this early; they had spent their half-day off in this bedroom.

Their working patterns for Olympus often saw them

apart for days on end. It had become second nature to grab every opportunity to show how much they meant to one other. The cold shower woke her up, and her mind was on full alert when she descended to the ice-house control centre in the lift.

In the nine months that Artemis had worked at Larcombe, there were many crises to face. But, she wouldn't swap her current role for her old job in the police service for love or money, despite the dangers that Rusty confronted whenever his missions took him into the big, evil world. They were together, that's what mattered, and she always believed she made a difference here with Olympus.

Giles greeted her with a smile when the lift doors closed in their smooth and silent manner behind her, "Good morning, Artemis. I hope you're fighting fit?"

"After a fashion," she grinned back, "so, what time did Maria Elena leave? Or is she still in the stable block?"

"Provided the alarm wakes her in time to get to the main house to collect Hope before nine, she'll be fine,"

With the preliminaries dealt with, they set to work. Over the months, it had become plain they made a good team. Giles was a computer wizard able to sift through masses of data gathered from the Olympus systems and isolate specks of gold dust. Giles's expertise enabled the organisation to work with maximum effect.

Artemis had been a bright, ambitious young detective sergeant with more ability than her role ever demanded. Since being at Larcombe, her acute, intuitive intelligence had sprouted wings. She thrived on the pressure; and enjoyed the challenge of making the disparate elements they uncovered fit into place. When they put their heads together, answers to insurmountable problems soon got resolved.

As they set to work on what lay behind the recent murders, little did they realise the extent of their instigator's threat to the rule of law across the nation. Unchecked, the controlling hand behind them threatened the existence of the Olympus Project itself.

"Let's analyse what Orion told Hayden," Giles began. "We have a series of unexplained deaths in towns and cities over a short space of time. Every victim was involved in criminal activity. Not every death featured in news reports as being a murder."

"Murders aren't as common over here as in the States," said Artemis. "So, because the deaths occurred in different regions, no one police authority joined up the dots. I'm afraid a death here and there from a wide range of causes becomes the norm. No massacres took place in one location; just individual killings scattered across half a dozen regions."

"A few might be ruled as suicide in error or merely accidental at a coroner's court," added Giles. "Only when you stand back to look at the big picture do you see there might be a sinister pattern."

"Well, that's Orion for you," smiled Artemis. "He's an old-school detective, brought up the right way. When his career started in Birmingham, he didn't have the politically correct, modern policing mantra drilled into him. His nose told him something lay behind these deaths. You can't teach that."

"I think you accept he was on the right track, don't you?" Giles asked.

"We'd be foolish not to," said Artemis.

She brought a map of Great Britain up onto the screen in front of them. Another keystroke added the sites of the reported deaths. Once they connected them, as Orion suggested, the letter 'H' was emblazoned across the screen in red. It was clear for all to see.

"Well, there's our link," said Giles, "we've seen that 'H' before, haven't we?"

"Hayden didn't appreciate the potential significance when Orion reported it," said Artemis. "He and Kelly didn't attend the morning meetings when we discussed Hannon and the Irish connections."

"I propose we divide the background analysis of the victims to the rest of the team," said Giles. "Somewhere in their past lies the reason for their elimination. If a criminal organisation is vying for overall control in the country, then whoever is at its head is likely to want to remove potential opposition."

"I agree," said Artemis, "we can then concentrate on the letter 'H'. Let's not dismiss other alternatives in favour of what we know out of hand. That might be a mistake. What else might it represent? Could it be a coded message to the criminal underworld? Are there other letters yet to appear? Have we missed letters from a series of earlier deaths?"

Giles thought for a while.

"I'll put one agent to work on those strands, Artemis. They can search for previous deaths of known criminals to see if the locations throw up a connection and set up search routines to alert us to any new news reports. You're right. We mustn't assume we have the answer within our existing data."

The likelihood of two instances *not* being connected where the same individual letter got used on matters under scrutiny in the ice-house had to be remote. That was even less likely when they cropped up only three weeks apart. For the rest of the time before the morning meeting, they continued to hunt for Ardal James Hannon.

The financial genius had dropped out of sight by the end of 2009. That happened only months after Hannon left the merchant bank where he worked. Rumour had it he planned on setting up his own business, but no company existed under his name. Nor did Hannon appear in the 2011 census. Whatever he called himself these days, it wasn't Ardal James Hannon.

"He lived in Cricklewood, didn't he?" asked Giles.

"Yes, in a four-bedroomed first-floor flat. It sold for two and a quarter million in February 2010. The buyers were a Saudi Arabian family. They still live there."

"Do we know which estate agents handled the sale?" asked Giles.

"I'll check," said Artemis. "I can always contact the present owners to see if they know."

"If you're ringing them, ask if Hannon left a forwarding address," said Giles.

"If only it were that easy," Artemis sighed. "Hannon slipped out of circulation for a reason. He would not send his friends personalised cards with 'My new pad' on the front."

"Henry said after hearing of the note left in Shanklin that Hannon had the credentials to be the mastermind behind the more structured tactics being adopted by a network of criminal gangs today."

"If he did set up on his own," said Artemis ", the most likely business would be another private bank, would it not? That's where his expertise lies. He worked for four years in merchant banks in the City. His private bank offers the perfect cover for the money laundering required to facilitate the operations of his underworld friends' finances. We need to trace banks set up in either late 2009 or early the following year."

"By their nature, private banks stay beneath the radar. They seek neither accolades nor notoriety," said Giles. "They are owned by a family, a partnership, or an individual. The one thing they guarantee you as a client is privacy. Apart from Coutts, or Hoare and Company, I doubt if the man on the street could name one. Hannon's bank operates in a mere handful of markets, and with his business acumen, it could be wildly profitable."

"I hope so," said Artemis, "because that might attract attention from his rivals. A new kid on the block, outperforming the competition, inviting questions on where the money is coming from, rumours of sharp practice; that might expose him. On the other hand, we might find a helping hand from the City of London."

"We had better put a report together for the morning meeting," said Giles, checking his watch. "There's still time to chase up the estate agent and locate new businesses that fit the profile."

"I'll work on the report on our progress while you follow up on the new banks formed within our time frame. We might be at work at silly o'clock, but London estate agency staff won't have left home yet."

"Fair enough," smiled Giles, "but I get the easy job next time. I started here in the ice-house before you arrived, remember."

"Ah, but it's a much more pleasant place to work now, isn't it?" Artemis replied.

They worked in silence on their respective tasks, and before they left the ice-house, they checked on the progress of the other agents. They were satisfied things were on track.

When the two colleagues reached the surface, they began the walk towards the main house. Henry strode out with a renewed purpose in the distance. Giles pointed him out to Artemis.

"Do you think he'll be his old self today?"

"He's missing Sarah Gough," said Artemis. "Who imagined they might get on so well?"

Maria Elena had crept out of the stable block ahead of them. She soon realised her chances of making it back to the main house without being spotted had disappeared. She waited for Giles and Artemis, then fell in step with them.

"Good morning, Artemis," she said, grabbing Giles's hand and hoping nobody noticed.

"It's okay, Maria Elena; there's no need to pretend. Everyone at Larcombe knows you and Giles are crazy in love."

"Oh," said the Spanish nanny, "and we've been so careful. I don't want the mistress to think bad of me. Athena might inform my parents and dismiss me."

"Very unlikely," said Artemis, "she and Phoenix have known for ages. They're cool with it. Just relax and enjoy being together."

Maria Elena gave Giles a quick kiss on the cheek and left them to walk across to the far end of the building. It was the fastest route to the apartments and Hope's nursery. She glanced at her watch. If she ran, she had time to drop into her room for a quick change of clothes.

"You're right, of course," said Giles, watching his lover run towards the side door. "Maria Elena changed everything for me here at Larcombe. I never thought for a moment of leaving Olympus because the cause is righteous, and our methods are appropriate to the scale of the crime. But, as I lay relaxing in the sun after my emergency appendix operation, I did question whether I gave too much of myself to the Project. Regardless of how lousy I felt, I had wanted to throw myself into my job. It could have been fatal if you hadn't insisted I get myself checked out. I lived alone, with no one to care for or have concerns for me. Athena and Phoenix, you and Rusty, were in solid, loving relationships. I realised that if I wanted to give my best when I returned, I had to open my mind to the idea that a relationship was at least possible. Despite our job and how all-embracing it can be, I had no idea Hope's birth at New Year would deliver the perfect woman for me in the shape of Maria Elena. These past months have been wonderful."

"I think that's the longest speech you've made since I arrived here," said Artemis. "We're happy for you both. Let's get upstairs to that meeting room, or we'll be late."

The two colleagues climbed the stairs, two at a time, and arrived at the doorway just as Phoenix approached.

"Good morning," he said. "Athena will be along in a minute. Maria Elena must have been running behind schedule, I guess."

Phoenix spotted the look between them as they darted into the room ahead of him. They behaved like school kids, trying to suppress a giggle. He could have told them that the nanny arrived with seconds to spare if they had given him a chance.

Athena's delay was because Hope had been sick during the night and was running a temperature. She had called for one of the medical staff as he was due to check on her within the hour. Athena wanted Maria Elena to be aware of Hope's condition and prepare for another episode.

Athena had dealt with Hope when her cries had first woken them. Then, on the second occasion, it had been Phoenix who got up to clean her up, change her bedding, and settle her back to sleep. The last thing he had suggested to Athena before trying to get back to sleep had been to call Maria Elena to warn her to wear old clothes.

Athena soon bustled along the corridor to join them. The morning meeting was underway.

"Can we have a report on the query posed by Orion, please?"

"We were wary of assuming 'H' was the same person, who left the message for Phoenix," said Giles. "So, we've got people double-checking for earlier letter clues. In addition, we've set up search routines to capture any potential cryptic clues relating to sudden deaths that may occur in the future."

"We're digging deeper into the deaths reported before Easter," Artemis continued. "To uncover the reason 'H' targeted them. We are now ninety-nine per cent convinced we're dealing with the same person. Orion has spotted a genuine connection between the killings. It relates to the growing network of organised crime in the country. Someone is guiding that expansion and encouraging a more professional and business-like approach."

"Those who oppose him are being eliminated," said Giles. "When we have completed our analysis of the victims' backgrounds, we expect to have learned what they did or said that put them on his hit list."

"Do we have any leads on the present identity of 'H'?" asked Phoenix.

Artemis leant forward with her elbows on the table.

"In most cases, I worked as a detective alongside Orion. He always told us to start with the bleeding obvious. If we had even a scrap of knowledge relating to the case, we should squeeze that until the pips popped out rather than hunting for fresh leads. Several names surfaced when we investigated why Gavin McTierney's death caused someone to seek retribution. Every one of them was born in Ireland. In their youth, they ran together in street gangs; McTierney came to London to become a gangster. Ardal James Hannon, the financial whiz-kid, followed him. He's the only 'H' we have that fits the bill. So we're pursuing that lead before we search elsewhere."

"As you will recall," said Giles, "he disappeared from Cricklewood in 2009. We're chasing the estate agent who sold Hannon's flat a few months later. He will have bought something near the centre, as we know he intended to set up his private bank. He's a man who wishes to be at the heart of things. To keep his finger on the financial pulse of the City of London. I'm waiting for details of the banks set up between late '09 and the following year's summer. There will only be a handful. The bank Hannon operates will perform far better than its competition."

"It sounds as if we're nearly there," said Athena. "Well done, you two."

"So, Hannon has adopted a new identity," said Henry Case. "Because of the cryptic clues spotted by Orion, we believe he's changed the name, but not the letter?"

"That makes sense," said Phoenix.

"I know you're busy, Giles," said Rusty, "but can we dig even deeper on Hannon? At first, it appeared his role was the money man for several gangs across the London boroughs. He worked for a series of merchant banks, and it's clear he excelled at his job. But, if he's behind a callous campaign of killings to further his grand design for a connected network throughout Britain, he's now got a much darker side. That must have been evident in Dublin when he was a teenage tearaway. No profiler ever suggests someone becomes a serial killer overnight. These tendencies have existed for years. They must have surfaced in the past. We need to find them; to better understand who we're facing. My gut tells me he's dangerous, a maniac who will stop at nothing to further his ends."

"That makes sense, too," said Phoenix.

Athena had been listening intently without yet adding her thoughts.

"I'm happy we're making progress. If this 'H' is as dangerous as we fear, the search routines from the ice-house to find new victims may prove to be the most beneficial over the coming weeks. His actions to date were controlled and targeted. I believe he intended them to send a message to criminal gangs wherever they operate, but they were also a message to the authorities. It served as a warning; to toe the line and follow his lead or pay the price. For the police, it was a notice of intent. This network or grid of interlinked gangs is a genuine threat. If he gets the different ethnic groups to work together, it will be more than a match for a police service shrinking in numbers and ill-equipped to fight organised crime. Too many officers are assigned to cold cases, chasing idiots driving using mobile phones. Policing sporting events and festivals. Those are luxuries, not necessities at dangerous times such as these."

Nobody around the table disagreed with what Athena said.

"Heaven help us if we have another spate of terrorist attacks," added Phoenix, "the authorities would be swamped. To support the police, they might need to draft in what's left of our armed forces."

Rusty groaned.

"We were stretched to the limit when I still served in the SAS," he said. "They've suffered budget cuts, year on year, since then. So I'm afraid they wouldn't be much help."

"It sounds like it's left to us to sort out again," Henry said.

"When will our first new intake be arriving for training," asked Alastor.

"In just over a month from now, on the first Monday in June," replied Athena.

"They'll be ready to go into the field on the first of September," said Rusty, "no sooner. They will undergo an intensive twelve-week course, regardless of how fit, skilled, or talented their military records might indicate. The training I have designed for Kelly and Hayden to carry out will deliver us a fresh set of agents capable of tackling any scenario."

"How many new agents will that give?" asked Minos.

"Twelve," said Rusty. "I know; that's a small number. Since Olympus began, we have only taken the best of the best. The pool we are sourcing our agents from gets smaller by the year. I can't influence that. I'm sorry."

"Don't apologise, mate," said Phoenix, "the government remains blind to the threats it faces. We know it's quality, not quantity, that counts. An Olympus agent is worth half a dozen street criminals any day of the week."

Minos raised an eyebrow. That was quite a reaction from one of The Stooges.

"Would you care to explain why you take issue with that, Minos?" asked Rusty.

"There are between fifty and sixty thousand criminals in gangs around Britain at any time. We have up to two thousand Olympus agents in theatres across the globe. We have less than five hundred available to us on these shores. Training fifty new agents per year, no matter how good they might be, will be of little help."

"Olympus can only do what it can afford, Minos," said

Athena. "The next item on the agenda today is the review you and Alastor have been undertaking on the four new potential Olympians. After that, we need a fresh injection of funds. We understand that the twelve people who sit around the top table, controlling the Project's missions worldwide, are not our only financiers. Erebus always reminded us we have friends who prefer to remain in the shadows. It's fair to say over the past six years, many of our sleeping partners have seen their investments suffer. Either because of the banking crisis in 2008 or the slow bleed of low-interest rates on their savings each year."

"Maybe we need to discuss this at the next Olympus meeting, Athena?" Phoenix suggested. "For now, let's ask Giles and Artemis to return to the ice-house to follow up on the leads they identified."

"Good idea," said Athena. "OK, you two find this bank and Hannon's new identity. Then, assign one of your team to find out what this stress point was in his history. Something flicked a switch in his brain, turning him from a mild-mannered accountant into a power-crazed maniac. That could be the key to revealing his ultimate aims."

Giles and Artemis were halfway out the door, eager to get on the trail of Ardal James Hannon and his new identity.

"Before we hear Minos and Alastor's report," Athena continued, "let me add to what Phoenix suggested. The time has come to re-evaluate our global strategy. Zeus is protective of his role in that theatre. He has been guiding it since Olympus formed. Phoenix and I will need to tread with care. If the immediate threats we face centre in Britain, we could consider switching overseas agents from dormant trouble spots. However, that throws up a logistical nightmare. Our agents don't enter a war zone the day before a mission and get evacuated to safety after completing their tasks. They live and work in areas identified as potential flashpoints. Often, they married local women and had families. There are fifteen hundred sleeper agents abroad, but few are available for transfer back home without careful extrication."

"Erebus explained this when I arrived," said Phoenix, "we must guard our true role at the Project. Someone in Moscow should quit working for a small international company to return to their country of birth without comment. But someone always asks questions. In countries that contain known flashpoints, this is inevitable. Even if the agent's work colleagues accept he's merely received a better offer elsewhere, government spies will stick their nose in to see what's happening."

"I agree," said Athena. "If we identified one hundred agents as surplus to requirements where they work now, sooner or later, someone would uncover their links back to Larcombe Manor. So we must avoid that whatever happens."

"So, we must manage with what we have available on the ground and add to their number in modest increments," said Minos. "That's not ideal, but perhaps Zeus can help. We would be switching experienced agents back home instead of sending freshly trained personnel into the front line. If the current hot spot is here in Britain, the more experienced our agents, the better."

"We'll take our concerns to Zeus at the next meeting," said Athena. "Phoenix and I will attend the Manchester venue on the first Wednesday in July."

"Only a full-blown crisis will bring that date forward," said Phoenix. "Let's hope one isn't lurking around the corner."

"Someone had better tell Hannon to behave himself then," said Rusty. "Based on his actions before Easter, he could well take further steps to achieve supreme control of this network."

"Shakespeare wrote that something wicked this way comes, didn't he?" asked Henry.

"Macbeth," replied Athena.

"Literature never was my strong point," sighed Henry.

"Better than you think, Henry," said Athena, "and the quote sums up the situation well, I fear."

Chapter Five

There was a brief pause in the meeting. Those seated around the table absorbed the import of what might pass for a light-hearted exchange but was a clear definition of the threat posed by the evil financier.

Athena cleared her mind of negative thoughts. She moved to the next item on the agenda without delay. She asked Minos and Alastor to take them through the detailed analysis of the histories of the four candidates to be Olympians.

Her two most senior colleagues delivered their report.

The decorated war hero Ludovic Tremayne, who would assume the code name Achilles, was everything the initial checks carried out by Zeus on his background had suggested. His credentials had been straightforward to verify. Minos had concerns over the moderate sums he offered the Olympus fighting fund. As a former Major in the Blues and Royals, Alastor had been more impressed with the counter-intelligence knowledge he brought to Olympus. Tremayne's wife, Rosalind, was active in the community as a local academy parent-governor and did volunteer work for several charities.

"One name to add to the list?" asked Phoenix.

"Tremayne gets our vote," replied Alastor. "Even if he's not mega-rich, the other attributes he brings to the table will be invaluable."

Next, the Two Stooges scrutinised the second candidate, Jean-Paul St. Clair. The prospective Daedalus had the funds to make him attractive to Olympus. There were no doubts on that score. St. Clair's business acumen, steely determination, and inventive mind appeared to be the icing on the cake. Minos paused and thought for a moment.

"I sense a 'but' coming," said Athena. "Have you found a flaw in his character?"

"Since he sold his business for three billion pounds, Jean-Paul has lived across the border in Wales. The age gap between him and his glamour model wife Simone could drive them apart. The amount of time she spends in their flat in Paris is on the increase, and last winter, she used the Chamonix lodge for eight weeks."

"There are no children, though, if I remember right?" asked Phoenix.

"No," replied Alastor, "and Simone has remained alone on her travels. So there doesn't appear to be a third party involved in the separation if that's what it has become. Indeed, Jean-Paul has visited Paris and Chamonix in the last six months. On those occasions, they got on with no apparent discord. So you might say it's an amicable distancing if they are growing apart."

"Careful, Alastor," said Rusty. "If that phrase ever gets out, I can think of a few celebrities' marital breakdowns it describes. It might go viral."

"In their world, a twelve-month marriage is equivalent

to a golden wedding for normal couples," snorted Henry Case.

"The separation isn't official then," asked Athena.

"Not at this stage," replied Minos.

"What are you recommending?" asked Phoenix.

"St. Clair shows no weaknesses to rule him out," said Minos. "Simone may be unhappy living with a billionaire in Monmouthshire day in, day out, yet Jean Paul's reaction to him and his wife living apart feels in tune with his Gallic roots. One can imagine him shrugging, accepting the situation, without resorting to tantrums or extravagant gestures. We suggest Daedalus is a candidate who adds diversity and a wealth of talents. The discord with Simone is a distraction Olympus could do without, but the man himself is just the person we're seeking."

"A cautious yes, then," said Athena. "I hope you've been leaving the best to last with our two female candidates?"

"Not entirely," said Alastor. "Piya Adani has youth and a healthy bank balance in her favour. Since her father's death, she has challenged many taboos she encountered in the business world. Piya hates the label of feminist, but if Ambrosia joined the Olympus upper echelons, she would challenge the existing order. Her ambition knows no limits."

"You might have a rival, Athena. So your succession to the top job when Zeus stands aside may not be automatic," said Phoenix with a smile.

"I've never thought that far ahead," said Athena. "I'm more concerned with what effect this challenging attitude might have on the whole group. We have three women among the eight current Olympians. After what happened last year, we need to promote harmony, not discord. We need team players, not loose cannons. Can Piya Adani be a team player, or not, Minos?"

"Piya's a leader, and a proven winner, Athena," the former Judge replied. "I believe Zeus has selected her not to cause division but to inspire each of you to question policies which hitherto have been, for the most part, male-dominated. Alastor and I believe she will bring a breath of fresh air to proceedings. Hera, with her seniority, might need to temper her exuberance from time to time, but Ambrosia still smells sweet to us."

"Fair enough," said Athena, "so that leaves us with Dawn Prentice. What have you unearthed on Aurora?"

"Enough to discount her out of hand," sighed Minos.

"Zeus had her checked out before he put her name forward at the last meeting," said Phoenix, surprised. "She had her problems in the past, but she was clean and committed to ridding the streets of the scourge of drugs. So what on earth happened?"

"As you know," said Minos. "Dawn Prentice worked for a charity helping recovering addicts. After over eight years of staying away from her old life, the wealth she inherited from her late parents a year ago attracted attention from unsavoury characters in her past. Dawn's ambition was to use her fortune to help combat the spread and use of drugs. It was the magnet that drew Zeus to her. He believed she had conquered her demons. She was another fascinating candidate in the spirit of the new blood he wanted to introduce to Olympus. Unfortunately, the new dawn for Aurora proved to be false."

Alastor then took up the story.

"The massive lottery win in 2010 received widespread publicity. Dawn's parents enjoyed the limelight their fifteen minutes of fame afforded and then spent their windfall modestly. They travelled the world, but there were no grand houses or fast cars. In the months that followed, the media at the lower end of the market exposed Dawn's past life, what they used to term the gutter press. Of course, they sensationalised her story, but she appeared to weather that storm and continued her work with the charity."

"The tragic death of her parents got reported in full, too," continued Minos. "Dawn was their only child, and it didn't take long for the same newspapers to sniff out a story. That triggered a change in her attitude. Her friends at the charity said she became withdrawn and less engaged in their work. The events that followed suggested blackmail."

"Dawn's old friends had caught up with her?" asked Rusty.

"At least one of her old drug dealers had got back in touch, threatening to uncover sordid secrets from Dawn's past life. So when she was at her lowest ebb, she sold her body for a fix. In return for keeping quiet, Dawn had to finance the import of large quantities of Benzo Fury and Meow, Meow. There's no evidence that Dawn has used these drugs, nor was she involved in dealing. However, we consider her candidacy to be too risky to support."

"Excuse my ignorance," said Rusty, "but are these the designer drugs, those legal highs that cropped up over the last five years?"

"Yes," said Alastor, "the correct term is NPS, or new psychoactive substances, rather than legal highs. They contain one or more chemical substances which produce similar effects to illegal drugs such as cocaine, cannabis and ecstasy. These substances are not yet classified as controlled drugs, although preliminary discussions have been conducted. Often you will see them advertised as incense or plant food to get around the law. The ingredients on the packaging may not represent what the product contains."

"Even if it did," continued Minos, "there hasn't been

enough research on their potency yet. Nobody can gauge any adverse effects from human consumption, nor how they react if taken with other substances or alcohol. The internet is driving the accelerating rate of legal highs hitting the European drugs market. They trade across the dark web. The authorities are struggling to cope with the rate at which new synthetic substances emerge, and designer drugs that have contributed to deaths are escaping detection."

"I sense you're about to tell us Britain is leading the way again," said Rusty. "Only six weeks ago, you told us we led the way in cocaine use."

"Our average mortality rate due to overdose is more than twice the average for Europe," said Alastor. "The total number of new psychoactive substances available exceeds three hundred and fifty, with new products emerging daily. The open sale of so-called legal highs on the internet has increased its availability to distributors and consumers. The potency of designer drugs means small quantities of the substances can convert into multiple doses. That means small, easily transported packages of innocuous-looking powders slip through customs checks unnoticed. Once here in the UK, they convert them into thousands upon thousands of individual doses."

"The dealer who approached Dawn Prentice wasn't working alone," said Minos. "He was part of a gang operating on both sides of the Channel. As heroin usage dropped, they searched for a product to replace it. They didn't want their lucrative criminal income to falter. Dawn had to hand over the funds to import the substances; the gang's supply chain manufactured and packaged the final product. Then the distribution link in their organisation got it to the consumer."

"Why haven't these drugs been banned?" asked Phoenix.

"At the outset, they weren't even illegal," said Athena. "Many still aren't, although they often contain a banned chemical. It's complicated, and a total ban could cause difficulties. For instance, it might lead to more drug-related deaths if people drifted back to heroin."

"Whether they're legal or illegal, they are far from harmless," added Alastor, "and can have similar health risks to cocaine, ecstasy and speed."

"One imagines young people engage in this madness?" asked Henry Case.

"The majority are youngsters," said Minos. "I have personal experience, as you know, with my son Harry. I often compare the actions of teenagers consuming a cocktail of alcohol and drugs with playing catch using a live grenade instead of a ball."

"I'm sorry, Minos," said Athena, "this matter must have brought back painful memories."

"It doesn't get any easier, Athena," he replied, "but Alastor is right. One can understand why the young lady felt she needed to bury these past indiscretions. She gave that money with no intention of personal gain from the drugs it brought into the country. Yet, her elevation to an Olympian must be opposed. We were fortunate the loss of the Titans from their number was managed with such aplomb that the media didn't question their deaths. We left no clue that might lead them to our door. Dawn Prentice will have other skeletons, no doubt. They will surface in time; that is inevitable. Her potential to become Aurora is a weak link. I fear that is something Olympus cannot afford at present. The next revelation from her past might not be a drain on her bank balance. It might cause her to start using drugs again."

"Understood, Minos," said Phoenix, "better safe than sorry. Athena and I will continue to work on your report on the four candidates. You arrived at your recommendations in your usual thorough and measured manner. I doubt very much if we will disagree with your conclusions. Thank you for your efforts. Well, you know what they say, Athena, three out of four ain't bad."

"That may be, but it means Zeus must look elsewhere, and Olympus will not have the financial resources available for which he will have budgeted. We will discuss this after the meeting. I may need to warn him before our trip north to Manchester so that he can start the hunt for a replacement for Dawn Prentice."

"What else do we have on the agenda?" asked Henry Case.

"Didn't you read the copy I sent you last night, Henry?" asked Athena.

"Er, um, I must have," Henry blustered, "but I can't recall the details."

"I don't reckon you read it, Henry," grinned Rusty. "There was a date for your diary mentioned towards the bottom."

"A date?" asked Henry, now somewhat red-faced.

"We have invited Sarah Gough to christen Hope here during the late Summer Bank Holiday weekend," said Athena. "We are awaiting confirmation she can accept."

"I see," said Henry, brightening up considerably, "well, that's terrific. I shall be happy to accept an invitation should I receive one."

"Don't worry, Henry," said Phoenix, "we wouldn't leave you off the list."

"Whether Sarah came to Larcombe or not," added Rusty.

"On that happier note, we'll call it quits for today, gentlemen," said Athena. "Tomorrow is another day. We must hope for a resolution in the hunt for our elusive 'H'."

Rusty and the others left the room. Athena and Phoenix continued to look through Minos and Alastor's findings.

"Am I ultra-cautious after our experiences?" asked Phoenix. "Of the three candidates we ratify, only one fills me with confidence."

"Achilles, I presume?" asked Athena.

Phoenix nodded.

"Why the reservations on Daedalus and Ambrosia?"

"I know how difficult it can be to give something one hundred per cent concentration when there's an issue in your private life," said Phoenix. "It can lead to mistakes. His problems with Simone will need resolving before this chap St. Clair can fully commit to Olympus. As for Piya, well, I don't doubt you can handle her if she mounts a challenge for the leadership. It might be way off but just read her history. She stepped up after her father died to run their company. She took no prisoners. It wasn't only the competition that felt the icy blast as she swept them aside. She removed a whole level of management one Friday at the company's headquarters without warning. Many of the people she fired that day worked for her father from day one. That move suggests she's ruthless. Nothing stops her from getting her way."

"Are you proposing we tell Zeus not to consider her then?" asked Athena.

"Piya has many positives in her favour, without a doubt, but she could be a disruptive influence," said Phoenix, "I think we should tell Zeus to proceed with caution."

"Fair enough," said Athena, "in the end, it's his decision. I'll send him our summary of the checks for each candidate and include our concerns over Daedalus and Ambrosia. I know he will be disappointed for Aurora, but there's no way we can support her candidacy. Let's hope he has another possibility up his sleeve. Zeus is a wise old bird. He may have anticipated someone falling at the last hurdle."

"Anything else?" asked Phoenix, "or can we check if Hope is feeling better?"

"I asked Maria Elena to text me if an emergency arose," Athena admitted. "I ignored my rule on switching mobile phones off when in a meeting. I'm sorry. I've heard nothing, so the doctor will have diagnosed it as a typical twenty-four-hour bug infants pick up with frustrating regularity."

"I hope so," said Phoenix, "so, what else is on your mind?"

"When we discussed the first intake of new trainees earlier, it was obvious several of you were unhappy at the apparent slow turnaround. Rusty designed the twelve-week course, and both Kelly and Hayden tell me they support its content and duration. When I challenged the numbers, Rusty explained why he had set the limit at fifty. He has asked for your two friends in the ice-house armoury to supplement the training team. They've given excellent service since their arrival here, but Rusty believes they're too valuable to leave below ground forever."

"I agree," said Phoenix. "Bazza and Thommo are ex-SAS, the same as Rusty and hundreds of our agents. They would make excellent trainers. So, what's the problem? I sense you don't want them assigned to help with Kelly and Hayden. We could double our annual throughput."

"It's something Erebus mentioned not long before he

retired to Ibiza. Don't take this the wrong way, darling, but you aren't getting any younger. That goes for a high proportion of our agents."

"I'm not ready for the pipe and slippers just yet, Athena," complained Phoenix.

"I accept that, but Erebus made a valid point," his wife continued. "That first intake included servicemen who served in the Falklands, as Erebus did. Others fought in the first Gulf War. We have over two hundred agents at home or abroad who are now in their mid to late fifties. A lot, including you and Rusty, are in their mid-forties. We must prepare for the time when the older ones won't act on the front line. Erebus suggested I start a programme of assessment for the oldest agents. We must consider bringing them to Larcombe in batches of twelve alongside the recruits. Thomas and Longdon's new role would be to check that their performance still reached our required standard."

"The first two that fail will take their place in the icehouse, I presume?"

"We can assign two temporary armourers from the staff here on the estate. There's more to the suggestion Erebus made, I'm afraid."

"He was full of ideas, wasn't he?" said Phoenix.

"Erebus had the best interests of Olympus at heart. In that same conversation, he said how ironic it would be if our agents suffered from PTSD. The mind is such a delicate instrument. Our sleeper agents overseas have spent as much as seven years leading a double life undercover. Seven years in which their minds and bodies have been ageing. The assessment will test how sharp their bodies are, but we must assess them for other factors. We have to devise a programme that tells us whether we need to pull them out of the front line because of stress or early signs of dementia."

"Are you serious?" asked Phoenix. "The whole reason we chose these guys was because they were the best of the best."

"No one is safe from the group of diseases that affect the brain. It's not a consequence of growing old, but the risks increase with age. For example, we received a call last month from Cairo. There's a strict protocol for contacts from agents to HQ. The wife of our agent in Cairo had discovered his passwords. She worried when he hadn't returned home after attending the courtroom where over five hundred members of the Muslim Brotherhood got sentenced to death following an attack on a police station."

"How old is this agent?" asked Phoenix. "Has he been in Egypt long?"

"He's fifty-four years old and was posted to Cairo in 2008. His most active period occurred in 2011 when the revolution began. It has been a volatile country since that time. He worked for an engineering company as his cover, and until last month we had no cause for concern."

"What happened to him?" asked Phoenix.

"He turned up, confused, after two days. His wife had no clue where he had been. When we asked how she got hold of his passwords, she said he had written them on a piece of paper by the phone around Christmas time. After that, he had trouble remembering them."

"Your point a fair one, Athena," said Phoenix. "We need to initiate a programme to assess the fitness and well-being of our older agents as a matter of urgency. It's another item to bring to the attention of Zeus and the others. The problems are mounting."

"Let's get back to our apartment now, to check on

Hope, and look after her," said Athena. "Perhaps we can allow Maria Elena a brief respite. Then, after we've grabbed a bite to eat, I plan to switch off for a while. There's much to consider."

They went along the corridors to their rooms. When they entered the sitting room, Maria Elena sat in the window seat. Hope lay on the rug in the centre of the room.

Athena stopped and watched. Hope rolled over towards her favourite teddy bear.

"That's the first time I've seen her do that," cried Athena, "what a clever girl."

"How has she been?" asked Phoenix.

"She's okay now, Senor Phoenix," said Maria Elena walking to the middle of the room to meet them. "You wouldn't know she had been sick as a puppy only six hours ago."

Hope was now lying on her stomach, arching her back slightly to see who was talking. When she saw her mother and father smiling at Maria Elena's comment, she smiled broadly, revealing a tiny white tooth poking through her bottom gum.

"Another first," said Phoenix. "At least she's happier than she was in the middle of the night. I didn't see that tooth when I cleaned the sick from her face."

"Nor me," said Athena. "We'll pop into the kitchen to get our lunch, Maria Elena. Then, if you keep an eye on Hope, we'll be back to relieve you. We'll be here for the rest of the afternoon, so I'll call you if we need you again today."

Maria Elena sat by Hope and played with her. Giles was working until six o'clock. She had better enjoy her time with the little one if she had to spend her afternoon alone.

After the three family members were alone, they found

that time had flown past. It was soon time for Hope's next feed, and then she went to the nursery for her afternoon nap. Next, Phoenix and Athena turned their attention to thoughts of Manchester and the next Olympus meeting.

"If we stick to the schedule, it's over eight weeks until the meeting in July," Athena said as they snuggled together on the settee. "You said only a full-blown crisis could bring it forward. If I contact Zeus to talk about Aurora and the other issues, do you think that will sway his decision?"

"It might," said Phoenix, "but I fancy something that posed an even greater threat to the status quo is required. There's no sign of that at present, so let's hope I'm not tempting fate."

Chapter Six

Friday 25th April 2014

Giles Burke and Artemis had stayed underground in the icehouse until after eight o'clock last night. The reaction of their partners was somewhat different when they surfaced and returned to their quarters.

Maria Elena was not happy to be denied time with her partner. Meanwhile, Rusty spent time in the pool, swimming one hundred lengths, and overlooked the time.

When the two couples got to talk to one another, the discovery of the private bank dominated Rusty and Artemis's conversation. But, unfortunately, Giles was not at liberty to discuss Olympus matters with his girlfriend, so he had to set his mind to getting back in her good books.

Giles could pass the good news on to Athena, Phoenix, and the rest at the morning meeting.

"What progress have you made, Giles?" Athena asked when the meeting started.

"I concentrated on the newly formed private banks,"

said Giles, "and it wasn't difficult to find. The Glencairn Bank opened in December 2009. It's small but aggressive — the same as its owner; the link to Hannon is in the name. Glencairn Park is an open space with a children's playground that marked the birth of many friendships among the Dublin boys who later gravitated to a life of crime. The name serves as a beacon to Irish families in the criminal underworld. It tells them that here is a haven for your money-laundering, tax avoidance schemes, and investments."

"Discovering the name Hannon is now using is proving more difficult," said Artemis. "The estate agent who handled the sale of his flat was uncommunicative. They put me through to the office manager, who told me she had been with the firm for fifteen years. As I probed her for details of the Hannon sale, it became obvious that someone had bought her off. I did, however, talk to the buyer. The Saudi Arabian gentleman proved more helpful. Of course, he had no forwarding address, but he recalled a scribbled note for the cleaner he had spotted on a calendar on the kitchen wall. On one occasion, he and his wife visited the flat, checking their white goods fitted in and measuring for curtains. He told me the note had asked his cleaner not to bother coming next week, as he was away in Ireland. The note had the initials 'HH'."

"This was in 2010, I suppose?" asked Phoenix. "So, he wasted no time shedding his old skin. First, he dropped out of circulation before Christmas; then, he adopted a new name in the New Year. Does knowing the initials help regarding the bank, Giles?"

"I don't have many contacts in that world, Phoenix. I'm in the dark. These people don't mix with those outside the small world where they work. That explains why they get portrayed in the media as being so out of touch. Remember Jeremy Faversham? Massive annual bonuses, a lavish lifestyle, and he robbed his investors blind."

"Faversham paid for his crimes," said Rusty.

"There are other ways to discover who 'HH' is," said Artemis. "We've left messages on internet forums designed to draw out someone who might know who he is and have a grudge against him. We chose our wording with great care. If there's a whistle-blower, he will seize this opportunity to get his own back. The Glencairn Bank has seen rapid growth in the time it's been operating. Its owner must have stepped on plenty of people to get to his current elevated position. We could drown in replies."

"Have we identified the trigger that turned our merchant banker into a power-crazed maniac?" asked Phoenix.

"Not yet," admitted Giles, "but my money is on the forums to answer that. As Artemis suggests, anyone who suffered will use the anonymity of a forum to stick the knife in. The internet can be a force for good as well as evil. People reveal more online than in face-to-face conversations. For whatever reason, they believe nobody's listening. The amount of data we gather from sites similar to these in the ice-house is staggering."

"How long do you keep that data?" asked Henry Case.

"We filter out the vast majority of it," said Giles. "We could make a fortune blackmailing the husbands and wives who admit to affairs. However, that's not our line of business. We retain any item that features one or more of our keywords. For instance, while we dealt with the Milton Keynes terrorist cell, we searched through reams of chatter passed to them from Pakistan. When we added that data to the rest we gathered through surveillance, it gave us a clear picture of how they were planning their attack."

"I only wondered if you might have captured chatter about the meteoric rise of 'HH' without realising it," said Henry.

"Good to see you're back on the ball, Henry," smiled Phoenix. "What do you say, Giles? Is that possible?"

"It will be worth checking, that's for certain," agreed Giles.

"No time like the present," said Athena. "Artemis can return to the control centre and get things moving. You should trawl through the old material you have on file and continue fishing in new waters."

Artemis got up to leave.

"Good fishing," said Rusty, "let's hope you get an early bite."

"Promises, promises," she replied as she walked to the door.

The other items on the agenda kept Giles, and the rest occupied until lunchtime. When Athena called time on proceedings, the agents broke up for the weekend. Athena and Phoenix remained on call if something turned up in the search for the elusive banker.

In the City, their target was finishing work for the week. His thoughts were not of a few days relaxing in the Spring sunshine but of retribution. Since that phone call from Sean Walsh concerning the Old Bailey court case, he had been itching for the action to start. Walsh had found everyone with a direct connection to the case except the exact whereabouts of Maurice Kelly and his wife, Deirdre. They were in the witness protection programme.

Hugo Hanigan was not prepared to accept they couldn't find and kill them. So he ordered Sean Walsh and other gang leaders to continue hunting for them, weekend or no weekend. As Hugo left his office to return to his penthouse suite, he looked forward to the morning newspapers. In a few days, what he liked to think of as his reign of terror was due to begin.

Saturday, 26th April 2014

Artemis had worked late into the night. Giles had helped her for a while after returning from the morning meeting. Since he and Maria Elena were away for the weekend, he felt he should make up for the lost afternoon on Thursday when he had worked a double shift underground. After Giles left her toiling away alone, Artemis found a lead. Something that led her right the way to Glencairn Park and the trigger they sought.

Their ploy had worked. The anonymous messages hinted at an unscrupulous new banker who might use dubious methods to make huge profits in the futures market. The exchanges attracted interest—the name they wanted featured on message board after message board.

When she returned to her apartment, Artemis nudged Rusty awake. It was late evening, and he had nodded off in front of the television.

"Oh, you're back," he said.

"You're sharp," Artemis countered. "I've got the news."

"Let's get something to eat first," said Rusty. "I started making a meal earlier, but I took a ten-minute break when you didn't come home."

As they tucked into a ham salad, Artemis told him what she had learned.

"The forums came up with the name in no time. Hugo Hanigan is our man, although only one or two replies called him by his first name and surname alone. To a man, they referred to either Hugo Bloody Hanigan or Hugo Effing Hanigan. He's not well-liked, as you can tell."

"Just as Giles predicted," said Rusty, pouring two glasses of white wine, "but why, Hanigan?"

"I checked through Hannon's background and made a few calls," said Artemis. "His mother and father split up when he was thirteen. Ardal lived with his mother in a less well-off neighbourhood than the one the family had occupied. There was animosity between his parents over custody. His mother switched back to her maiden name, which had been Sorcha Hanigan."

"The mist is clearing," said Rusty. Artemis gave him a gentle dig in the ribs.

"Mother and son moved home several times before he finished his schooling. Sorcha was desperate to hold on to her boy. Anthony Hannon thought his son got influenced by the kids he mixed with on the streets in the rougher districts she now occupied. He wanted Ardal to move in with him, and his new wife, in their large house in the suburbs. If he had got his way, Ardal might have lived a far more worthwhile life."

"It's still very misty around Glencairn Park," said Rusty.

"I'm getting to that," said Artemis. "I worked hard on this; allow me the pleasure of showing off for a change. As I said, Sorcha relied on Anthony for everything during the marriage. As soon as the law said he could, he cut the purse strings to provide for his son. Anthony didn't want Ardal to suffer. He wanted to force Sorcha to give him up. When Ardal left Dublin to move to London, Sorcha slipped further into debt. She was too proud to ask him for financial help. He was unaware of how bad things had become. He was making his way in the City of London and doing well. Trips home became fewer and farther apart. When old friends such as Gavin McTierney called, he fell in with their plans and laundered their drug money. The ties that bound them from their days on the streets were all-powerful."

"So where's his mother now?" asked Rusty, offering to refill their glasses. Artemis shook her head.

"You can have another one if you wish. I'll finish my news, and then I'm having an early night. Athena needs to hear this first thing in the morning; Sorcha was the trigger. Ardal returned home for a weekend in September 2009. His mother wasn't home when he arrived and didn't answer her mobile. Ardal called his father, something he hadn't done in years. Anthony told him his mother had borrowed money from the wrong people. Their interest rates were unreasonable. Their punishment for non-payment would be brutal. He had no idea where Sorcha had gone. He suggested Ardal try her parents, who lived in Bangor. Ardal drove to the large town on the coast and found his mother. Once the truth was out in the open, he gave her the money she needed to get these thugs off her back. Sorcha promised never to let herself get into such trouble again. Soon, she found it impossible to manage on what little money she received in benefits. She had few qualifications, so her part-time work was menial and low-paid. The debts mounted yet again. The loan sharks soon circled the tiny flat where she lived. A dog-walker found her body bludgeoned to death in Glencairn Park in early May in 2010."

"And there we have it," said Rusty, "great work, Artemis. Hannon took his mother's maiden name, Hanigan. That ties in with the note left for the cleaner in Cricklewood. Sorcha's death was the trigger that unhinged him. Everything that's followed connects to that. It explains the bank's name; it wasn't only the connection to the children's playground and where the street kids played together. Everything is in homage to his mother. Why Hugo? Any ideas?"

"His grandfather, from Bangor. It was his middle name. When the police notified them of their only daughter's murder, Martin Hanigan suffered a heart attack and died."

Rusty drained his wine glass.

"An early night, did you say?"

"Mm. Do you think I will get a reward for doing so well?" said Artemis.

"From Athena?" Rusty replied, getting up and holding out a hand.

"No, you big ape," she said, slipping an arm around his waist, "from the man I love."

"When you said that Athena needs to hear this first thing," said Rusty. "Could we let them sleep a while longer before we disturb their Saturday morning?"

They walked into the bedroom. Events across the country meant a leisurely weekend for anyone at Larcombe was out of the question.

Hugo Hanigan was up bright and early. He wanted to see the headlines. There was no chance of this being hidden away in the middle pages or becoming a footnote to a news bulletin. His TV screen showed a reporter outside a semi-detached house in the suburbs. He turned up the volume to listen to what he had to say.

'A small barbecue grill still stands in the enclosed rear garden; drinks and snacks sit unclaimed on a side table. The plastic chairs strewn across the lawn are the only sign a party ended in bloody violence. Last night, a group of twelve friends and neighbours had gathered at this modest house in Battersea Close, Brent Cross, for a housewarming party. At eight o'clock, the party-goers moved indoors as the temperature dropped. A few stayed outside, smoking. A black van drove into the cul-de-sac and parked at the end, facing the exit. Neighbours say its headlights were blazing, the engine was running, and two hooded men got out. They walked to the side gate of number twenty-two behind me and kicked it open. The men disappeared from view. Seconds later, people heard loud bangs. At first, they thought it was fireworks. Even the guests inside the house were confused. Then people from the garden came running indoors, screaming and splattered with blood. Two more shots rang out above the chaos that followed. The neighbours watched the house's front door thrown open, and party-goers spilt out onto the street, shouting and running for their lives. The gunmen ran back to their van, jumped inside, and sped away. Those inside the house, cowering behind sofas, or hiding in the bathroom, emerged to help those who got shot. A woman of twenty-five and a man of twenty-seven received treatment from paramedics who arrived at eight-seventeen pm. Both got hit in the stomach and legs. Then they both received a single shot to the head at point-blank range. "This was an execution," a police spokesperson told me when interviewed. The reporter continued with his report. The attack came only days after the male victim, Simon Greaves, served as a juror in the Tommy O'Riordan trial at the Old Bailey. The gang leader was found guilty of the murder of a former colleague, Michael Devlin. O'Riordan is due for sentencing on Monday. Simon Greaves worked at Heathrow Airport as a baggage handler. His wife Dani was the second victim. She ran a mobile hairdressing business. While Simon and Dani were out, her parents looked after the couple's daughters, Maisie and Roxy. They had attended a housewarming party held by new arrivals to the street. A neighbour told me the family is distraught, "Simon was just doing his civic duty. This ain't right," she said. Now back to the studio.'

The newsreader thanked the reporter and wrapped up the item by saying a Metropolitan Police detective described the shooting at the barbecue as indiscriminate. Despite suggestions from eyewitnesses, they maintain the target was unclear at this stage. They assured the public that incidents such as this are infrequent. They stressed there was nothing concrete to suggest the murders were related to the court case, but enquiries continued.

Hugo laughed at the inadequate police response.

"Even when it's staring them in the face, they still can't see it," he stormed. "I ordered the attack. I chose the victims. One of them helped find my mate Tommy guilty. The wife's death was necessary to get across the message. Nobody crosses me and gets away with it. So wring your hands as much as you want, mourning the poor young things and those sweet kids with no mummy and daddy. Get used to it; this is just the beginning."

Alone in his apartment, yelling at his large-screen TV, nobody heard Hugo ranting and raving.

Around the country, people turned on their televisions or collected their newspapers, and the horrific pictures and reports from Brent Cross threatened to dominate the conversation over the coming weekend.

At Larcombe Manor, Athena and Phoenix watched as the drama unfolded. Hope was much improved, so much so that she had wanted to be up at the crack of dawn. While the couple entertained their lively daughter, Artemis and Rusty continued to sleep.

"And so, it begins," said Phoenix.

"That poor young couple and their daughters," said Athena. "How terrible."

"We need to get everyone in for a meeting," said Phoenix, heading for the shower. "I'll get washed and dressed, and then I'll start making calls."

"We haven't got Maria Elena on hand, remember," Athena called after him, "she and Giles are in Devon. So please apologise to her for the short notice. Ask Kelly if she can babysit Hope for the morning."

"Good idea," called Phoenix. "If they're serious about starting a family, she needs the practice. I hope Little Miss Lively doesn't put her and Hayden off kids for good."

Everything was in place within thirty minutes. Kelly and Hayden were now taking care of Hope, who looked at ease with being introduced to her new babysitters. Why her mother made such a big deal of it, Hope couldn't imagine. These two had been at the wedding reception. Did they think she didn't remember faces?

As soon as the call came, Rusty and Artemis realised that something significant had occurred overnight. So they got ready as fast as they could and skipped breakfast.

"We need to hear what Athena has to say first, and then I need to pass on my news," Artemis said as they hurried along the corridor from their apartment.

"My guess is it will be pertinent," said Rusty.

Henry Case bumped into Minos and Alastor on the staircase as they, too, made their way to the meeting room.

"Any ideas, chaps?" he asked.

"Brent Cross murders, at a guess," said Minos. "There's

a chance they connect to a gangland court case from last week."

"Blimey, I missed the news today," said Henry.

Phoenix and Athena hurried to the meeting room. The seven agents arrived together. Once inside, Athena took control.

"Last night, in Brent Cross, a young couple was killed. Simon Greaves sat on the jury in the Tommy O'Riordan case at the Old Bailey. O'Riordan was found guilty of murder on Wednesday; he's due in court for sentencing on Monday. The Met police won't confirm the two things are related yet, but after the killings in the week leading up to Easter, I believe 'HH' is behind this."

"Hugo Hanigan," said Artemis.

"You confirmed his identity then?" asked Athena, surprised at hearing the name.

"I worked late last night and uncovered his new name. I worked out how the Glencairn Bank got its name and identified the trigger that started this violent campaign within the gang network."

"You've been busy. Fill us in on the details," said Athena.

Artemis told them what she had discovered.

"Hanigan is the driving force behind the network, as we thought," said Phoenix. "The earlier murders were designed to send a chilling message to the gang memberships. We should anticipate his crazed mindset will expect the nation to sit up and take notice of him. He wants people to realise the stranglehold the network can exert over every aspect of life around the country. He's dangerous."

"If Hanigan ordered these murders last night, then we should act at once," said Minos. "It's unlikely they would target a single juror unless they nobbled him. Did Simon

Greaves receive payment to deliver a 'not guilty verdict, I wonder? We must check, Artemis. If not, then the other jurors are at risk."

"I agree," said Phoenix. "Artemis, contact the ice-house, please, and get someone on duty to check whether Greaves's bank account shows evidence of a large deposit. Get them to find the names and addresses of the other jurors too. The Met police might drag their heels deciding whether there's a connection, and Hanigan could have hit squads lined up waiting to take more of them out."

Artemis left the room to call one of the team on the day shift underground.

"I know the Judge who sat on this case," said Minos. "I hope he and his family aren't in any danger. Reuben Finkelman was two years behind me at Cambridge. Our paths often crossed while I was a High Court Judge, and he climbed the ladder."

"We'll send agents to give twenty-four-hour cover, Minos," said Athena, "the rule of law is sacrosanct. We may operate outside it on occasion, but only when necessary. We can't allow criminals to interfere with due process. O'Riordan must receive the sentence on Monday morning that Judge Finkelman will consider over the weekend. Hanigan must not halt that."

"I have to admit, I haven't been following this case, Minos," said Phoenix, "what have I missed?"

"O'Riordan is from the same estates in Dublin as McTierney, Hanigan, and the rest. Many Irish families moved here before, during, and after The Troubles. Not every family contained criminals. Hanigan may seek retribution on behalf of a comrade or a loved one. O'Riordan is a gang leader operating in the borough of Kilburn; his drug money passes through Hanigan's bank. One of his cronies, Michael Devlin, was a police informant; his evidence led to several low-level villains going to jail. O'Riordan believed Devlin was the lowest of the low. So he tortured and shot Devlin in a scrapyard owned by one Maurice Kelly. Kelly was the only witness available to the prosecution; his evidence was crucial in the guilty verdict. Maurice and his wife, Deirdre, appear to be in the witness protection programme. So, if that's secure, which one prays it is, they should have nothing to fear from Hanigan."

Artemis had returned to the table. The wheels were in motion.

"I think we should at least check," said Athena. "don't you?"

"I'll follow that up, Athena," said Rusty.

"Where do we go from here?" asked Henry Case.

Athena considered things for a moment.

"I propose we research whether we provide cover for the Finkelman family until the police are on the same page. We get confirmation the Brent Cross murders link to the O'Riordan case. Then, using the same logic, we guard the remaining jurors until the Met assumes responsibility. They must never learn we were ever there. Then, if Rusty confirms the witnesses are still in hiding and not in immediate danger, we turn our attention to Hanigan. We know who he is and why he's behaving as he is these days. We have yet to track him to his lair. He needs to be dealt with, and the sooner, the better."

Brave words, but were Olympus too late?

Chapter Seven

Saturday, 26th April 2014

In the capital, Hugo Hanigan watched the aftermath of the Brent Cross murders unfold. The police had swarmed over the street. They had parked incident vans, erected tents on the back lawn of number twenty-two, and dozens of officers in paper suits crawled around doing fingertip searches.

"It's a charade," he laughed, "what do they think they'll find? Buried treasure, or a weapon, spent casings, maybe incriminating fingerprints? Do me a favour; I don't employ buffoons. Anyone that naïve deserves to be in prison. It was a professional job. They would better spend their time protecting the others on my list."

Hugo phoned Sean Walsh for an update.

"Have you found Kelly yet?" he asked.

"We've had a tip-off that he went north to Newcastle. So I've got our people asking questions in the right places on the streets."

"Good," said Hugo, "the sooner we find him, the happier I'll be. Have our other teams reported in yet?"

"I should get news within the hour. One had a legal matter to sort out in the country, and the other was visiting a young lady in south London.

"Excellent," said Hugo, "call me when you receive confirmation that things went to plan."

"Keep watching the TV. You'll hear before I can get hold of you," said Walsh, with a laugh, and ended the call.

When Artemis returned to the ice-house, it didn't take long for her to confirm Simon Greaves as an honest citizen. O'Riordan's gang colleagues hadn't paid him to pervert the course of justice.

Artemis called Rusty to tell him the news.

"I thought that would be the case," he said, "you don't get many instances of jury tampering — no more than a hundred trials a year where it's attempted. Judges only order jury protection on a maximum of ten occasions a year. London courts receive close protection from the Met, but the possibility of interference increases the further you go into the countryside."

"I can't say we saw much evidence of it while I served at Portishead," said Artemis, "then again, we didn't suffer much gangland crime. Nor many cases where intimidation was a factor. From what I picked up over the years, attempts come to light after the trials have ended."

"We've started mobilising our teams to give short-term cover for the eleven remaining jurors," said Rusty. "How's the list of names and addresses coming?"

"I've just received the details, Rusty," Artemis replied, "I'll send it through straight away."

"Athena may have to add this expense to the list of things she discusses with Zeus," said Rusty. "Providing twenty-four-hour protection will be expensive. But, at least the trial is now at an end. The Met has to stump up for monitoring juries in sensitive cases for weeks, sometimes months, in long-running trials. That's on top of protecting the witnesses. Not everyone goes into witness protection like this guy Kelly."

"Although interference levels are low, it's on the increase, isn't it?" asked Artemis.

"Yeah, and no big surprise," said Rusty. "It's because of the funds available to drug traffickers and other serious criminals to thugs to carry out their dirty work. If you add recent newcomers from parts of the world where interference in the criminal justice system is commonplace, this problem will only worsen."

"The joys of the open borders policy," said Artemis. "Have you received that list?"

"Ah, yeah," said Rusty, "thanks, I'll let you get on. I'm getting together with Phoenix to liaise with our units in London. The sooner we can find these jurors, and Minos's Cambridge chum, to check they're safe, the better."

"Bye, darling," said Artemis. "I'll see you tonight."

Rusty collected the details of the people they needed to locate and protect. Then, he called Phoenix, told him he was ready, and his friend suggested they meet in ten minutes in the orangery.

"Here we go again," said Phoenix when he arrived. Rusty sat, waiting for him.

"Where do we start?" asked Rusty.

"Let's assign the jurors to our guys in London. It shouldn't take them long to put surveillance teams in place. Do any of them live outside the city boundaries?"

"Not the jurors, no," replied Rusty, "but his Lordship lives in Surrey."

"It's always dangerous to assume," said Phoenix, "but as the first victim was a juror, we'll protect those first and then get to the Judge. So where do we stand regarding the witness protection couple?"

"I was checking up on that before Artemis called with these juror details," Rusty replied. "I hadn't made much progress. Official sources are tied up tight, which is a blessing. It's a shame Giles isn't available this weekend. He's got the skills to hack into those official sources, find what we want, and get out again with nobody being any the wiser. Artemis is excellent, but she's not Giles Burke. I'll ask her if any of the others underground on this shift can access the 'dark web' with the same ease."

"If we need Giles back here, we'll call him," said Phoenix. "He can give Maria Elena one here. He needn't drive down to Devon to do it."

"Let's see how we get on with the first job," said Rusty. "As soon as we've got that in place, I'll contact Artemis."

They split up the list of jurors between them and phoned the team leaders of the agents in London. Once done, they had to wait for news their charges were at home and surveillance had begun. They ordered team leaders to intercept and eliminate anyone who looked suspicious and kept hoping for the Met police to arrive. The sooner their resources could be freed up and moved elsewhere, the better.

"While we're waiting, let's concentrate on Maurice Kelly and his wife," said Rusty.

"I suppose we should be grateful it's difficult to find where they've put them," said Phoenix, "that means it will be just as hard for Hanigan. The system aims to keep the most vulnerable court witnesses safe, but concerns exist over the level of support provided after the trial ends. Those concerns get voiced on both sides by witnesses and police chiefs. Did you know these witnesses must sign an agreement, or they don't receive full protection? They don't receive a copy of the agreement they sign either, and they're not entitled or able to seek legal advice concerning the content."

"What happens then if there's a dispute?" asked Rusty.

"The stock reply from the police is always don't worry, everything will be taken care of, but often that is not the case. The police only care about conviction. Both sides of these procedures need sorting out. When they're trying to encourage more people to come forward to give evidence against serious and organised crime, that's essential."

A phone rang on the table; it was Rusty's. He picked it up.

"Surveillance is now in place in Deptford. The juror is in his driveway, washing his car. His wife just got back from having her hair done, by the sound of it. The street is quiet for now."

"That's one guy less to worry over," said Phoenix.

As they continued discussing the shortcomings of the witness protection scheme, their phones buzzed with updates.

Jurors' names got ticked off the list, as the surveillance teams confirmed their whereabouts and were safe.

"Eight accounted for, three to find," said Phoenix as the clock ticked around to one o'clock.

"We had better call the kitchens for our usual lunchtime treat, Phoenix," said Rusty. "We're stuck here for a while. We need these last three sorted, and then we can move on to the Finkelmans and the Kelly."

"That's a great idea, Rusty," said Phoenix. "I'm starving."

Neither had eaten breakfast because they had rushed to the meeting as the Brent Cross murder was headlining,

They pored over the notes relating to the three outstanding jurors, looking for why Hanigan might have targeted them. Nothing sprang off the pages. They were ordinary, working folk who received a summons to do their civic duty. Each was as normal as the guy in Deptford, who washed his car on a sunny Saturday morning.

They were as ordinary as Simon Greaves, the airport baggage handler. Yet that poor sod had been gunned down with his wife. Hanigan was a maniac; nobody was safe. So what was holding up these last three phone calls? Did these people work at weekends? They could have taken advantage of the weather and gone away for two days.

"Are you getting worried?" Rusty asked Phoenix.

"I've done the same as you; I bet," he replied, "I've gone through a checklist of places they could be if they're not at home. It's the weekend. They could be on their way to a football or a rugby match. They could be on a golf course. Recheck the notes, and call Artemis if we're short of information. She can send their social media data to the agents involved so they have extra options to locate them. They might be on the ball, but we should have thought of this angle earlier."

"Yeah, we assumed after a stressed-out few weeks at a major trial they wanted to sit at home with their feet up relaxing," said Rusty. "It takes all sorts. People relax by throwing themselves off tall buildings with just a piece of cloth the size of a duster to keep them safe until they land on terra firma."

"Yeah, it takes all sorts," said Phoenix.

Rusty called Artemis.

"We may need more data than we asked for on these jurors, Artemis," he said. "Can you dig through their online profiles to see what they might be up to this weekend? Their teams haven't reported in yet, so they must be having trouble tracking them."

"No problem, Rusty," she replied. "Tell me which teams I need to update, and I'll send the information through as soon as I get it. It will save you from relaying it to them. I'll bring a copy over to the house later."

"Thanks. We're in the orangery," Rusty told her, "waiting for lunch to be delivered."

"Coffee and bacon rolls, no doubt?" she groaned, "they'll be gone before I can get there. See you later."

Rusty ended the call. It rang again at once.

It was the lead agent on the team assigned to Ruislip in West London. Peter Downs, forty-six years old, worked for Lloyds Bank in the town. There was no sign of him at his home address. They had tried his place of work, but he wasn't on duty this Saturday.

"You should receive a message from our people in a short while," said Rusty, "we're analysing this guy's social media accounts. It may give us a lead on where he's gone."

Rusty listened to the team leader's reply.

"Okay, keep searching, and if you get any more tips, let us know."

Rusty ended the call and gave a big sigh.

"A nosy neighbour came out to see why our guys were outside her house. So much for being careful. She reckoned Peter Downs hadn't been home since late last night. Downs lives alone. He drinks with work colleagues on Friday nights and then picks up a curry. The neighbour saw him go indoors at half-past nine. At midnight, she lay in bed, reading, and a vehicle's headlights swept across her bedroom window. She didn't leave the bed to look, but she heard noises and what sounded like a scuffle. She put her light out and dropped off to sleep. Nothing disturbed her after that."

"Damn," said Phoenix, "it sounds like someone could have lifted him."

A phone rang. It was Phoenix's turn to answer.

"What have you got for us?" he asked.

Rusty watched as Phoenix closed his eyes. It was not good news. The door behind him opened, and their lunch had arrived. A steward brought it over and laid the tray on the table.

"Sorry to interrupt, sir," he said, "but there's a ton of trouble in London. It's breaking news. They're running a special bulletin. You might need to return to the main house where you can watch the TV."

"Any idea where the boss is?" he asked.

"She was in the gardens with Miss Hope and the new training officer, Kelly Dixon, when I delivered this tray. They were sitting on the patio, enjoying the sunshine."

Phoenix had finished his conversation.

"Grab everything, and let's get back," he said to Rusty. He pointed to the tray. "I know you've carried it over here, but can you follow on behind us? We'll be in the meeting room upstairs, and we're still starving."

The steward nodded.

Rusty and Phoenix hurried across the lawns towards the Manor. They could see Athena in the distance. When she spotted them, she jumped up, said something to Kelly and ran to meet them.

"What's happened?" she said.

"We've got two jurors confirmed as missing," said Phoenix. "One team still has to report back. We need to get in front of the TV screen, pronto."

"Where did your team report in from just now," asked Rusty.

"Lewisham," said Phoenix, "a young girl from the jury. Melissa Sanders, twenty-five, went out to a nightclub with a party of friends and never made it home. Her family reported it to the police. Our team are staying nearby to monitor the situation. We have three jurors involved in incidents now, maybe four. How long will it take for the police to join up the dots?"

"Have you had any contact with the team that hasn't reported in?" asked Athena.

Rusty checked his phone.

"Still nothing, Athena. They're in Bromley, looking for Grenville Benjamin, the thirty-seven-year-old dentist. He's married to David Spears, same age, who owns a flower shop on the High Street in town."

"Call the team again," she said. "I need to know what they're doing. A dentist should be at home at the weekend, even if his husband might be working. Who knows? Benjamin could help in the shop on a Saturday if they've got weddings and parties to supply. Let's find out, shall we?"

They had arrived at the meeting room. The steward was leaving.

"I've turned the TV on for you, ma'am," he said, "and brought the lunch tray across for the gentlemen. Shall I fetch extra coffee and sandwiches from the kitchen?"

"That would be great, thanks," Athena said. She turned to watch the news unfolding on the screen.

"I can't reach them, Athena," said a concerned Rusty. "It's gone straight to voicemail."

Phoenix picked up his phone and dialled without taking his eyes from the TV screen.

"I know you're keeping watch on your assigned juror, but we need someone to get across to Bromley to find out what's happened to our team. You're the closest, a twenty-minute drive away. Call me the second you locate them."

"Was that the nearest team?" asked Athena.

"Croydon," Phoenix nodded. "Their little old lady juror has walked the dog and is now watching the racing on TV. We can relax the surveillance and get a new guy to keep watch. The team leader will make the call, disturb someone's afternoon, and then drive to Bromley. The old lady will be okay on her own for half an hour."

"This doesn't feel right, Phoenix," said Athena, watching the TV screen. "I'm getting anxious."

"That's the special bulletin over then," said Rusty as the programme ended and the regular afternoon schedule resumed. "We need to switch to the 24-hour news channel. It will be on a loop, but at least we can get up to date."

Rusty flicked to the rolling news, and they caught the start of the report on the fate of Peter Downs. They listened in silence to the stern-faced male newsreader: -

A vicious gang kidnapped Mr Downs from his home in Ruislip late last night. They drove to the Colne Valley Regional Park. There he appears to have been tortured and killed. Joggers discovered his body this morning, lying half in and half out of the water. The forty-six-year-old bank employee had been shot several times in the knees and finished execution-style with a single shot to the back of the head. DCI Geoff Titmus, who is leading the inquiry, spoke to our reporter at the scene: -

"This gang must be caught because they've used extreme violence and are dangerous, vicious people. They forced their way into Mr Downs's property at midnight, bundled him into a vehicle, and tortured him for six hours. Our preliminary 'time of death' is eight o'clock this morning. Two members of the public discovered the body at a quarter past nine while out running. We're tracking the movements on CCTV of a black or dark blue van that travelled between the town and the country park just after midnight. We are keen to talk to anyone who noticed any vehicles in Ruislip similar to the one I described. That was either earlier on Friday evening or when they returned home early on Saturday morning. Several men were involved in the attack. We believe the gang targeted this victim; it was not a random assault. We do not have a motive currently, but there are possible links to another ongoing investigation."

Neighbours of Mr Downs told our reporter he had just completed a spell of jury duty at the Central Criminal Court, the Old Bailey. He hadn't spoken of his experience except to say he was glad it had ended. The ongoing investigation DCI Titmus referred to is the slaughter yesterday evening of Simon and Dani Greaves at a barbecue in Brent Cross. That was a strong hint that jurors who deliberated that case, finding the gang leader guilty of murder, are being targeted and murdered. We await confirmation from the Metropolitan police that a link exists between the two incidents.

Athena muted the sound on the television as the programme moved on to the weather and sport.

"I feel helpless sat here," she said, "we need to be taking action, yet I'm at a loss to know where to start."

"We're off the pace, Athena," said Rusty. "Hanigan has selected his targets. Although we now have teams covering most of the jurors, the fact that two are dead and one missing means we're too late. Somehow we need to anticipate his next move and get in front of him."

"Where does Reuben Finkelman live?" asked Phoenix, "and perhaps, more important, what is he doing this weekend?"

"He lives near Beaconsfield, in south Buckinghamshire," said Rusty, checking notes he had received from Artemis. "The family have a six-bedroom detached house in Forty Green, valued at around four and a half million. As for where he's spending the weekend, I'll get Artemis to check."

"Do that, Rusty," said Athena. "I'm calling Zeus right away. We need to hold an emergency meeting early next week. That full-blown crisis we discussed has arrived. We can't sit on our hands any longer."

Rusty called Artemis in the ice-house.

Phoenix called Giles Burke in Devon to order him back to Larcombe Manor. There could be no quiet weekend for any of them. Giles had seen the news reports and promised to be back on duty in two hours.

"Tell Artemis that Giles will be with her by four this afternoon," Phoenix called to Rusty.

"OK. The Finkelmans flew to their Jersey home after the trial," said Rusty. "Four family members travelled from Denham Aerodrome by chartered helicopter. Reuben, his wife Miriam, and their twin daughters Ruth and Rachel. Their flight schedule shows they are returning to Denham early on Sunday evening. They have a regular reservation for dinner at the Beech House restaurant in Beaconsfield. The Judge will drive into London for O'Riordan's sentencing hearing at the Old Bailey in the morning. Artemis has confirmed that nothing has happened to the family on the outbound flight or since they have been at their holiday home in St Ouen."

"Rusty and I will get a team to Denham to meet the helicopter," said Phoenix. "We'll make sure the Judge gets home safe and sound, enjoys his evening meal, and gets a good night's sleep in his bed. Then, we'll escort the car that picks him up on its journey into the capital in the morning."

Rusty nodded at the screen behind Athena. She was concluding her telephone conversation with Zeus.

"Something new has hit the fan," he said.

It was Melissa Sanders, the third missing juror. A reporter stood outside her Lewisham home. Athena turned up the volume. A different reporter this time, but a similar depressing report: -

Melissa Sanders enjoyed a fun-packed Friday night in several cocktail bars and nightclubs in Lewisham. When she decided to return to the home she shared with her parents at around two o'clock, she left her friends and walked to a nearby taxi rank. The police have viewed CCTV images from the town centre, and Melissa was spotted still waiting for a taxi at ten past two. Several people in the neighbourhood may have seen her. The police are keen to speak with them. The nightclub's own CCTV showed two men of Middle-Eastern origin leaving thirty seconds after Melissa Sanders. At fifteen minutes past two, Melissa was no longer standing by the taxi rank. There's no evidence to suggest she was picked up by a registered cab. At some point in those five minutes, Melissa disappeared. Whether these two unidentified men were involved in her disappearance is uncertain. The police are due to issue e-fit photographs of the men they wish to interview later today. For the time being, Melissa's parents and the rest of her family and friends can only hope and pray for her safe return. DCI Geoff Titmus, who is heading the investigation into the brutal murder of Peter Downs in Ruislip, was unavailable for comment. We wished to ask him whether Melissa Sanders is the third juror in the Thomas O'Riordan murder trial to have been abducted. The nation's capital is waiting for an answer.

"They haven't heard the news concerning Grenville Benjamin yet," said Athena.

"When do we meet Zeus and the others?" asked Phoenix.

"I'll be in London on Tuesday at our usual venue," said Athena. "Whether you join me will depend on how long it takes to find the missing jurors, protect the Judge, and guard Maurice Kelly and his wife. Hanigan can find these people at will. He has terrific resources at his disposal."

"In the past, criminal gangs were parochial and competed against one another within city boundaries," Phoenix replied. "What happened in other parts of the country rarely concerned them. Hanigan is a different breed of criminal. He is intelligent, ruthless, and able to work with different nationalities within organised crime. Their intelligence network is impressive and may even be more extensive than our own in some instances."

There was a knock at the door; the steward had returned with fresh coffee and several plates of sandwiches. A mobile phone rang as he left.

Phoenix picked up his phone from the table, looked at the screen, and paused before answering, "It's our Croydon team calling from Bromley."

"What did you find out?" he asked the team leader.

Athena and Rusty poured cups of coffee while they watched Phoenix listening to the team leader's report. He sat stone-faced, staring at the wall in front of him. Finally, he placed the phone on the table.

"Our Croydon team arrived at the home Grenville

Benjamin and David Spears shared. The street was quiet; there was no sign of movement at the property. They checked with the flower shop and learned Mr Spears had finished work today at one o'clock. He had received an urgent call from Mr Benjamin, asking him to return home as soon as possible. The car our surveillance team had driven had been parked fifty yards up the street from the house; it was empty. The passenger side door window had been smashed; there was no sign of the agents. The team leader decided to enter the property. They found four bodies in the lounge, bound and gagged with their throats cut."

"Oh no," said Athena, "what a nightmare."

"Hell," said Phoenix, "we need to act fast. Hanigan is clever. If he, or his hired killers, call the police, they will discover the dead juror and his husband, plus two bodies that don't belong. We must protect Olympus, whatever it costs. The police mustn't prove a link between the two foreign bodies and Larcombe Manor. We have only one choice; I'm calling the Croydon team to instruct them to remove our men and set fire to the lounge. With luck, we can burn the house to the ground. The remains of two men in the ashes will confirm the death of yet another juror and his husband. We may get away with it if we act at once and leave no clues."

Athena nodded. She was thinking of the dead agents; they had to notify their families. Next, she needed to arrange a visit from one of the Olympians. Then, two more agents to replace. If Hanigan and his collection of thugs continued unchallenged for much longer, there was no telling how much bloodshed there might be. These were testing days, indeed. She recalled the phrase Henry had quoted on Thursday, something wicked this way comes. She shivered at the thought.

"The wheels are set in motion, Athena," said Phoenix after completing yet another call, "we'll remove the bodies and set the fire. They'll take the car back to base with them. We must pray the police aren't on their way. We can only wait and hope."

Chapter Eight

A few minutes before four o'clock in the afternoon, Giles Burke entered the control centre in the ice-house. Artemis had been on duty since her lie-in with Rusty was interrupted by the summons from Athena.

"I'm sorry, yet another Saturday is in ruins," smiled Artemis. "Events in London have caught us unawares."

Giles shrugged.

"Maria Elena struggles to understand. She appreciates that the Project is important, but we have never told her the full story. So far, she's so engrossed in looking after Hope that she hasn't questioned what she knows about the charity. We'll get through it, don't worry. This relationship is strong enough to survive the odd crisis. At least, I hope so."

"Rusty and I are comfortable with things, too," Artemis replied. "He had to be one hundred per cent sure I was committed to us being together before he uncovered the truth concerning Larcombe Manor. That was an interesting evening. I can tell you."

Artemis updated Giles on the events that had unfolded

since last evening. He had seen various news reports and connected the dots to Wednesday's trial verdict.

"What does Athena want me to work on first?" Giles asked.

"Find out where Maurice Kelly, and his wife, Dierdre, were moved to in the witness protection scheme. We have to get to them before Hanigan and his hired assassins. We need your hacking skills this afternoon, Giles, and your superior knowledge of the dark web."

"Right," said Giles, "time to get my hands dirty."

He went to his workstation, fired up his computer, and started work.

In a flat in Lewisham, Melissa Sanders awoke. At first, she wondered where she was. The room was unfamiliar. Her watch showed five o'clock, and the date told her it was Saturday. Then, as her head cleared, the horror of what had happened over the past fifteen hours came flooding back.

Melissa remembered leaving the club to get a taxi home. She had been alone, with no sign of a taxi, and she had started to get anxious. A man Melissa had seen in the nightclub had approached her. She thought his accent was Turkish, but she couldn't be sure. He asked Melissa if she needed a ride home. She had moved away from him, saying she was waiting for a taxi. The man continued to annoy her, telling her his friend was picking him up and dropping her off at home would be no trouble. What happened next was a blur. Melissa wasn't sure whether she was drugged, but a car pulled up at the kerb, and they bundled her into the back. A man got in beside her, and his colleague drove them to a house in a part of the borough she had never visited. There were pleasant parts of the area where she had lived all her life, but places better avoided too. This flat was in one of the rougher parts of town.

The details of the first hour of her ordeal were simpler to remember. What came next was something Melissa wanted to push to the farthest corners of her mind. Somewhere from which it could never escape. Once they got into the flat, rough hands grabbed her, and the men stripped her of her clothing. Melissa resisted as long as she could. She had then been punched and kicked. She was semi-conscious when the first man raped her. As she fought back again after he withdrew from her, he had then pinned her arms to the bed while his colleague took his turn. They spoke in a foreign language. Melissa had feared for her life.

They left her on the bed, curled up in a ball. She had been in pain and crying. The men sat laughing and drinking on the floor beside her. They had continued to take turns raping her until morning. Then, finally, the driver of the car fell asleep. The other man had tied her hands to the bedstead and continued drinking until he passed out. She had struggled with her bonds, but it was no use. Melissa couldn't remember when she had fallen asleep, but it was now five o'clock, and she was alone.

Melissa worked away at the ties that secured her. Her arms felt tired, her body ached, and they had cut her lips and eyes when they hit her last night. It was six o'clock when her efforts paid off. She freed herself, gathered her torn clothing from the floor, and dressed. A mirror on the dressing table told her she looked a mess.

She listened by the bedroom door to hear if the men were in the flat. Then, she crept to the window to see if she recognised their car in the street. If it wasn't there, maybe they had abandoned her, and she could creep downstairs and find her way home.

Melissa opened the door. Facing her was one of her attackers. He held a gun and pointed it straight at her head.

"Thanks for last night," he smirked, "but my boss doesn't want you to see tomorrow."

Melissa realised her nightmare was over. She slipped to the floor. The last thing Melissa saw was a bright orange cushion pressed to her face. She didn't hear the gunshot that ended her life.

In Bromley, a fire crew still worked at the scene of the blaze they had attended at the home of a local dentist. Members of the Metropolitan police had just arrived.

"What do we have here then, gents?" asked DCI Geoff Titmus.

"We received an emergency call from a neighbour at three this afternoon. They had seen flames up to the ceiling in the lounge. There was a lot of smoke, too, by the time we arrived. We got delayed by traffic. The fire destroyed the lounge. There's considerable smoke damage to the rest of the ground floor. The first floor, loft space, and roof escaped relatively unscathed."

"Why am I here, then?" asked the senior policeman.

"Unless my twenty-eight years fighting fires in London counts for nothing, we have what's left of two dead bodies in the burnt-out lounge," said the fire chief. "You can check for yourself. You'll do well to hang on to your lunch, though. It smells crispy in there."

"Not another one," groaned Geoff Titmus. "We were alerted by our control centre that the address of your fire was familiar to us. This home belonged to one of the jurors in the O'Riordan trial, Grenville Benjamin. They butchered him, the same as Simon Greaves and Peter Downs. That's five deaths in total inside the past eighteen hours; three were members of the same jury. There's another one missing too. She is a young girl, but she could have pulled a bloke. She'll creep home in an hour or two if we're lucky."

"I don't envy you," said the fire chief.

"Yeah," said Geoff. "Saturday afternoons are not just writing out speeding tickets and keeping sets of football supporters from tearing each other's throats out."

"We'll stay here for an hour or two," the fire chief added. "Your people will be able to get inside the building tomorrow morning to carry out the forensics you'll need."

"There was me thinking I might go to church," grumbled Geoff, "it looks as if I'll be working."

Sunday, 27th April 2014

Phoenix and Rusty were up early. They were en route to Beaconsfield later to check out the Finkelmans' home in Forty Green. They didn't want to escort the family from the nearby airfield this evening, only to watch them blown to smithereens as soon as they walked through the door.

There were plans to make and details to discuss. Phoenix always enjoyed this part of any mission. Before they concentrated on the Judge, however, there was another matter that they needed to consider.

"Yesterday afternoon in Bromley made this personal," said a grim-faced Rusty. "Even if we can't strike at Hanigan, for now, I need to find the bastards who murdered our boys."

Phoenix nodded.

"Giles is combing through every CCTV feed within a five-mile radius of the dentist's house. I called him before I walked across to meet with you. I disturbed Hayden Vincent too. I don't see why we should be the only buggers up this early."

"Our procedures on surveillance need immediate revision," agreed Rusty. "A nosy neighbour in Ruislip spotted one team, and the Bromley killers clearly identified the other. They also crept up unseen to break into their car and capture our agents. It was sloppy. We're short-handed; we can't afford to lose people without firing a shot in anger."

"Whoever killed our men in Bromley will pay," said Phoenix. "You can take that to the bank."

"Did Giles make progress yesterday evening on hacking into the witness protection programme," asked Rusty.

Phoenix smiled.

"What do you think? He's almost there, from what he said this morning. The Crown Prosecution Service doesn't have robust enough firewalls to keep Giles at bay. Money is tight in these times of austerity. The CPS has cut over half the staff it employs to look after witnesses. Only around forty Witness Care Units now remain in England and Wales. The police were supposed to take on greater responsibility for support, but their numbers had reduced by twenty per cent. Their system isn't wide open, but the framework gets weaker with each round of cuts."

"So, we might have an address by the time we've wrapped up our babysitting duties later?" said Rusty.

"We live in hope," said Phoenix. "Although, don't count on us going to cover Maurice Kelly and his wife. I want to persuade Athena to let us catch up with the killers of our friends from Bromley."

"Amen to that," said Rusty.

"The more I read of this CPS shambles, the more frustrated I get," said Phoenix. "Victims' rights are at the heart of the modern criminal justice system. With the current voluntary setup, that will never happen. On top of what I said earlier, the CPS's legal teams have seen their numbers cut by a third. As a result, the number of occasions where they keep key evidence from the defence teams has shown a dramatic rise. So trials are jeopardised. Criminals often walk free to offend again."

"Two steps forward and three steps back," said Rusty. "That's progress in this modern world for you."

For the next thirty minutes, the two friends made plans for Judge Finkelman's safekeeping. From the second his helicopter touched the tarmac at Denham to watching him take his place in the courtroom at the Old Bailey.

Both of their mobile phones rang.

It was Athena. She summoned them to the meeting room.

"Hoping for good news, but steeling myself for another tragedy," said Phoenix.

He and Rusty trotted back to the main building. They caught up with Henry, Giles and Artemis, who had just returned to the surface.

"Any clues why Athena called this meeting?" asked Rusty.

"Another body," said Artemis.

Minos and Alastor sat with Athena when they reached the room. The TV was on, and as they took their seats, a reporter was speaking: -

The body of a young woman got dumped by the side of the A21 on the outskirts of Bromley. She had been severely beaten and shot in the head. DCI Geoff Titmus, the officer in charge of the investigations into the deaths of jurors from the Thomas O'Riordan case, has just issued this statement from outside New Scotland Yard,

"Melissa Sanders has become the fourth juror from last week's murder trial to be killed since Friday night. Six people have died in total in the most brutal attack on the criminal justice system in living memory. The remaining members of the jury and their families are now under the protection of the Metropolitan police. We will hunt these killers with all the resources we have available. In the past hour, we took eighteen members of the O'Riordan gang into custody for questioning. We ask the public to co-operate with us in finding and arresting the groups of men responsible for these killings. At this time, we believe separate teams of two or three men were responsible for each murder. My team will be reinforced from today by the team led by DI Jonathan Barclay from Kilburn. DI Barclay arrested Tommy O'Riordan in Marbella. His team brings detailed knowledge of gang structures within the local community from which these hit squads will have come. The message I send to those criminals is that we will find you. You will face justice. There's no hiding place for people who commit crimes as heinous as these. Thank you."

There will be further reports throughout the day, the reporter continued. I have just received a message. The Home Secretary and the Prime Minister are due to issue statements within the hour.

Athena turned off the television.

"That poor girl," she said, "we couldn't protect her."

"Let's concentrate on what we have learned from that report," said Phoenix. He was acutely conscious of his wife's emotional state. Athena may be in charge at Larcombe Manor, but she was also a woman and a new mother. Phoenix knew she would soon rediscover the resolve that first attracted him to her. She was vulnerable for the moment. He had to step into the breach and spearhead the fightback against Hanigan and his network of thugs.

"The police have realised the deaths were linked to the murder trial and have assumed responsibility for protecting the remaining jurors. We can order our teams to stand down. They can transfer to other duties. Rusty and I will leave soon to inspect the Judge's home and start getting him and his family home safely. The police don't appear to think the Judge is in danger, nor is the only person to give evidence against O'Riordan. We must find where the latter is and get teams to protect him, whatever the cost. Giles, and Artemis, we're relying on you."

"The police could be loath to show their hand," said Henry Case. "They may have protection details but don't wish to reveal that to the criminals. The deaths this weekend will have alarmed the public. Every murder in these boroughs leaves the police facing a wall of silence. Even when cases reach court, witnesses are often too terrified to speak. It won't help matters. Jury service is never popular; many try to avoid it. After this weekend, the vast majority will wonder whether they're risking their lives by answering the call to do their civic duty."

Athena wiped a tear from her eye. She was ready now to continue.

"I have requested an emergency meeting with Zeus to discuss this crisis. I shall go to London on Tuesday. It's hoped that as many Olympians as possible will attend at such short notice. We must present a united front against Hugo Hanigan and this gang network. They have murdered two of our people. We must take direct action."

"Will this be the only item on the agenda?" asked Minos.

"I intend to give him your report on the four candidates, Minos, and our thoughts on how we might increase the numbers of our home-based agents. We have a desperate need for more personnel."

Phoenix outlined the approach he and Rusty had discussed: -

"The second Giles and Artemis discover the whereabouts of Maurice and Dierdre Kelly; we will send teams to supplement their protection. The police have re-housed them somewhere in the UK, but their resources are stretched to the limit. If a similar assault gets carried out, then they will be overwhelmed. The orders to our teams will be to eliminate any hit squad, regardless of the potential risk of a trail leading back to Larcombe. The authorities need success. If they add Reuben Finkelman and Maurice Kelly to the list of those killed, the rule of law could fracture. One big push by Hanigan could see it demolished. Every criminal in the country would think they were free to commit any crime they wished. Nobody would speak out against them, no juror would be safe from their reach, and money might even secure a High Court Judge's murder, if necessary. The possibility of that horrific scenario ends here. Is that clear?"

"Crystal," said Rusty. "Phoenix, will we be travelling alone today?"

"With Athena's permission, I want to ask Kelly Dexter and Hayden Vincent to come with us," said Phoenix. "They've got stacks of experience in the field. Tonight is our first opportunity to achieve that first success we need. If one of Hanigan's teams strike between Denham and Beaconsfield, or from there to the Old Bailey, we need to be ready."

"Kelly and Hayden have offered to help in any way they can, Phoenix," said Athena. "They aim to step away from the front line, which is why they became our lead trainers, but this weekend has affected everyone. Hayden served in Afghanistan with an agent murdered in Bromley. He wants an opportunity for revenge."

"Thank you, Athena," said Phoenix. "We'll pick them up on our way to the ice-house. Then, as soon as we're tooled up for the trip, we'll get to Beaconsfield. We should be there in two hours with less traffic on a Sunday afternoon."

"I think that's it for now," said Athena, "Giles, good hunting this afternoon. Contact me the minute you find our witness. I'll see most of you in the morning. Phoenix, could we can talk before you leave?"

"Sure," said Phoenix. "We'll go to see Bazza and Thommo first to collect the guns, ammunition, and equipment we need. Then I'll come to the apartment to say goodbye to you and Hope."

The room emptied, and Athena sat alone with her thoughts. Phoenix and Rusty were going into danger yet again. Every time he left her, it seemed the risks grew worse than ever. Hanigan was the most significant threat Olympus had to face. If only Erebus were still here to advise her on what she should do. Athena turned on the television. There was still no good news.

The latest news report on Melissa Sanders was uncomfortable to hear: -

Miss Sanders suffered severe internal injuries. She was covered from head to toe in bruises and had two fractured ribs. The police say she sustained a prolonged degrading attack by two men. They have issued e-fits of the men they wish to interview. They created them from the CCTV images captured inside the nightclub Melissa visited in Lewisham town centre on Friday night and nearby, where she waited for a taxi. This is from DI Barclay with the investigating team: -

"These e-fits are a good likeness of the two men. They are of Turkish or Turkish Cypriot origin. They are in their mid-thirties, both around six feet in height and of muscular build. We urge anyone with information on this attack to contact Crimestoppers on the number on the screen."

Athena had heard and seen enough; she walked back to the apartment. Maria Elena sat in the window seat, reading.

"Hope has just gone to bed for her afternoon nap," she said, standing up and walking to the middle of the room. "Is everything alright?"

"No, Maria Elena, it's far from alright," sighed Athena. "But, if we can get through today and tomorrow unscathed, then perhaps we can turn the corner."

"Shall I stay?" the nanny asked.

"You can have an hour or two to yourself," Athena replied, "I'll see you this evening at six o'clock."

Maria Elena left the room. Athena remembered that Giles was hunting for Maurice Kelly's new address in the ice-house.

"Ah well, she'll soon find out for herself," she thought. "It can't be helped."

Athena walked to the nursery and, making as little noise as possible, turned the door handle. She stood in the doorway and watched her daughter's chest as it rose and fell in innocent slumber.

Phoenix found her there twenty minutes later.

"We're ready," he whispered.

Athena and Phoenix walked back into the lounge, and she clung to him.

"Don't worry," he said. "Rusty and the others will be with me. I'll be home by lunchtime tomorrow."

"I can't lose you," she said, her head lying against his shoulder. He could feel the dampness of her tears seeping through his shirt.

"I know," Phoenix replied.

They kissed and held one another tight for several minutes.

"Good hunting," whispered Athena.

"I'll see you tomorrow," said Phoenix, "give Hope a kiss from me when she wakes."

With that, he left the room and hurried to the front door. Two vans from the transport section were waiting outside, their engines idling. Have waved to Kelly and Hayden and then jumped into the passenger seat of the lead vehicle.

"Drive," he said to Rusty.

Hugo Hanigan checked his mobile phone for the sixth time. There was still no call from Sean Walsh. He must have been among the people picked up by the police earlier today. The fools were wasting their time.

The jurors he had planned to target were dead. The other deaths had been collateral damage. Hugo couldn't fathom why the police hadn't announced that two plain-clothes police officers had died in the Bromley house fire. That puzzled him. Why else would two armed men sit in a car fifty yards from a juror's home?

As for Sean Walsh and whoever else they had grabbed in their frantic attempts to show they were pro-active, they would get nothing from them. Nobody would dare to talk. Not if they valued their lives and those of their families.

Hugo looked at his watch. It was three in the afternoon. The chartered helicopter ferrying the Finkelman family back from Jersey would take off at five o'clock. It was due to land at Denham Aerodrome around six.

A team stood by to intercept the family when they appeared in the doorway with their hand luggage. No one on board was to be left alive. An incendiary device would destroy the helicopter and leave a lasting memory in the minds of every person in the UK.

Hugo smiled at the thought.

Then he considered his next move. The Newcastle address was still unknown to him. Sean had been so close to discovering it. Now he had to wait for the police to release him. They had no reason to keep him for long. If they were stubborn enough to refuse to accept 'No comment' as a genuine response, he might need to devise an audacious plan to release Walsh and senior gang members the Met had arrested.

Hugo rechecked his phone, this time for a number for Colleen O'Riordan, Sean's sister. He thought she might know who the police had grabbed, but better still, she might be able to put him in touch with Sean's contact in Newcastle. They needed to find Kelly. Another couple of deaths before the Old Bailey opened for business in the morning. That would be the icing on the cake.

The country would be on its knees before he had finished.

They would show him respect then.

Chapter Nine

Sunday, 27th April 2014

Rusty made good progress as he drove through scattered showers along the M4 and left the motorway at Junction seven. As he had thought, traffic was light. They reached Forty Green, two miles outside Beaconsfield, at a quarter to five. Kelly Dexter parked behind him thirty seconds later.

"Right," said Phoenix, "we passed the Judge's house four hundred yards back. I saw no signs of anyone loitering. I'll walk back alone to make sure the coast is clear. I'll call you if we've got company. Just give Kelly and Hayden a heads-up to stay in the van for now."

"OK, Phoenix," replied Rusty.

Phoenix strolled along the road to the fine-looking Finkelman property. He wore a white hard hat and a hi-viz jacket and carried a clipboard. Any cover to explain why he wandered around on a Sunday afternoon was better than none. Although these large, detached houses offered seclusion and stood well back from the road, there were always nosy people around.

Phoenix reached the driveway to the house. He checked again in both directions, but nobody was in sight. He walked quicker now and skirted around the side of the building. Phoenix peered inside the double garage. Phoenix looked for telltale signs someone had been here since Friday when the Judge and his family had left for Denham Aerodrome. There were none that he could see. A final check outside the house satisfied Phoenix that everything was well. No nasty surprises awaited the Finkelmans when they returned home.

Phoenix returned to the van.

"No worries," he said, "let's get to the airfield. We must recce the approach roads and the airfield before that chopper lands."

"We'll be there in twenty minutes, give or take," said Rusty, driving towards the M40. The closer the two vans got to Denham, the wetter the roads became. It was a passing shower that showed no sign of being in a hurry to blow away.

Although that made visibility a problem, it kept dog-walkers and other pedestrians indoors for the time being. After that, spotting vehicles or people on foot who posed a threat would be less complicated. Every little helped.

Phoenix called Hayden and told him to get Kelly to park the van and await further orders. Rusty and Phoenix drove past the entrance to the airfield and looked for any signs of unwanted visitors.

"Not that my knowledge of small airfields is that great," said Rusty, "but it's quiet. A light plane is lining up to come into land. I see two men near the main building on the tarmac, who might be ground crew judging by their uniforms. They're sheltering from the rain for the moment, not taking much notice of the plane. I can't see anybody in the tower from here. How many people did your research tell us there might be here today?"

Phoenix sighed.

"This is a busy little place during the week. At weekends, it varies. I hope it's the quietest it gets all week at six on a Sunday evening."

Phoenix kept looking around for danger signs and continued reading from his notes.

"This airfield lies on a well-drained gravel plateau and is easily accessible from Central London. They store and maintain one of the Helicopter Emergency Service helicopters here."

"Bloody good job they do, don't they?" said Rusty.

"Too right," replied Phoenix, "they might be busy later. As for the tower, a duty officer supervises flying operations, so he's up there somewhere, even if you can't see him. There is no full Air Traffic Control service, but he provides pilots with flight information, weather forecasts and the rest. The airfield is in close contact with customs, border control, and the police."

"Terrific; we can expect company if we have to engage with the enemy," muttered Rusty.

"There are only two entry points we need to watch," Phoenix continued. "The one we used and one on the far side. There are loads of hangars on the north side of the airfield. Those have several businesses running out of them. Flying schools that offer pilot training and aircraft hire firms for fixed and rotary-wing aircraft and companies providing maintenance. Monday to Friday, this place must be buzzing."

"Ten to six," said Rusty, checking the clock on the dashboard. He was happy that it was Sunday and civilian casualties would be minimal.

"The rain has stopped," said Phoenix. "We'll get a good view of any vehicles approaching from the other side. We'll make our move as soon as we see the helicopter approaching. I see one of your ground crew guys walking over to that row of parked cars to the right of the main building. I guess he's got a spare set of the Judge's keys. There he goes. Straight to the brand-new Mercedes. That car will be waiting for them as soon as they reach the bottom of the steps. No doubt they pay well for the door-to-door service."

"I think I can make out a chopper through the clouds," said Rusty, "it's showtime."

"When they land, it will only take two minutes before they're in the car," said Phoenix. "Call Kelly, and tell her to turn the van around and stay in position until she sees the Mercedes approaching. Then, she should move in front of it, and we'll cover the front and back door as we escort them home."

The dark shape of a helicopter loomed over the landing area. Rusty and Phoenix were mesmerised for a few seconds by the flailing rotor blades. The noise was deafening. The helicopter hovered, descended, and with two gentle bounces, stood stationary on the tarmac.

"There!" shouted Rusty, slamming the van into gear and gunning for the gateway. Phoenix rang Kelly in a frantic call to get her and Hayden to provide support.

A beat-up transit van was speeding from the north side of the airfield.

The helicopter pilot, Keith Stott, chatted to his passengers, asking them to wait until after the blades had stopped before leaving the aircraft. Then, as he did on every trip when he flew them to Jersey, he reminded them not to leave any belongings behind. Reuben Finkelman and Keith Stott had a good relationship. Keith was one of the family.

Keith opened the side passenger door and lowered the steps. He saw a transit van only fifty yards away and closing fast.

A sudden movement to his right made Keith step back, putting a protective arm across the chests of Ruth and Rachel, who were eager to get to the car.

"Wait," he cried. "I'm not sure what's happening."

Rusty's van shot across the tarmac in front of the helicopter and alarmed the pilot. With a screech of brakes, Rusty protected the pilot and passengers from immediate danger. A second van blocked the entrance. Kelly and Hayden had arrived.

The three gangsters in the beat-up transit were heavily armed; they came out firing. The appearance of the two vans had been unexpected. It was supposed to be an easy kill. Drive across the airfield at speed, rake the doorway with automatic fire, finish anyone still breathing, and then toss the incendiary device into the passenger compartment.

Simple, they'd told them.

It would be far from simple.

The four Olympus agents were now out of their vehicles and finding cover wherever they could. Keith Stott had moved his passengers back inside, where they crouched by the seats. He remained by the doorway.

Two gangsters were using old AK47 assault rifles, and Rusty thought he heard the sound of a Skorpion submachine gun spitting lead. The same weapon Phoenix had used less than two months ago to take out Gavin McTierney.

Compared to the Olympus agents, these guys were amateurs. They sprayed bullets left and right. The van blocking the chopper doorway received dozens of hits in its bodywork, but it served its purpose as a barricade.

Rusty and Phoenix took careful aim with their SAS C8 carbines. Hayden lay in the prone position armed with a Heckler and Koch G36. Kelly Dexter stood with her weapon of choice, the MP Shield, behind her van's open driver's door.

A volley of well-placed shots rang out. The reply from the gangsters became sporadic at once and then stopped. The airfield fell quiet once more. The three attackers lay dead on the tarmac.

Rusty and Hayden ran forward to check the bodies and kick away any weapons. Kelly got back inside the van and started the engine. She could see the duty officer in the tower, standing by the window, phone to his ear. From that angle, he couldn't see her van — time to leave. The cavalry would soon be on its way.

Phoenix reached the door of the helicopter. The Finkelman's cowered inside on the floor; Ruth and Rachel looked shocked and in tears.

"Keith's hit," cried Miriam Finkelman.

"I'll look after him," said Phoenix. "You and your family need to get your things and run to your car, sir. We'll escort you home from here."

Reuben Finkelman urged his wife and daughters forward, and they dashed across the tarmac to the Mercedes. Miriam clung to her husband's arm.

"Who are you?" the Judge shouted over his shoulder, "Special Forces?"

"We're just glad to help, sir," replied Phoenix, "the young lady will lead the way."

Kelly Dexter drove through the aerodrome entrance,

followed by the Mercedes. Hayden and Rusty ran back to the helicopter, where Phoenix bent over a body.

"What's the damage?" asked Hayden.

"A stray bullet straight through the heart," Phoenix replied. "There's nothing more we can do here, I'm afraid. But, we must follow the Judge's car in case a backup hit squad is lying in wait up the road."

The three agents jumped into the bullet-ridden van. Rusty offered a silent prayer; the engine started first time.

"That was lucky," Rusty said, "it's just cosmetic. We can write it off as wear and tear."

He barrelled through the gateway and sped after the other vehicles. Twenty minutes later, they parked on the grass verge outside the Finkelmans' home. Kelly was waiting.

"The ladies are upset," she said, "they were asking after the pilot. I think he's a friend of the family."

"He didn't make it," Phoenix replied.

"We've shown our hand now, mate," said Rusty, "unavoidable, but what do we tell them?"

"I'll wing it," said Phoenix, "the old man thinks we're SAS, so I won't shatter his illusion. The Judge is alive, and so is his family. He should be grateful enough to keep quiet for now. We'll disappear as soon as I've informed him of the pilot's death. I'll tell him we'll be back in the morning, but he won't see us. If he co-operates, we can avoid getting mixed up with the authorities, which will arrive en masse in the next few minutes. So Kelly, you and Hayden get back to the M4 and head for home. Rusty, keep the van ticking over; I don't think the gunfire did any favours. Time to put Plan B into operation."

"I didn't know we had a Plan B," said Rusty.

Phoenix grinned, "You know me, mate, I love planning.

Telephone our transport section in London. Tell them I need the replacement van. They will have it ready for us. We'll stay up here overnight and escort the Judge into the city in the morning."

"Are you sure you won't need us?" asked Kelly.

"The Judge has an official driver organised. I checked with Giles before we drove here. After the weekend's events, he tells me the Met will send the Judge an armed escort. We'll give covert support. I doubt if Hanigan's thugs will attempt a strike in the city in broad daylight, but if they do, we'll be ready."

Kelly and Hayden said their goodbyes and left.

"The three gunmen were dead when you checked, I take it?" asked Phoenix.

"Yes," said Rusty. "I only hit one. I think Hayden got the other two. The G36 leaves its signature. Do you know what he said when we stood over the bodies?"

"What?" asked Phoenix.

"That was for Davy," replied Rusty.

"Good," said Phoenix, "he wanted a chance to avenge the death of his colleague. But, what nationality were they?"

"Eastern European, at a guess. Two might be Polish, the other from the Balkans somewhere," said Rusty.

"He's got every nationality dancing to his tune, hasn't he, this Hanigan?" said Phoenix.

He left Rusty and walked towards the house. Reuben Finkelman came out of the front door to meet him in the driveway.

Rusty was making the call to the transport section in London.

"We owe you our lives," said the Judge, offering his hand.

"I'm sorry, sir," said Phoenix, shaking his hand, "but

your pilot was fatally wounded. There was nothing we could do. He deserves much of the credit; his quick thinking prevented your daughters from exiting the helicopter. Things might have been far worse."

"That's why I popped outside. I didn't think Keith looked too good. We've known him since the girls were toddlers. He was a good chap and a brave one."

"We will stay close by until the morning, sir, then when your transport arrives, I understand the Met will send an armed escort to escort you. No doubt you watched the news over the weekend. You must reach the Old Bailey in one piece in the morning. Our role will be to shadow your car unseen to prevent another attack."

"I've never known times like these," the Judge said, blowing out his cheeks. "it's Chicago in the Roaring Twenties. I understand your position. Your unit goes into action; you do the deed, then disappear. My lips are sealed. Who's behind this, officer? Do we know?"

"Not part of my brief, sir," Phoenix replied. "Yes, you described our role to perfection. Ours not to reason why, and so on…."

"Right, I'll let you get on, and thank you again."

With that, Reuben Finkelman returned indoors.

Phoenix rejoined Rusty by the van.

"Have the transport boys been in contact yet?" he asked.

"Another ten minutes, mate," said Rusty. "Is his Lordship cool with things?"

"I reckon so," said Phoenix. "Let's hope so. We'd better move this heap of metal further up the road. He's had a bad enough day without us killing the grass on the verge outside his home."

"We're not leaking oil, are we?" asked Rusty, looking underneath the van.

"No, but in ten minutes, when the lads from Chiswick deliver our replacement, they'll need peace and quiet to alter a few things on this one. When they finish that, they can torch it. Plan B involved confusion tactics. If an attack occurred at Denham and we got forced into the open, I wanted to fool the police into believing two rival gangs arrived to claim the bounty for wiping out the Finkelman family. Inter-gang rivalry isn't such a difficult pill to swallow. So we must deflect their investigation away from following the trail to our door. We'll leave the Met to determine why the surviving gang didn't follow through and finish the job."

"Fingers crossed, it will work, mate," said Rusty. "Right, let's shift this van."

Phoenix and Rusty pushed the van up the road to await the replacement vehicle. Meanwhile, Giles Burke returned to the surface at Larcombe after a good afternoon's work in the ice-house.

After hours of fruitless effort trying to hack into the various systems that contained the whereabouts of the Crown's vital witness, he had suddenly found the key. Minutes later, at a quarter past four, he and Artemis were staring at an address in Russell Street, Jarrow,

"A terraced house, not far from the centre," said Giles. "Modest accommodation compared to what Maurice Kelly was used to, I imagine?"

"I doubt he's too happy with being shut away up there, with little opportunity to get out to enjoy the sights," said Artemis.

"It's all rather bleak up north, isn't it?" said Giles. "Dark, and satanic, covered in industrial grime."

Artemis wasn't sure whether Giles was being sarcastic, but as a Durham lass, she sprang to the North East's defence.

"There are twenty places of interest I could name within ten miles of where they're living," she said. "Monasteries, museums, galleries, and countryside walks by the side of the Tyne. There are lots of beautiful spots up there."

"Easy tiger," laughed Giles. "I haven't forgotten where you were born. I still think it will be alien to the Kelly's."

"I'll call Athena," said Artemis, "tell her the good news. Then, she can order teams to move the Kelly family to a safe house. There are people on the outskirts of Newcastle, only fifteen minutes away."

"The sooner, the better," said Giles. "I'll make my way out of this system now, closing every door behind me. We don't want anyone to know we've been here. Then I'll get back to hunting Hanigan to see if I can't unearth an address for him."

Artemis called Athena, who assigned agents to rescue Maurice and Deirdre Kelly before they came to any harm. The two teams of agents reached Russell Street, Jarrow, at twenty minutes to five.

Although nobody answered the knock by the agent who stood at the front door, the agent who slipped unnoticed along the passageway further up the terrace found the back door unlocked. Maurice and Deirdre Kelly dozed on a battered sofa in front of the small TV. They were missing the end of another repeated property show on BBC1. The agent let his colleague inside the house.

The former scrapyard owner and his wife were soon awake to find themselves secured and bundled into a waiting van. They would thank their rescuers later, but for now, Maurice thought this was it; his past had caught up with him. Both he and Deirdre would pay for testifying against Tommy O'Riordan.

The agents and their passengers drove away from Russell Street at fourteen minutes to five. They sat in a safe house in Newcastle by ten past the hour. They learned what was happening to them, except who their saviours worked for, and Maurice and Deirdre Kelly could breathe again.

At six o'clock in Jarrow, a car pulled up outside the terraced house on Russell Street. The timing was impeccable. It aimed to coincide with eliminating the Judge and his family in the south. Two masked men smashed the door to the house off its hinges with their guns at the ready.

They stood in an empty house. The television now showed the latest news programme. On the top of the set, the would-be assassins found a note.

'Gone on a long holiday. Sorry we missed you.'

"Bastards," shouted one of the gunmen, "how did they know we were coming? We only knew the address for thirty minutes. We need to tell the people in London."

The other gunman dialled a number.

"They must have left in a rush. The TV's on, and their stuff is still here. So what do you want us to do?"

On the other end of the phone, Colleen O'Riordan wished she didn't have to make the next call. Hannon, or whatever he called himself these days, frightened her. She remembered him as a snotty-nosed weakling when they were children. He was a different kettle of fish these days. He had been crazy ever since his mother had died. Colleen told the Geordie guy to stand by in the house until she called back.

Colleen walked to the drinks cabinet and poured herself

a drink. She delayed facing up to what she needed to do for as long as she dared. Her Tommy was going to jail for a long stretch in the morning unless these killings changed matters. She understood only too well who had ordered the deaths of the jurors. Hannon had phoned her earlier for her brother's Tyneside contacts. He needed the address for Maurice Kelly. With Sean in custody, he had persuaded her to ring up the Geordie mob. The slimy sod didn't want to talk to the hired help.

After a long swig from her double vodka and tonic, Colleen took a deep breath and made the call. It was now twenty-five past six.

"Hello," she said. "I'm sorry, but they found nobody there when they got to Russell Street. They want to know what to do."

Hugo Hanigan was spitting feathers.

"Have you seen the television?" he screamed.

Colleen looked over her shoulder; she muted the sound. A news helicopter was sending aerial pictures of an airfield. An aircraft stood on the ground, surrounded by police cars and other vehicles from the emergency services. Colleen switched on the sound.

In Jarrow, someone was also watching the small TV in what had been Maurice Kelly's front room. The masked gunmen sat side by side on the sofa and listened to the reporter: -

At around six o'clock, the helicopter below me landed at Denham Aerodrome, having flown in from Jersey. It was carrying a local family returning from a weekend trip to the island. Two sets of gunmen clashed here on the tarmac. Fifty yards away, surrounded by police incident tape, forensic officers are piecing together what happened. Three dead bodies, covered by white sheets, are still on the ground beside a transit van. The other gunmen drove off towards the M40. A stray bullet hit the helicopter pilot in the gunfight, named locally as Keith Stott, who ran an air charter company from Denham. Mr Stott died at the scene from his injuries.

As the news helicopter circled the airfield, the fire engine turned around and drove out of the gateway with its flashing blue lights visible.

Another emergency call for the fire brigade, it appears, the reporter continued. We hope to speak with the police officers attending the scene. There are several questions to answer. Was this a dispute between two local gangs that resulted in an innocent bystander dying in the crossfire? Or was it something more sinister? The car belonging to the helicopter's passengers is said to have left at high speed. The family escaped the mayhem. Mr Stott made regular trips to Jersey with Beaconsfield resident Judge Reuben Finkelman. Was this yet another attempted murder relating to the O'Riordan case? Mr Finkelman was the judge in the now infamous trial at the Old Bailey. He's due in court tomorrow morning for the sentencing hearing. Has a bounty been placed on the High Court Judge's head? Was this why the rival gangs arrived just as the helicopter landed? I'll hand you back to the studio for more news and the weather. Ah, just before you go. I can see a pall of black smoke in the distance. It looks near the M40 approach road, a few miles outside Beaconsfield. For now, back to the studio.

In Jarrow, the gunmen looked at one another.

"We might as well get off home, lad," said one, "for definite, it's gone tits up tonight."

Colleen O'Riordan held the phone in her lap. She took another long drink.

Hugo Hanigan stared at his wide-screen plasma TV.

The ceramic bowl he had launched at the screen at the end of the news report stuck in the smouldering remains of the top-of-range model that had cost him fifteen hundred pounds.

"Who's trying to stand in my way?" he yelled. "When I find them, they're dead meat. Who sent that rival gang to Denham? Why did they kill my crew and let the targets get away? How did Kelly learn my gang were on their way, and where have they gone? When's Sean Walsh going to be released from custody? Who's got the brass balls to challenge my leadership of The Grid."

Hugo Hanigan had plenty of questions to wrestle with on Sunday night but no answers.

At Larcombe Manor, Athena received the news she needed to hear. Olympus had successes to celebrate, at last.

The Newcastle lead agent reported that Maurice and Deirdre Kelly were settling into their new surroundings well. The safe house was smarter than Russell Street, and Deirdre Kelly, for one, looked forward to getting new clothes to replace those she had abandoned.

The news channels kept Athena up to speed with Phoenix's progress. The Finkelmans were safe. The helicopter pilots' death had been unfortunate, but more casualties would pile up before this fight ended.

The van fire kept the authorities guessing. It was the van seen on the tarmac near the helicopter. So far, the police couldn't get to examine its burnt-out shell. However, they identified the three gunmen killed in the Denham shoot-out. All three were known criminals in their country of birth. In the past five years, they had used Britain's open-door policy to transfer from Europe to carry on their criminal activities.

Kelly Dexter had called earlier to say she and Hayden were home safe. Athena had thanked them for their help at short notice. She promised to avoid sending them on a direct action again. Olympus needed them alive and well to train the new agents they required.

Athena decided on an early night. She turned off the lights in the lounge and walked through to their bedroom. Her phone rang. It was Phoenix.

"I thought I'd ring to say goodnight," he said.

"I'm glad you're safe," she said, "was it bad?"

"We've been through worse," Phoenix replied. "Rusty and I are sleeping in the van tonight. We'll follow the Judge into the city in the morning. I'll call you as soon as we leave to return to Larcombe."

"Take care," said Athena.

"I'll do my best," said Phoenix. "Oh, can you call Artemis and tell her Rusty says hi."

"The last of the red-hot lovers, isn't he?" said Athena, "okay, but I'll embellish it. The poor girl will feel neglected."

Athena called Artemis, who answered at once. She must have been waiting by the phone.

"They're both safe and well, and send their love," said Athena. "We can expect them home by lunchtime."

"Thanks for ringing, Athena," said Artemis. "I'm shattered and wanted to get to bed, but I stayed up, just in case. Today could have gone far worse, but two families are alive tonight, thanks to Olympus's actions."

"Indeed," said Athena, "success at last. I'll see you at the morning meeting, Artemis. Goodnight."

As she passed the nursery door, Athena looked inside at Hope on the way to the bedroom. "If Daddy does his best, that should be good enough," she whispered.

Athena lay alone in their bed. But sleep didn't come easy.

Would tomorrow bring more success? Or did yet more trials lie ahead?

Chapter Ten

Monday, 28th April 2014

Judge Reuben Finkelman awoke at six o'clock. His wife, Miriam, lay asleep by his side. Reuben felt every one of his fifty-eight years on this earth today. The trauma of yesterday's events at Denham returned with each moment his eyes were open. He put on a dressing gown and went downstairs to make his breakfast.

Reuben drew back the curtains in the kitchen and the lounge. That was his routine. The morning looked to promise a dry and settled start to the week. He hoped he survived to see the weekend. Their much-loved garden he saw from the kitchen window was unchanged. The manicured lawns leading to the roadway he viewed from the lounge windows looked calm and serene, as always.

Those people who saved him and his family last evening were invisible, as promised.

Keith Stott was still dead.

His twin daughters, Ruth and Rachel, remained nineteen years old and would carry their memories of yesterday to their graves. He and Miriam had raised them as best they could, trying to protect them from the wickedness of this world. In seconds, that ended.

His years as a High Court Judge had prepared him for times such as these. He faced the results of the horrific things one human being could do to another regularly. While they had relaxed in St Ouen, he had left Miriam and the girls in the kitchen in the holiday home they treasured. He wanted to walk to the headland and gaze out over the bay.

Reuben had needed to be alone to consider the evidence. Review what he had seen and heard in the courtroom over the past weeks. There were various options open to him. Then, as Saturday afternoon passed over him, he had come to his decision. It had been five o'clock when he had returned to the house.

The smells from the kitchen wrapped him in a warm blanket. Memories of his childhood flooded over him.

Images of his mother and father filled his head; memories of sunny days running on the beach with his brother and sister on the south of the island at St Brelade's.

As Reuben stood in the kitchen, a little over thirty-six hours later, the smell of the breakfast, he had prepared only stirred images he'd prefer to forget. Yet, one that remained firm was that of Thomas O'Riordan, who had stood in the dock before him when the guilty verdict was delivered.

None of the arrogance left O'Riordan, who still behaved like a cock-of-the-walk. His family had screamed abuse and made threats. They had vowed revenge on Maurice Kelly.

Reuben Finkelman had seen and heard it before. His career had led him to this defining moment.

Today was his opportunity to stand up for his profession's principles. It was his chance to deliver a sentence to wipe that supercilious smile from the gangster's face.

Reuben hoped it sent a message to whoever ordered the slaughtering of the jurors that justice would prevail no matter what threats it faced. He left the kitchen and walked across to his study. He wanted to read through the notes he had prepared once more.

Reuben crossed out the introduction but felt the rest of his short speech was satisfactory. However, it was incumbent upon him to ask O'Riordan if he had anything to say before passing sentence. Experience told him O'Riordan wouldn't weaken and beg or apologise. His superior air maintained to the end.

As he raised his eyes from the desk for inspiration, Reuben saw the crest of his old college hanging on the wall. Many years had passed since Reuben studied at Churchill College, Cambridge. Finally, inspiration struck; he would paraphrase a speech from the great man. That should send the message he wanted. He took up his pen and wrote the final paragraph: - *'We shall go on to the end; we shall fight with growing confidence and growing strength, we shall defend our Island, whatever the cost may be, we shall never surrender.'*

"That's it," he said with a satisfied sigh.

Reuben went upstairs, ready to face the day ahead. Miriam and the girls surfaced at half-past seven. They were quieter than usual as they sat in the kitchen. The front doorbell rang at five to eight. An armed officer faced Reuben when he answered. By his side stood a senior officer, whose epaulette badge identified him as a Commander.

"We're here to escort you to the Central Criminal Court, your Lordship," the Commander said.

"I'll just collect my things and say goodbye to my family," said Reuben.

Two minutes later, the limousine containing the Judge pulled out of the driveway. It arrived sandwiched between two vehicles from the armed response unit. They headed to the M40 and travelled into the heart of the city.

Phoenix and Rusty shadowed them throughout the journey.

"A pleasant morning for it," said Rusty.

"Uneventful," said Phoenix, "just how we prefer it."

Reuben Finkelman attempted to relax in his limousine one hundred yards in front. Other journeys to work had involved just him and his driver. There was no cavalcade. There were no armed guards. It must have been his imagination, but he thought every pedestrian, every motorist did a double-take as they passed. Instead of gliding by unnoticed, he was now the centre of attention. It unnerved him.

As the journey sped past, Reuben ticked off the landmarks in his head. The White City was on his left, and soon they approached Little Venice. The group of cars had to stop at traffic lights. Little did the Judge realise that a few hundred yards away, the gun Tommy O'Riordan had used to murder Michael Devlin lay at the bottom of a canal.

Soon they turned the corner and passed University College, the British Museum and the London School of Economics. In front of them stood the Central Criminal Court. One hour, door to door from Forty Green, with no sirens or flashing lights, thank goodness, and no drama. Reuben gathered his things and went to leave the car.

"Stay inside, please, your Lordship," ordered the Commander, appearing on the pavement in front of him. "We'll move the crowds out of the way for you. No point taking undue risks at this late stage."

"Sorry," said Reuben, "force of habit."

Two minutes later, the armed officers received clearance to rush the Judge inside the building. Reuben found himself in his changing rooms in no time; it was a few minutes after nine. They called for him before ten; O'Riordan was first on his list for today. Reuben Finkelman was ready and waiting.

With the van parked in a nearby multi-storey, Phoenix and Rusty were yards away from the main entrance in Newgate Street.

"Court Two in this old part of the building has a history, doesn't it," said Rusty.

"It's a high-security case," said Phoenix, "even more so after the weekend events."

The two agents kept their eyes on the street. There were plainclothes officers everywhere, trying to look nonchalant, and all their efforts ended in miserable failure. Any sudden noise, such as a slamming van door, and they jumped out of their skin, putting a hand to their earpiece.

"Bless them," said Rusty, "this has been a tough ask for them. It has stretched the Met to the limit since it kicked off Friday evening."

"Time has run out for Hanigan," said Phoenix. "His thugs failed twice yesterday, and having many of his senior henchmen in custody will have hampered his efforts. Making a frontal assault on the Old Bailey is unlikely, but we'll stay on watch until we hear the judge has delivered the sentence."

"Tommy's going to prison, no matter what," said Phoenix. "The Met will escort him at high speed to Belmarsh. Do you think they'll try to intercept the van?"

"Who knows, with Hanigan?" said Phoenix, "a madman is capable of anything. We'll wait and see and then play the cards we've got."

The minutes ticked away towards ten. More armed police arrived from the Territorial Support Group in two vans. They prevented any vehicles from getting near the building. The clock at St Sepulchre's church chimed the hour. The only sound to be heard as the ringing faded was the flapping of pigeons' wings it disturbed. It was as if the capital held its breath.

Inside Court Two, proceedings had begun. Tommy O'Riordan stood suited and booted in the dock. The public gallery was half-empty. Only Colleen, the two children, and the gangsters' closest relatives were granted entry.

Judge Reuben Finkelman addressed the court, never taking his eyes off those of Thomas O'Riordan. As he had thought, the Irishman refused to offer mitigating circumstances when his final chance to speak arrived. Finally, Reuben could deliver the sentence. When the words whole life order escaped his lips, he watched with satisfaction as the colour drained from O'Riordan's face, and his head dropped to his chest. It was rare days such as this that made Reuben's job worthwhile.

The public gallery's reaction was as expected. The only person to remain silent was Colleen, who stood, turned, and walked away, followed by her family.

News of the verdict filtered through to those standing outside on the pavement. Reporters were gathering and trying to break the police cordon. The prison van sped out of the side road, and the TSG vans set off to ride shotgun.

Phoenix and Rusty watched them go.

"Does the Judge have other cases today?" asked Rusty.

"I believe they rescheduled his cases," said Phoenix. "Either way, the Met will get him home safe. He'll have a guard until the threat level diminishes."

"Looks as if we can get off home then?" asked Rusty.

"I want to hang around for a few minutes yet," said Phoenix. "We haven't heard from the family yet. But, no doubt, they'll be on the steps with their brief talking of an appeal. It was a disproportionate sentence and the usual garbage."

A sudden crowd of people appeared at the entrance. Cameras and phones flashed, and there was shouting as the O'Riordan family spoke to anyone with a microphone. Phoenix had called it right.

As the defence solicitor painted his picture of the justice delivered in Court Two this morning, Phoenix watched the faces of the family members. Only one woman appeared at odds with the bile pouring from the mouths of the others. Colleen O'Riordan never spoke.

Questions got fired at her, but she stood, as if in shock, her face impassive.

Phoenix sensed this was a woman who felt wronged.

Life as a gangster's wife had its financial benefits. However, Phoenix imagined Tommy had treated Colleen as more of a trophy and a skivvy than a revered partner.

Her life could go in two ways. She could crumble as the luxurious trappings she had enjoyed fell away and the protection offered by the gang removed. Or she could take Tommy's place.

She was a Walsh by birth, and her brother, Sean, was her husband's lieutenant. With her husband in prison, in all likelihood, until he died, Colleen might have a taste for the good life and fight tooth and nail, not to have it torn from her. However, her family history suggested she was tough enough.

As the family's cars drove away back to Kilburn, Phoenix wondered whether their paths might ever cross again.

"Time to make tracks," Phoenix said to Rusty, "our work is over."

They returned to the car park, retrieved their van, and drove home to Larcombe.

The morning meeting ended while they parked by the transport section garage. Phoenix wanted to catch up with what had been discussed. Rusty reminded him that a quick visit to the armoury was necessary to return the equipment they had withdrawn.

Once they had travelled underground, Bazza and Thommo were eager to discover what had happened at the Old Bailey.

"We're mushrooms in here, mate," said Bazza. "We get fed shite now and then, but nobody tells us a thing."

"That will change soon, Bazza," Rusty said, "when you join the training team."

"We've been below ground so long," said Bazza. "Thommo reckons we'll need sunglasses for the first few weeks until we get accustomed to the bright light."

"O'Riordan got a whole life order," said Rusty. "The Judge was pissed at being shot at last night. Someone had to pay."

"Life feels right for how he dealt with Devlin," said Thommo, "he can't have any complaints."

After checking in the guns and ammunition and telling the armourers more details of their mission, Phoenix and Rusty left the ice-house and walked back to the main building.

They met Artemis, Giles, and Henry, heading in the opposite direction.

"Welcome home," said Artemis. "I hope you had a successful mission?"

"It had its moments," said Rusty, squeezing his partner.

"What did we miss this morning?" asked Phoenix.

"Athena took us through the arrangements for tomorrow," said Giles, "she's glad you will be free to go with her to London. The news from Newcastle was excellent. Maurice Kelly and his wife transferred from the safe house early this morning. They will spend their retirement in a remote cottage in the centre of the Irish Republic. I can't say more because even we didn't hear. Zeus alone has received an email with the details. There's no way Hanigan will ever find them."

"That will make him madder than ever," said Phoenix, "troubles often come in threes, don't they? Two attempted attacks failed yesterday; O'Riordan's sentence was number three. Now there's the fourth failure. Maurice Kelly has disappeared again. This time for good.

"Nothing else?" asked Phoenix.

Giles shuffled his feet.

"Sorry, no joy yet finding an address for Hanigan," he said. "Artemis suggested we find an old picture of Hannon from somewhere and put an agent outside the bank. Then, if we can spot him leaving, we could follow him home."

"We know from experience that Hannon is cute," said Phoenix. "Look how long it took us to find his new identity. You can bet he used the 'right to get forgotten' loophole to cover his tracks. I doubt we'll find much more than a grainy, unrecognisable face on a photograph from his schooldays in Dublin."

"We've had the General Data Protection Regulation to contend with since last month," said Henry. "Another mealy-mouthed piece of legislation from the European Courts."

"Look, Giles, I'm not saying don't bother," said Phoenix, "but don't build up your hopes. When we meet with Zeus and the others tomorrow, we'll see if we can think of a way to draw Hanigan out into the open."

"OK, Phoenix," said Giles, "we'll keep searching for clues. If a usable photograph surfaces, we'll put a tail on him later."

Phoenix and Rusty left the others to return to the icehouse and passed the stable block on their way to the main house.

"While I'm here, I'll drop in on Kelly and Hayden," said Rusty. "I'll fill them in about this morning and thank them for last night."

"Good thinking," said Phoenix. "Thank them from me too, and assure them that unless something drastic occurs, that was their final mission. We need to protect our senior trainers regardless of the costs."

Phoenix made his way upstairs and found Athena playing with Hope.

"Good morning, my two lovely girls," he said.

The reward for Phoenix was two beaming smiles.

"It's great to have you home, darling," said Athena.

"We saw the others on our way over from the armoury. They brought us up to speed."

"I've heard from Zeus since the morning meeting ended," said Athena, handing Hope over to her father, "he told me Apollo wouldn't be joining us until tomorrow. He's visiting Davy's family and that of the second agent, Clyde, killed in Bromley."

"What do you have planned for this afternoon?" asked Phoenix.

"Maria Elena will get here in forty-five minutes, and I have admin work to catch up on for the charity. We can't afford to get caught by a Charity Commission spot inspection. Then I want an early night. We'll be leaving for London at eight in the morning."

"I'll hold you to that early night," Phoenix said. "I think I'll go for a swim, clear my head, and then prepare notes to present to the other Olympians in the morning."

When he returned from the pool, Phoenix closeted himself in the orangery and set to work. It was time for Hugo Hanigan to suffer another series of setbacks.

Meanwhile, Sean Walsh and the other gang members in London were released from custody at six o'clock in the evening. The interviews had revealed nothing. DCI Geoff Titmus and DI Jonathan Barclay had expected as much. Nevertheless, they went through the motions because their superiors ordered it.

Television reports and daily newspapers continued to wring every drop of emotion out of the public over the deaths of the jurors. News teams attended every candle-lit vigil—the familiar pattern developed with each terror incident, natural disaster, and tragic loss of life.

Each one was more elaborate than the last, and each masked the truth that nothing tackled the root causes. As a result, the Irish, Jamaican, Eastern European and Asian gangsters returned to their respective homes.

In his penthouse, Hugo counted the cost of the past twenty-four hours. Maurice Kelly had gone to ground. Hugo had threatened the local gang leaders on Tyneside there would be a price to pay if they didn't find him. He had doubled the amount on Kelly's head.

The Judge was off-limits now. A drive-by had shown his home being guarded twenty-four-seven by armed police, and the chance of that headline-busting strike had gone.

Despite his efforts to prevent Tommy from getting sent to prison, he had failed. The life sentence had stunned Hugo, but he knew he had to go forward without Tommy's strong presence at his side. At least Sean was free, and they needed to talk soon. Tommy was just one man from The Grid. All said and done. Any sign of weakness encouraged another gang leader to threaten the hierarchy they had introduced over the past year,

Hugo tried to think who might have authorised the clash at Denham Aerodrome, which thwarted his crew's attack on the Judge. He needed Sean to consider that first thing in the morning.

Hugo rang Sean, but his son told him his parents weren't at home. Instead, they had gone to be with Colleen O'Riordan. She had received bad news today, and the family had gathered around her in solidarity.

Hugo ended the call. He knew well enough that she had received bad news, and so had he. Colleen was a lush. She had been drunk when she talked on the phone with him last night; it didn't take a genius to fathom that. Hugo thought of ringing the O'Riordan home but decided it could wait until the morning.

Hugo picked up the TV remote and remembered that he hadn't sorted out a new set because of bank business and the sentencing hearing occupying his time. So the remote joined the ceramic bowl in the screen.

Tuesday, 29th April 2014

The car waited at the front door at eight am. Phoenix and Athena left Maria Elena with Hope and hurried downstairs to head for London. Traffic was heavy, and it was ten-fifty when they arrived outside the venue. Once inside the conference room, they met with Zeus and Hera.

"Congratulations on a well-executed mission yesterday, Phoenix," said Zeus.

"Teamwork, as always," said Phoenix, "but it was not flawless. Unfortunately, the pilot Keith Stott died. I wish we could have avoided that."

"So, do we all," said Hera, giving Athena a welcoming hug.

Phoenix thought about how things had changed since the first meeting he had attended. The atmosphere had shown a dramatic improvement. Duncan and Celia Eliot were old friends now. Dionysus joined them a minute later, and then James and Elizabeth came bustling through the door together, looking very pleased with themselves.

Sir James Grant-Nicholls and the Duchess did the rounds of the other Olympians, shaking hands with and air-kissing the appropriate colleague. Heracles and Aphrodite were excited over something; that was evident.

"Are we ready to begin," said Zeus, with a knowing wink in Athena's direction.

"Well," said Elizabeth McLaren, "Sir James and I want to share our news with you all."

"So, three or four trips in his private plane with your knees touching has done the trick. Is that what you're telling us?"

Several pairs of eyes turned on Phoenix.

"We prefer to think it was more elegant than that, Phoenix," said Heracles.

"We have spent more time in each other's company on the ground than in the air," the Duchess of Lochalsh continued. "Last Friday, James asked me to marry him, and I accepted."

"Congratulations to you both," said Athena. "This calls for a celebration, don't you agree, Zeus?"

"We only have soft drinks," said Phoenix, who had wandered to the side table.

"I'll rectify that," said Dionysus, leaving the room to order champagne and glasses.

Zeus looked at his watch.

"We need to get on with our busy programme," he said. "Can we agree to a start time of half-past eleven? We won't take a break until after one o'clock."

There were no objections. The champagne arrived, and the Olympians toasted the happy couple.

"I wish Apollo were here," said Dionysus, joining Athena and Phoenix. "Until we add to our number, we are soon to be the only two here without our wives. There has been a significant change in the past year."

"For the better, I hope?" asked Athena.

"Without a doubt," replied Dionysus, "but new blood would be most welcome."

"We'll discuss that later," said Athena.

It was eleven-thirty, and Zeus called the meeting to order.

"As we had to call this emergency meeting, I won't run through the financials today, nor the updates on our overseas actions. Important though those items are, we must concentrate on today's current crises. We have seen the events in London since Friday evening, and our direct actions have prevented several deaths. However, we lost two agents in Bromley on Saturday afternoon. Apollo is with the families now. I expect him to join us after lunch. Phoenix and his team averted a disaster at Denham Aerodrome last evening. We retrieved Mr Kelly from witness protection. Right from under the noses of his guards and the likely attack from The Grid."

"The grid," asked Heracles, "what do you mean?"

"Capital G," replied Zeus. "I have no idea what they call themselves. It sums up the resultant framework of interconnected gangs that has been growing in strength for a while. From now on, The Grid is how we shall refer to them."

"Hugo Hanigan is the figurehead," said Athena, passing folders around the table for each Olympian to study. "This report details everything we have learned about him. To date, we haven't found his home address. That's frustrating. We will continue the hunt."

"I have a few ideas on how we might flush Hanigan out into the open," said Phoenix. "He's the madman who organised the murders before Easter and those this weekend. He's dangerous in the extreme, and I believe these attacks were to make the people of this country sit up and take notice. He wants the world to fear the name, Hugo Hanigan."

"How do you intend to flush him out, Phoenix?" asked Aphrodite.

"I propose a series of direct actions against regional elements of this Grid. We might be poking a sleeping lion with a short stick. To eliminate Hanigan, first, we must find where he lives."

Zeus stood up and paced the far end of the room.

"I'm conservative in my approach on most occasions, Phoenix, but the time has come for action. Athena tells me the training programme for new agents is ready to start. Also, she has asked for extra personnel at Larcombe, so you can have two agents released to serve as senior trainers.

That will double the number of successful candidates we can produce. So you have the green light on that one, Athena, effective at once."

"Thank you, Zeus," said Athena, "that's most welcome."

"Also," Zeus continued with a wry smile. "I have ordered one hundred overseas agents home to bolster the people we have available for the actions Phoenix is proposing. They have had little to do recently, as their trouble-spot has become less volatile. Your second set of trainers can give them a quick refresher course before they hit the streets. I insist, Phoenix, that you warn me why, where, and when you intend to strike. You will receive a green light on every occasion unless I know a bloody good reason it might be unwise."

"That's no problem, Zeus," said Phoenix. "You can expect my first call within seventy-two hours."

"We need a change of pace," said Zeus, taking his seat at the head of the table, "this pro-active mood I'm in is exhausting. What news do you have for us on the four potential candidates we put forward at the last meeting, Athena?"

Over the next hour, Athena took them through the reports that Minos and Alastor had compiled. Apollo arrived halfway through, fetched himself a coffee, and sat at the table. Zeus nodded to him to acknowledge his presence. Apollo sat and listened as the discussions continued.

When they concluded, the positives outweighed the negatives.

Ludovic Tremayne would assume the code name Achilles with no reservations. Dawn Prentice's name must drop from the list of possible candidates. They needed to uncover another candidate to take the guise of Aurora.

As for Jean-Paul St Clair and Piya Adani, they became Daedalus and Ambrosia from now on. However, Zeus, as expected, remained cautious over the character traits exposed. He needed time to consider. Achilles would get an invitation to the next meeting in Manchester in July. As for the other two, they would hold back their letters while Zeus, and Larcombe, continued to test their suitability.

"What do you intend to do concerning the replacement for Dawn Prentice?" asked Phoenix.

"I had other names to put forward," said Zeus, "but I believed these four the best candidates. I won't reconsider those I discarded; we can't accept second-best. I'll start a new search. We will carry on with either nine or eleven Olympians until we find the right people."

"Well, I guess that's it," said Athena. "What a most positive meeting."

Apollo spoke for the first time.

"I'm sorry for my late arrival. These family visits are necessary but stressful, as you know. I hope someone can bring me up to speed with what happened before I got here?"

Daedalus tapped Apollo's sleeve.

"When the others leave, stay with me; I'll run you through everything."

"There is one low-priority item I wished to raise," said Apollo, "regarding rumours I picked up on my travels. I donate money to amateur boxing clubs across the country. I would never have been a world champion unless I had received the opportunity to learn the noble art. My troubled teenage years could have led me on a different path. The ex-boxers who mentored me gave me discipline and respect for my body and opponents. They saved me. Now I use my wealth here at Olympus to help save small regional clubs threatened with closure. I paid recent visits to gyms in Reading and Newbury. One name cropped up in both, which made me ask more questions. The name was Dean Laker. He's said to be a nasty piece of work who is a serial stalker and abuser of young women. I want that confirmed, and if it is, that we teach this Laker a lesson. I understand this pales into insignificance against matters you've discussed today, but I would appreciate your help."

Athena looked at her husband. Phoenix nodded.

"We may have just the people for the job, Apollo," she said. "We'll take on the task, and it won't need any resources from Larcombe. Our man will find the proof."

"Thank you, Athena," said Apollo. "That's terrific."

Zeus looked around the table to see if any other business was forthcoming. He saw nothing, so he brought the meeting to a close.

"Onwards to Manchester then," he said, "and happy hunting between now and when we meet again."

After they said their goodbyes, Phoenix called their driver to come and collect them. He and Athena left the conference room.

Apollo and Daedalus were deep in conversation. Zeus and Hera were chatting with Aphrodite and Heracles about their wedding plans.

"We couldn't have hoped for such a positive outcome today," said Athena.

"Zeus surprised me," said Phoenix. "We've got the go-ahead to strike at the heart of the Grid. We'll prod the sleeping lion until he breaks cover. Then I plan to make sure he doesn't live to see his dream of a nationwide crime syndicate come to fruition."

Chapter Eleven

Wednesday, 30th April 2014

Phil Hounsell struggled to find a good reason to be at work today. It wasn't the weather. That was changeable, unlike the warm, dry spell they had experienced lately. He and Erica took the kids to the seaside at Burnham-on-Sea last weekend. They enjoyed twelve hours of sunshine, with little more than a breath of breeze. It was perfect weather for wandering along the promenade and then sitting on the sea wall, eating fish and chips. The Hounsell family found simple pleasures often the most satisfying.

No, the monotony of the jobs Hounsell Security Services received these days squeezed the will to live out of him. The hunt for 'mispers' was time-consuming and mostly fruitless. To confirm a poor wife's husband was up to no good when he swore he was working late could be soul-destroying. It might pay his staff's wages, but it wasn't fulfilling.

As he watched the grey clouds scudding across the skies,

he longed for the thrill of the security jobs that came their way in the early days. Even though the treacherous Sixties pop singer Honey B almost cost him his life, Phil would have swapped a few days of excitement for the boredom their work schedule promised. He scanned the jobs he and his operatives needed to carry out on the whiteboard in front of his desk and gave a deep sigh.

"Should I ask, boss?" asked Wayne, his senior colleague.

"Don't you find these jobs repetitive, Wayne?" said Phil.

"We're working with no sign of things drying up," shrugged Wayne, "so that's a positive. Things can be repetitive, but that's life. I go shopping every week at Sainsbury's. When I grab hold of a trolley on a Friday evening, I can't believe it's been seven days since I did the same thing. I find myself analysing every one of my activities the same way. When you start getting older, your life slips into a rut."

"Thanks, Wayne," said Phil. "I hoped you might cheer me up, but you've made me more depressed than ever."

The office phone rang. Phil grabbed it; he was praying for a lifeline.

"Hounsell Security Services, Phil Hounsell. How may we help you?"

It was Hayden Vincent at Larcombe Manor. Olympus was calling. Maybe things were about to improve?

"Good morning, Orion. We have a job for you. A name has come to us concerning a serious case of harassment. We need surveillance carried out. If you can confirm our informant's suspicions, please send your supporting evidence in whichever format you collect, and we will take the matter forward. That would end your involvement. If you agree to accept this mission, you will receive a full background report in the next hour and payment on completion. What do you say?"

"Yes, please," replied Phil, trying not to sound too eager, "we're not short of work, but variety always helps."

"Understood," said Hayden.

"Another job, boss?" asked Wayne.

"Larcombe has someone suffering aggressive harassment that needs a helping hand. Unfortunately, I haven't learned much more, but my inbox will receive the full details soon."

"It might be tricky to carry out effective surveillance if this person gets harassed in their workplace, boss, unless it's a business. We could send one of our lads in to pick up a zero-hours contract for the duration."

"Let's not try to second-guess what they're asking us to do, Wayne," said Phil. "All will be revealed in time."

The file Hayden Vincent promised soon arrived in Phil's inbox. He downloaded it, printed out the relevant contents, and he and Wayne browsed through the details for the next fifteen minutes.

"Heck," muttered Wayne, "this girl has been through the mill, hasn't she?"

Phil nodded. Stalking had been a contentious issue while he was a serving officer. More so in the early days, with the police being more male-dominated than when he quit last summer. Only a tiny proportion of cases ever got recorded. Often the officers treated the woman involved as a nuisance, not a victim.

Over the years, he noticed subtle changes. At Portishead, officers such as Angela Chambers, and Zara Wheeler, for example, proposed initiatives for more training for officers to recognise the crime. They wanted to give support to those that suffered from it.

Things improved, but they had a long way to go yet, for the number of offences to reduce to any high degree. Only about half of the victims appeared to go to the police anyway. Which suggested they didn't trust the authorities to take effective action. That was another issue that needed confronting.

Eight months later, sitting on the other side of the fence, Phil read of the nightmare this young woman was experiencing and understood her frustration. It was clear the police had been unhelpful.

Olympus were alerted to her plight, and with the help of HSS, maybe her nightmare could end. How she coped in the aftermath was a different matter. Phil wondered what support structures existed for victims of stalking and aggressive harassment. He was ashamed to admit that he didn't have a clue.

"It looks as if Amy Grant was unlucky to find a lazy copper on duty when she plucked up the courage to report this Dean Laker at last, boss," said Wayne, interrupting Phil's reverie.

"Amy reported the number of occasions she spotted Laker stalking her. Although I bet that was only a fraction of the times he lurked nearby," said Phil. "As soon as she mentioned the online element, they told her not to check her e-mails so often. Or abandon the internet altogether. Not helpful, was it? I see they told her 'to come back when he does something'."

"The law changed eighteen months ago," said Wayne, "differentiating between stalking and harassment, didn't it? Officers haven't learned the difference yet; that's obvious. The training is inadequate. Things can escalate into real danger in a flash. I read somewhere that stalking's the only crime where if someone is going to kill you, they warn you first."

"It's vital the right training is in place," said Phil,

"because many stalking cases will involve physical violence. A significant proportion of domestic homicides identified stalking as occurring in the lead-up to murder. Guys such as Dean Laker are often serial offenders, and Amy Grant may not have been the first, and she won't be the last. The threat of violence levels increasing with each successive victim is always there. Murder is the outcome."

Phil and Wayne worked on the details of the case and formulated a plan.

Amy Grant was thirty-three years old. She had never married. She worked as a market researcher in a busy office in the centre of Reading, Berkshire. The man accused of harassing Amy was thirty-five-year-old Dean Laker. He worked in advertising in a role that didn't need him to be face-to-face with the public. That raised a 'red flag' in Phil's mind at once.

Amy met him through an online dating site and, at first, couldn't believe her luck. Her friends were getting married or in steady partnerships, but a five-year relationship ended months earlier. She was keen not to make the same mistakes again, and Dean Laker seemed different.

Dean Laker lived in his two-bedroomed maisonette. He was always well-dressed and insisted on picking up the bill when they went out. Laker was not how he appeared. Although warm and friendly at first, his jealous rages and controlling behaviour left Amy feeling trapped and isolated within weeks of their meeting. When she plucked up the courage to stop seeing him, he bombarded her with texts and e-mails. He followed her time and again. Dean turned up outside the offices where she worked. Amy suffered anxiety and panic attacks. Finally, she relented, and the relationship with Laker continued for the past few months.

"We need more research on this Laker fellow," said

Wayne. "I'll bet you a large, iced bun that the guy has previous."

"More than likely," Phil agreed, "you get started on that. I'll carry on checking the stuff Larcombe sent."

Life had been more straightforward for him and Erica when they started dating, but times had changed so much in fifteen years. Couples found it more challenging to find partners. Thousands used online dating sites in the hunt for true love. Relationships define people these days; many are socially isolated and rely on the internet's relative anonymity. When they went online, a person could manufacture an identity that bore no relation to their reality and exploit it to their ends.

Phil re-read Amy Grant's statement about her initial break-up with Laker.

'Dean couldn't accept the relationship was over and kept telling me how much he needed me. He pleaded for reconciliation and flew into a rage when I refused. I felt so embarrassed at yet another failed relationship that he wore me down, and I agreed to see him again.'

For Amy, alarm bells rang within weeks of her and Dean getting back together. At first, everything was sweetness and light, and she was flattered by the attention. He showered her with gifts and wined and dined her even more than the first time. She slept at his place often over the weekend and awoke one night to find him looking through her phone. Amy thought it rude and a touch weird but didn't challenge him. Amy still believed she had found her soulmate.

Only later did she discover Dean must have watched her entering her security passwords and realised he had been through her social media accounts and e-mails.

In the past couple of weeks, he had become jealous of

any online male friends and insisted she delete their contacts. Laker became a Jekyll and Hyde character. One minute he was charming and attentive, the next threatening and intimidating. Because Amy was desperate to make the relationship work, she kept making excuses for his behaviour.

Phil was aware recent statistics showed one in five couples now meet online. Why would Amy Grant, an attractive, intelligent professional woman and a good judge of people, suddenly let reason fly out of the window when picking a partner? Why did she accept such crass behaviour?

Phil supposed it was because everyone is extra-vulnerable when looking for love. If you meet someone through an online dating agency, you've already revealed yourself as available. You've given away personal information you might well hold back until you talked to them face-to-face several times.

These profiles people filled in online had much to answer for, Phil thought. Unless girls such as Amy limited how much of themselves they showed 'up-front', they risked being exposed to exploitation by a serial offender looking for a victim to control.

Amy Grant's experience might have been far worse if someone from the predatory sex offender category had seen her online profile. What she had gone through so far at the hands of Dean Laker disgusted Phil. Whatever retribution Olympus planned for him was his just dessert.

Wayne didn't take long to return with information on what they sought.

"Just as we suspected, boss," he said, "I Googled him and found his previous convictions straightaway. They got reported in his local newspaper. Laker moved to Reading from Newbury two years before he met Amy Grant. He was a serial stalker with a criminal record for harassment and violence against a former partner. For terrorising an ex-girlfriend, Dean Laker received an indefinite restraining order preventing him from contacting her. He received a three-month prison sentence, suspended for two years. That period had since run out. While dating Amy Grant, his profile was listed on three separate dating websites. It's obvious he had every intention of carrying on in the same manner."

Wayne's investigations revealed a catalogue of crimes going back a decade. They showed Laker had served a prison sentence for harassing and assaulting an ex-girlfriend seven years earlier. Before he moved to Reading, his last partner, Tina Fowler, confronted him over a newspaper report about his earlier trial. She, too, carried out a simple online search and uncovered the real Dean Laker.

Dean Laker was not the charming, presentable young man she fancied but a sad loser who preyed on unwitting, defenceless females. Laker tried to explain the news report away; he maintained it wasn't how it looked. Tina told him it was over. That only antagonised Laker further, and he began stalking her in earnest.

He hounded his ex-partner for weeks. He demanded the return of presents he had given her and turned up at the shop where she worked to intimidate her. Tina was forced to change her phone number and went home to her parents to escape the hassle. In desperation, she plucked up the courage to report him to the police for harassment. Laker was arrested.

"Stalking has become a serious crime," said Phil. "It's to do with obsession and fixation. Serial offenders steal peoples' lives."

"You've only got to see what these girls have experienced," continued Wayne. "Celebrities who attract stalkers are likely to get help and protection because of who they are. However, it must be harder to convince the authorities when you get stalked by someone you've been in a relationship with. It sounds so feeble when a girl goes to the police and says she's received a dozen long-stemmed red roses. Then tells them an ex-boyfriend met her outside her workplace and said they still loved her. Unless you record every instance of e-mails, text messages, and surprise gifts, it's difficult to convey the relentlessness with which a stalker pursues their victim."

"What do you think we need to do, Wayne?" asked Phil.

"Most of what we need is here, boss," he replied. "I reckon I could drive to Reading and spend a few hours watching Amy Grant and Dean Laker's movements. Then we can add a few dozen photographs of our own to the evidence and give your contact the green light. I wouldn't want to be in Dean Laker's shoes, that's for sure."

"You had better get moving then, Wayne," said Phil, "heaven knows what state their relationship is in today. Amy is still dating the swine, despite the black marks against him. What's that old saying?"

"There's none so blind as them that cannot see, boss?" Wayne offered.

"That's better than mine, mate; I was thinking love is blind," smiled Phil, "but that's perfect."

Wayne collected the keys to the company car, took note of the details of where Amy and Dean lived and worked, and then headed for the door.

"Camera, Wayne?" Phil called after him.

"Ah, better take a proper one instead of relying on my phone, I guess," said Wayne, walking over to one of the filing cabinets. "I was distracted. I wondered whether you might pop to the cake shop on the corner for that large, iced bun before I undertake a tiring drive or not?"

"Not," said Phil, "your snacking has already cost HSS enough money in expanding uniforms. Erica keeps making barbed comments about my waistline. You're a bad influence, Wayne Sangster."

"Ah well, I'll visit Reading Services for a comfort break. Then I can manage my stint of surveillance without needing a pee. I'll pick up a snack while I'm there."

With that, his colleague left, camera bag slung over his shoulder. Phil smiled to himself. Wayne was a character. The day he bumped into him at Glastonbury a year ago had been a lucky break. They developed a good understanding that weekend and had worked well together since he set up HSS.

Phil spent the rest of the morning collating the Grant/Laker investigation paperwork. First, he attached the newspaper accounts and various items Wayne had discovered during his online search. Then he got a new folder from the stationery cupboard, ready for the incriminating photographs and written evidence he hoped Wayne's surveillance yielded.

As he poured himself another cup of coffee, he offered a prayer. Phil prayed that his daughter Tracey would never endure the nightmare Tina Fowler and Amy Grant suffered. She was only six years old, but if time sped past as fast as it had done of late, she'd be a young woman before he knew what happened — the thought of how much older that would make him spurred him into action.

"When I dug out this new folder, that cupboard looked messy. Time for a tidy-up, I reckon. I need to keep busy, or I'll get depressed again."

While Phil was housekeeping, Wayne drove up the M4 towards Reading. He was listening to a presenter interviewing a celebrity chef on the radio. He knew he ought to change channels. They'd discuss recipes for cakes or something equally unhealthy for him any minute now. Wayne was feeling peckish and dreaming of iced buns.

Wayne looked at the clock on the dashboard and then switched to a music channel. That's what was needed – willpower. The sign to Membury services appeared one hundred yards in front of him. The draw of the sticky bun became too strong. He'd buy something here, and have a coffee, then drive on to Reading, and call in or a comfort break as planned. That was okay; Dean Laker and Amy Grant would still be at work.

The first day of the new working week had been uneventful for Amy. She left to walk to the office before the postman pushed his trolley into her street. That had been the norm since the previous weekend. Matters had moved on in the ten days since the latest 'sitrep' Phil and Wayne received.

Amy made another attempt to finish things with Dean for good. He had become even more possessive and demanding. So much so that Amy feared for her safety. Her office colleagues had commented after two or three early mornings in a row last week. They asked why she was so bright and early. Amy shrugged and said it was just the warm early summer weather.

The fact was it avoided having to face unwanted contact from Dean. She knew he would write her another long-winded letter, begging her to give him another chance. Leaving home early, switching off her phone, and avoiding checking social media until she got home in the evening gave her breathing space.

The letter, and sometimes flowers, or other gifts could then go into the bin together. It saved time. Amy tried finding a colleague to eat with at lunchtime and experimented with eating alone in a different bar or café after work. There were dozens to choose from on her way home. She varied the route she took each time to avoid bumping into Dean.

This past weekend had been the worst. The phone calls kept coming, and e-mails too. Amy left home early on Saturday morning and drove to her parent's place to find peace. They were surprised to see her turning up without prior notice; but happy to have her stay for the night. They fussed over her on Sunday, and her father took her to one side when her mother was in the kitchen preparing dinner.

"Are things okay, sweetheart?" he asked.

"Fine, Dad," she replied, "just boyfriend trouble. Time to move on again. Whenever I think I've found Mr Right, he turns out to be Mr Wrong."

"Don't settle for less than Mr Perfect," her Dad said, giving his daughter a rare squeeze.

When Amy reached home late on Sunday, Dean had been trying to contact her throughout the weekend. The tone of the messages he left on her phone had become angrier and more threatening. Amy couldn't sleep, as the slightest sound scared her into believing Dean was trying to break into her home.

Amy's working day ended. Her colleagues made their separate ways home. Nobody wanted to visit the pub up the road for a drink tonight. So she had to face making her way through the streets alone. Amy searched the street through her window in either direction to catch sight of her tormentor.

Wayne Sangster arrived outside Amy's office building

fifteen minutes earlier. It had taken him five minutes to find a parking spot that gave a clear view of the building and the surrounding street. His camera was at the ready, the zoom lens giving perfect images for him to capture should this toe-rag Laker arrive to carry on pestering Amy Grant.

The ex-policeman wasn't aware of the couple's relationship's further deterioration, but he was well-placed to record what took place. He waited and watched.

Dean Laker had been waiting in a café across the street from Amy's place of work. He had spent the weekend calling her, knocking on her door, and searching the streets. Who did she think she was? No way was he going to let her end it with him. He convinced himself her absence only meant one thing.

She must have found someone else — another poor sod fooled by her looks and lies. Dean wouldn't let them continue seeing the Amy Grant that he knew if she was hell-bent on leaving him.

With a twisted mind like Laker's, that didn't mean he would tackle any potential new boyfriend face-to-face. Oh no, he didn't have the guts for that. Instead, he was ready to do whatever it took to make Amy Grant as unattractive to other men as possible. As he sat in the café, waiting for her to emerge from her office, he had a bottle in his coat pocket. The acid it contained was to be her reward for messing with him.

Across the street, the door opened. Amy stepped onto the pavement, looking around her. She tucked her head into her coat collar and, keeping near the buildings, headed for the zebra-crossing.

Wayne spotted her immediately and snapped a picture of Amy for the record. It was evidence of someone frightened of her own shadow. A sudden movement on the pavement on his left-hand side startled him. The door to a café had burst open. A man was running. It was Dean Laker.

Wayne opened the door of the car and climbed out. He tried to snap a quick shot of Dean chasing along the street after Amy, but a moving target on a crowded pavement made things tricky.

Wayne wasn't a sprinter, but his copper's nose anticipated that whatever Dean's intentions were, they signalled trouble for the young girl. He set off in the direction the two of them headed.

Amy crossed the street and hurried through an alleyway leading to the park. This route was one of her favourites. Open spaces and young children playing, people walking their dogs. Everyday things she hadn't been able to do for ages.

She heard Dean shouting at her; she glanced over her shoulder. He was getting closer. Amy ran. Wayne was puffing and blowing but kept an eye on Dean. He was wearing a lightweight hoodie with long sleeves and gloves on his hands. He held something in his right hand. Wayne couldn't make out what.

Amy emerged from the alleyway and ran along the path through the park. Dean was ten yards behind her and closing fast.

"Stop trying to get away, bitch," he yelled.

Wayne saw Amy falter and tumble onto the grass; she looked to have twisted an ankle. He cursed. Laker was right on top of her now. Wayne saw him turn the lid of whatever he held and drew back his arm to throw it at Amy. A shiver ran up his spine.

"Amy!" he shouted, at the top of his voice, "cover your face. Turn away. For God's sake, turn away."

Dean hesitated.

Amy looked at the crazed look in his eyes and knew he meant her harm. She rolled away, shielding her head and face with her arms. Her screams echoed around the park.

Wayne had stopped running. He tried to steady his breathing. Click! He gave it his best shot. The image he captured was the evidence Olympus needed. It showed an apoplectic Dean Laker holding an opened bottle of acid in his right hand. On the grass in front of him lay Amy Grant. She escaped unharmed.

Passers-by crowded around. Dean looked back towards Wayne. He saw the figures approaching him from every side and started running in the opposite direction.

Amy was soon comforted. Fingers pointed back towards the large breathless man twenty yards away. Amy Grant wanted to know who had saved her from a vicious attack; and how he knew her name.

But explanations weren't part of Wayne's brief. He hurried away from the park and back to his car; it was time to head home to Bath. He would report to Phil Hounsell in the morning. His boss would then pass the damning photographs to his contact at Larcombe Manor.

Dean Laker could then receive the appropriate punishment.

Chapter Twelve

Thursday, 1st May 2014

Another morning meeting at Larcombe Manor was getting underway. Hayden Vincent hadn't received reports of yesterday's events in Reading from Orion. So, Athena began by apologising for Phoenix and Rusty's absence.

"This is the second day of planning the strikes ordered by Zeus against members of The Grid. They will continue their preparations in the orangery. They must ensure the necessary steps are in place to achieve the maximum effect with the least impact on Olympus financially and physically. I expect you to give them your full support and give whatever data they need."

"I've not had much input in these plans so far," said Henry. "I look forward to having guests delivered to the icehouse. My methods might persuade them to tell us where this Hanigan devil lives?"

"Phoenix will let you know when we require your services, Henry," said Athena. "For the time being, you must concentrate on keeping Larcombe secure. Advise Giles on how to block anyone from The Grid linking our impending strikes to the Olympus Project. You must protect our anonymity. We must not get careless."

"Understood, Athena," said Henry. "I'll batten down the hatches."

"Artemis and I are still coordinating the search for Hanigan's home address," said Giles Burke. "Phoenix was right. Hanigan is a slippery customer. He's been successful in covering his tracks. There's no record online of anywhere he might have laid his head since he sold that flat in Cricklewood."

"Any photographs available are useless too," added Artemis, "but an agent is watching the Glencairn Bank. He's not staying there the whole day. Gresham Street isn't long. A pedestrian loitering for any length of time would soon be spotted. He's inventive with his disguises and varies the time he visits daily. We hope to gather enough footage from his secret camera to build up a gallery of regular visitors. Hanigan may not attend the bank daily, but he will not be an absentee owner, that's for sure. We hope to narrow the choice to two or three faces in time. We can then follow these men home and continue the search online using those images."

"That's an approach with potential, Giles," said Athena.

"Has Phoenix given any sign when he might carry out the first strike?" asked Alastor.

"He won't say before the event. Rusty will know, but Zeus is the only contact necessary. Phoenix will identify his target. Zeus will then decide whether to authorise the strike. If his mood on Tuesday persists, the strikes will come thick and fast. We will be informed of the outcome as soon as the mission ends."

"Phoenix and Rusty are putting their heads in the lion's mouth," said Minos, "isn't that going to be a dangerous ploy?"

"Without danger, Phoenix doesn't feel alive," said Athena. "He's concerned for Hope and me when he leaves on a mission. He feels the best way to keep us safe is to face danger headfirst. He won't sit back and let others take risks for him."

"Rusty holds the same beliefs," said Artemis, "and if he's fighting side by side with Phoenix, he's certain they'll come through unscathed. They're a formidable pair."

Athena's mobile phone rang. It was Hayden Vincent.

"Orion has completed his part of the job, Athena," he told her.

"Gosh, that was quick. Excellent. Have someone pick up the target, please. Henry wants to entertain someone in Hotel California."

Hayden rang off and sent an agent to collect Dean Laker. His stalking days were over.

At HSS, Phil Hounsell received an email confirming that a five thousand pounds credit was now in their account. He decided a celebration was in order. Phil took five pounds out of petty cash and sent Wayne to the cake shop on the corner for large iced buns. Excellent staff are hard to find.

Only a few miles from Phil's office, the day-to-day affairs that comprised the Olympus morning meeting kept the senior agents occupied until lunchtime. Then they carried on their other duties in the main building or the ice-house.

In the orangery, the formidable pair continued to plan their attacks.

"This will be our primary target," said Phoenix. "Leroy Gordon and the crew he operates. The dramatic increase in gang warfare ties in with a brutal battle for supremacy in the local drug trade. Much of the violence has come from Gordon's activities. Born in Kingston, Jamaica, forty-four years ago, Gordon spent most of his teenage years in Croydon. He has moved the crack cocaine trade out of the inner cities and into the suburbs, where prices are higher. Gordon works exclusively with indigenous Yardie gang members and has made millions from the drug trade. He's responsible for the deaths of over a dozen members of rival gangs."

"Where did he move his operations to after he left Croydon?" asked Rusty.

"They never leave their home turf," said Phoenix, "not entirely. One town they descended on to open new markets was Guildford. Just an hour's drive away. Police reported that crack gangs targeted the town after a group of Jamaicans were arrested during a swoop. Their presence was due to Gordon, who uses the name Lay-Z on the streets. Lay-Z was an immediate suspect when a Guildford drug dealer Brett Stevens was found dead in a country lane near Godalming. Police arrested and questioned Lay-Z, but they released him without charge. He never stays anywhere long. He moves around between several addresses, one of which is the home of an elder sister, Abigail, in Selhurst, Croydon. Close to a football pitch."

"Crystal Palace," said Rusty, thinking the name meant nothing to Phoenix.

"They used to be the Glaziers," said Phoenix, looking at the glass surrounding them in the orangery, "because of the vast amount of glass in the original Victorian building."

"Blimey," said Rusty. "I never expected you to have heard of them."

"Don't worry, I haven't developed a sudden liking for sport; it was in the article I read on Selhurst. However, I wanted to be familiar with the place if we need to pick Lay-Z up from his sister's place."

Phoenix returned to his notes and continued outlining the profile of their target. Rusty shook his head. The man never changed. His attention to detail is unwavering. Rusty sensed they would both be working here late into the evening. When Phoenix was ready, they could call Zeus. If he gave the go-ahead, he and Phoenix would participate in yet another direct action tomorrow.

In Reading, Dean Laker sat at home in his maisonette. He had been in hiding since he ran away from the park. He phoned in sick for work, drew the curtains to shut out the world, and emptied his drinks cabinet. Dean looked a mess.

He had failed in his attempt to scar Amy Grant for life. People in the park had seen his face. That bloke who shouted the warning even took a photograph of them. He was stuffed. He needed to find another job and put this place on the market. It was time to move.

The door to his home splintered and crashed open. Two men burst inside. The drunken shambles of a man that Dean Laker had become was in no position to resist. They overpowered him in seconds. He was bound and gagged and dragged out to a waiting van.

He fell into Henry Case's hands after an hour's drive along the M4. In time, Dean Laker would become another poisonous blight on society taught by the Olympus Project that crime doesn't pay.

Later that Thursday evening, Sean Walsh sat in Hugo Hanigan's penthouse apartment for the first time. He admired the luxury that surrounded him. The artwork on the walls looked genuine, not the series of prints at home. The widescreen television looked brand-new.

The view from the floor-to-ceiling windows was stunning. The beating heart of the City of London lay before them. Sean could appreciate why the boss wanted this place. His aim was to lord it over the capital, to have it in a vice-like grip, controlling everything with the power The Grid gave him. When the nation's capital fell, the rest of the country followed. In confidence, Sean's best friend and brother-in-law Tommy told him this before things went pear-shaped.

Hugo fixed their drinks. He strolled over and handed Sean a lead crystal tumbler full of amber liquid.

"Jameson's for you, Sean?" said Hugo, sitting opposite him. "Do you want water with that?"

Sean looked at the gap between the liquid and the brim of the glass and decided whatever he squeezed in there wouldn't make much difference.

"I'm fine, thanks, Hugo. You've got a great place here."

"We work hard for our money in our way, Sean. Now Tommy is out of the picture; we need to move on. Do you have someone in mind to be your lieutenant?"

Sean had expected this to be why Hugo invited him up here, but he was smart enough not to let Hugo know.

"Heck, you want *me* to take Tommy's place? What an honour, Hugo. I won't disappoint you. A second-in-command, you say? Can I mull over that for twenty-four hours? We have a few people who might be suitable."

"A diplomatic answer, Sean," said Hugo. "We'll work together well. You have twenty-four hours, but don't let me down, Sean."

Sean Walsh took a drink. The whiskey stung his throat

and warmed his stomach, but Hugo's last comment reminded him how cold and ruthless he could be. A shiver ran along Sean's spine.

"When you've finished nursing that drink, you can go," said Hugo, no longer the genial host who welcomed him in earlier. "Call me tomorrow with that name. I'm flying to Ireland at the weekend on family business. The real work starts on Monday. With Tommy in jail, that grass Kelly in the wind, and the Judge slipping through our fingers, we're on the back foot. That's unacceptable. From next week, we come out fighting."

"Whatever you say, boss," said Sean, draining his glass.

He needed to get out. Underneath the sophisticated surface of this crow's nest in the sky lay something rotten. Even the wall paintings had grown more grotesque since their owner exposed his true black heart.

Tommy had been his leader and best friend since their schooldays. They airbrushed him from the gangs' history in a heartbeat. Hugo didn't mention Colleen once, either, while he was there. He showed no concern for his sister or her family.

When the guilty verdict had arisen, Hugo wanted nothing less than protection for one of their own. Only days later, Tommy was left to rot in Belmarsh. Family and loyalty meant nothing to the banker. It was money alone that mattered. Sean was well aware every gang leader within The Grid across the country enjoyed operating within Glencairn Bank.

That was a significant attraction for many. But, as Sean reflected on the situation further along the line, he realised because the banker controlled the money, there was no escape. They had to do Hanigan's bidding or starve. Worse still, he would have them killed if they stepped out of line.

As the gangster travelled in the lift, eager to get to the ground floor and into the fresh air, he was positive of one thing. He would even go to confession again if it meant he never had to return to that penthouse.

Friday, 2nd May 2014

Athena nudged her husband in the ribs.

"What time did you get into bed last night?"

"Eleven o'clock or just after," replied Phoenix. "Why, what time is it now?"

"Just before seven," said Athena, "I can hear Hope snuffling along the corridor. She's snotty-nosed with a cold. I might fetch her and use a flannel from the bathroom. It will be quicker to clean her with. I expect she's got it smeared over her face and hair."

"Do that and bring her in with us," said Phoenix. "I'm leaving in an hour. We can have family time before I get ready."

"Oh, you're ready to go," she said, surprised, "when did you speak to Zeus?"

"I texted him before eleven with the basic details, and he answered at once. He just sent back 'Go for it', with a smiley face."

"Is it you and Rusty on this mission?" asked Athena.

"We have two teams assisting us, one at each location," replied Phoenix ."Rusty and I plan to be back this evening. I'll tell you the details then."

"Be careful, darling," said Athena.

She got out of bed and brought Hope back from the nursery. Their little poppet was red-faced and suffering.

"Hello," said Phoenix, sitting Hope on his knee after Athena handed her to him, "have you got a code in da doze?"

Hope sighed and then sneezed, covering her father in flying snot and saliva.

Athena laughed. "Give her here," she said, "you shower and change.

Phoenix kissed Hope on her hot little forehead at eight o'clock and hugged his wife.

"See you both tonight," he said and headed downstairs to meet up with Rusty.

The next hour followed their familiar routine — a visit to the armoury to sign out the equipment. Phoenix had texted a request to Bazza last night, so it was ready for them to collect.

"Are you going anywhere nice, Phoenix?" asked Thommo, handing over the weaponry.

"If he told you, he'd have to kill you," said Rusty, "these missions have to be hush-hush. Our enemy has intelligence as good as we have here at Olympus, if not better."

"Which makes him a formidable opponent," said Phoenix.

"It's not that we don't trust everyone here at Larcombe," Rusty added. "Not since we removed that one bad apple. On these missions, we need to keep details locked up tight. Only three people know where we're going today."

"And I'm looking at two of them," said Bazza, "well, happy hunting lads."

The weapons, ammunition and equipment that Phoenix ordered took two trips to move to the surface. Once the van was loaded, they set off for their first destination. Rusty drove towards the M4 while Phoenix called the two team leaders he had assigned to the missions. He relayed their meeting points and time of arrival. He would divulge nothing more until they met.

The two men travelled up the motorway in silence. There was no musical accompaniment today. At Junction 13, Rusty turned off towards Newbury. He took the A339 through Basingstoke and Camberley before arriving on the outskirts of Guildford a few minutes before eleven.

"We're meeting our guys in the car park near the centre, Rusty," said Phoenix, "and then it's a ten-minute drive out to Westborough."

"Do we expect to find Lay-Z here?" asked Rusty.

"Not a chance," said Phoenix, "but the semi-detached house he often visits is where his boys are staying."

Rusty drove through the busy streets of Guildford and soon found the car park. It was almost full, but he found a spare spot in the end. He parked facing the entrance, watching the incoming vehicles.

"How many are we up against?" he asked Phoenix.

"Between zero and six," replied Phoenix. "Giles had the house watched over the past forty-eight hours. People come and go. The odds are they'll be there for the next few hours. Their busiest times are after dark."

"What's their background?" asked Rusty. "Home-grown, or from Jamaica, drug dealers, or the heavy mob?"

"Do you recall Scotland Yard issuing a warning over the increase in armed criminals entering the UK from Jamaica? Up to nine men, using false names, arrived in the country last year. They came to the UK to carry out violent robberies against suspected drug dealers and rich black people. At first, they went their separate ways. Two men lived in London and launched a crime spree that included murder and rape. The police caught them in no time, but the remaining seven are still at large. They have been linked to up to fifteen drug-related murders this year."

"So, they're illegals, and killers, then?" said Rusty. "Terrific."

"Yes, they used counterfeit documents and stolen passports to enter the country," said Phoenix.

"The term open borders doesn't cut it any longer, does it," said Rusty, "it's wide-open borders these days. Did these murders occur in inner-city areas?"

"Not all of them," said Phoenix, checking his notes, "one guy, thirty-five years old, was bound and gagged, then shot through the head at his home in Maidstone. Another was shot dead in front of his wife and two young kids in Southwark. A thirty-year-old woman got shot in the street in Wandsworth. This gang moved around, and they're not fussy. Murders occurred in both Thatcham and Basingstoke."

"You said they were a team of seven," queried Rusty, "but that can't include Lay-Z, though, can it?"

"No, Leroy Gordon came here legally with his family years ago," said Phoenix. "The Essex police stumbled across one of the gangs a month back. They stopped him for a minor driving offence. The traffic officers only intended to have a word. He was given a roadside swab test because of the strong smell of cannabis in the vehicle, and, of course, he failed. He couldn't produce a driving licence or insurance. They arrested him and got him to the station in Chelmsford. There they discovered he was here illegally. Plus, someone looking very much like him was wanted for questioning over a murder outside a fast-food restaurant in Peckham. Those traffic guys got a gold star for that one, even though it was a massive stroke of luck."

"This must be our guys driving in now," said Rusty as a

black Range Rover crept into the car park. He flashed his headlights once. The Range Rover returned the signal.

"Right on time," said Phoenix, checking his watch.

He got out of the van, walked across to the driver's window of the SUV, spoke briefly, and then returned.

"Right, let's go. Our guys will follow us to Westborough."

Within ten minutes, they parked on the corner of the street where the gang stayed. Rusty got out of the van and walked to the back doors. He removed a Men At Work sign and tools and placed them on the grass verge. He handed a hi-viz jacket to Phoenix as he returned to the cab.

The SUV drove past them and parked at the far end of the street. Phoenix called the team leader on his mobile.

"How's it looking?" he asked.

"A man is mowing the lawn at number 46. A lady is hanging out her washing at number 55. Two dog walkers are almost out of sight. Then, a young mother headed for the shops up the road with a toddler and an infant in a buggy. Little or no road traffic, as you can see from your end."

"Sounds as if we're good to go," said Phoenix. "Did any movement catch your eye at number 33?

The team leader laughed.

"Not my eye," he said, "but my ears. I think we're heading for Number 33. It has two flash cars on the driveway, the windows are open, and they've got reggae music blasting out."

"It suggests someone is at home, doesn't it?" said Phoenix.

"What are my orders?"

"Park the Range Rover. Rusty will meet you both halfway along the street. He's got hi-viz jackets for you and a 'Men At Work' sign to stick on the pavement by your van. It's only to keep the nosy neighbours satisfied for a few minutes. I'll join you in two minutes, and we'll pay a visit to number 33."

Rusty didn't need to be asked; he got out of the van and fetched the kit from the back. Phoenix watched the house, and the street, for movement while his friend walked towards the approaching agents. He carried the jackets, the sign, and the Enforcer.

Satisfied there was nothing to concern them, Phoenix got out of the van and headed for the target house. The four men gathered by the gateway to the next-door property.

"Nice houses along here, Phoenix," said Rusty. "How much do you reckon they cost?"

"You won't get much change out of three hundred and fifty thousand," Phoenix replied, "it might help us if we discover who owns it. I wonder whether they care what their tenants have been doing?"

The music continued playing inside the house. Even on the pavement, the agents could make out a strong smell of cannabis.

"No wonder they have the windows open," said Rusty.

"It can't do the neighbours much good either," said one of the agents.

"I expect they give the place a wide berth," said Rusty. "The time to worry is if they start laughing for no reason and develop a craving for Jelly Babies."

"We've been standing around here for two minutes, and nobody has moved," said Phoenix, "it's time to get indoors and take them out. I'll ring the front doorbell; you guys use the Enforcer to access the back door. No shouted warnings. Does everyone understand your orders?"

Something Wicked Draws Near

Phoenix saw three nods in response; he walked to the door and pressed the bell. The others ran to the back door. The music might have muted the tone of the doorbell, but someone heard it. The door opened an inch. A stoned-looking Jamaican in his thirties peered out.

"Wassup?" he asked.

Two heavy thumps on the back door made him turn away for a split second. Phoenix hit the door with his boot, sending the gangster sprawling across the hallway. He stepped inside with his pistol raised. One shot disabled the man on the floor.

Rusty and the two agents ran through the kitchen just as three men emerged from the front room. One carried a machete, and the other two stumbled towards the intruders. They found that running while stoned was tricky. The Olympus agents' pistols found their target. The three men hit the floor without landing a blow.

"Check upstairs," said Phoenix to the team leader.

He led his colleague upstairs, and thirty seconds later, they returned to the hallway.

"Clear, upstairs," he reported, "it was just the four of them."

"We've bound and gagged the first two," said Rusty. "Truss up others while Phoenix and I check out the front room."

"Carry out a search upstairs for the usual stuff," said Phoenix, "weapons, cash and drugs. We've been inside for just over two minutes. I want us out of here within the next three. Got it?"

"Understood," replied the team leader, running up the stairs, two at a time.

Under three minutes later, the four men left number 33. Phoenix closed the door behind him. The road signs and the tools returned to the back of the van, along with the hi-viz jackets. The dart-firing pistols were stored away. The men inside the house would wake up in an hour. They were secured so well; they weren't going anywhere before the police arrived.

The two Olympus vehicles drove away towards the A3 and then joined the M25. Phoenix and Rusty set off to Croydon. The team in the Range Rover had no further part to play in this mission. They left the motorway twenty minutes later and headed home.

"Why did you tranquillise them instead of killing them?" asked Rusty, "they're murderers, aren't they?"

"The police need successes, Rusty," said Phoenix. "If we left four bodies for them to discover, they could ask awkward questions. The need to keep the authorities, and anyone else, away from our door at Larcombe Manor is paramount."

"Yeah, that makes sense," said Rusty, "there was plenty of gear in the house, wasn't there? What else did I see you pick up from that desk in the front room?"

"I found the paperwork, but I left it for the police to follow up," Phoenix replied. "Guess who owns number 33?"

"Leroy Gordon?" asked Rusty.

"Abigail Gordon," replied Phoenix. "She's more involved in this than we thought."

Thirty minutes later, they drove into Croydon en route to Selhurst. Rusty glanced in his rear-view mirror.

"A blue Renault van slipped behind us at those traffic lights we passed."

"That's our men," said Phoenix, "when you get a chance, let him pass you. They've got the local knowledge. They're leading us into position. Parking's a nightmare around here, and we'll be better arriving at the Gordon gaff on foot."

Phoenix took a burner phone from the glove compartment and made a call.

"Hello? Is that Surrey police? I think you should take a trip out to Westborough. Number 33, Ash Drive. You can't miss it. It's the one with the windows open, reggae music playing all day, and the sweet smell of cannabis. No, I'm not complaining about the music or the smell. It's the drug factory upstairs and the dealing that goes on every day. It spoils the neighbourhood. I'd rather not give my name. You sort it out; that's good enough for me."

Phoenix ended the call, removed the sim card, and smashed the phone with the heel of his boot on the van's floor.

Rusty followed the Renault van for another two miles through Selhurst. He could see the football stadium up in front. Finally, the Renault turned off, pulled up, and parked on Auckland Road. Rusty parked behind him. He and Phoenix got out and greeted their new team.

"Which way is Abigail Gordon's house from here?" asked Phoenix.

"Back towards the stadium," replied the team leader, "but this road is far safer for parking. Then, when you get back, you're less likely to find your wing mirror smashed or your van's on bricks."

"It's a trek," the other agent said as they set off walking, "we're fifteen minutes away."

"That's not a trek," scoffed Rusty, "it's only a mile."

"An agent checked the property out over the past couple of days," said Phoenix. "Abigail volunteers at a local lunch club for Afro-Caribbean families. Lay-Z Gordon is a nightbird; he'll not be long out of bed."

"Will Gordon be armed?" asked the team leader.

"No question," said Phoenix, "this will need the four of us to be quick and accurate. Any hesitation and we could suffer casualties."

Four men arriving in the street where Abigail Gordon's house was situated would provoke interest. Even on a matchday at Selhurst Park. Someone would spot what Rusty was carrying by his side in as unobtrusive a way as possible.

The teams split into two. A few minutes later, Phoenix and Rusty entered Pembroke Road. The terraced house lay fifty yards in front of them. Their colleagues were on the other side of the road, hanging back twenty yards, waiting for a gap in the lunchtime traffic."

Rusty reached the door first; there was no polite bell press as in Westborough. He hoisted the big red key and smashed the door off its hinges. Lay-Z by name, he might have been, but the big Jamaican Yardie flew down the stairs in his underpants with a gun in his hand, screaming obscenities.

Rusty stepped aside.

Phoenix was ready with his PSS pistol raised, and before Lay-Z Gordon reached the bottom step, he had fired twice. Gordon was hit twice in the chest and died before he clattered to the floor. The silent killer had done its job. A car backfiring would have made far more noise. Rusty and Phoenix looked around the house. They found a small stash of drugs for personal use in Gordon's bedroom, plus over a grand in cash.

"Nothing incriminating in Abigail's room," asked Phoenix.

"Eye-watering, but not incriminating," replied Rusty.

After pulling the door to, as best they could, the two friends left the house and joined the other team.

"Sorry you didn't get to join the party, guys," said Phoenix, "We were lucky. Gordon was still in bed and had none of his friends staying with him. The two illegals still on the run must keep for another day. With luck, the police will arrest them for us."

The men walked back to the vans on Auckland Road. As the team leader promised, they both remained intact.

The London-based team set off towards their base to await the next call of duty. Rusty threaded his way around the M25 until he found the right exit to take them home to Bath. Three hours later, at half-past four, he swung the van through the stone pillars of the Larcombe Manor gateway. The rattle of the cattle grid stirred Phoenix, and he stretched his aching limbs.

"A good day's work, Rusty," he said, "I'm hungry, though. First, let Athena and Artemis know we're back safe, and I'll call in on the lads in the armoury. Once we stow the gear away, I vote we get to the cafeteria for a meal."

"That sounds like a plan," said Rusty. "I can't wait to put my feet up for a rest this evening."

There was a slight pause.

"Ah, I thought we could have something to eat, then we'd spend the evening in the orangery. I want to plan our next hit. We can't allow Hanigan any breathing space."

Rusty groaned.

"Whatever you say, Phoenix, but you're paying for the grub."

Chapter Thirteen

In Kilburn, Sean Walsh had come to his decision. He had only two names on his shortlist of candidates for a second-in-command, but he didn't want to let the boss know. There was nothing between the two men. So, he flipped a coin and made the call.

Hanigan answered.

"Sean, you have a name for me?"

"Seamus McConnell," replied Sean.

"Not a Dublin lad then, Sean? Portmarnock family, are they not? I hope you can trust him. The cream of my Irish gang leaders come from the same few streets in Dublin where we met as children. Ah well, on your head, be it. I'm flying out to Dublin tonight. I'll call you on Monday first thing. There's work to be done."

With the phone call he'd been dreading ended, Sean allowed himself to breathe again. Seamus was one of the best men he and Tommy had recruited. That reaction to his choice of lieutenant was typical of the boss. He thought of everything as being on a national scale for matters relating to The Grid. He was parochial, here in the capital, when it only concerned the Irish gangs. The power base belonged to the seven streets that had been their breeding ground.

Sean rang his sister to invite her to his place for Sunday lunch. He didn't want Colleen sitting alone in her house, festering over Tommy's fate. Their kids were back in Marbella too. Now the trial had ended. They were always happy to profit from their old man's criminal activities but never wanted to get their hands dirty.

Sure, they worked for a living, but when Tommy's money disappeared, as it was bound to do, they'd struggle to afford to live in the lavish style they did now. So Sean thought it sensible to tell Colleen to give them a wake-up call.

Colleen answered.

"I'll drive over on Sunday to pick you up," he said. "We want you to have dinner with us. Is one o'clock OK with you, Colleen?"

"I'm fine on my own, Sean," she said, "you don't have to worry. Yes, I'll come to you on Sunday. We need to talk about launching the appeal. We can't leave Tommy to rot in jail. That judge unfairly punished him because of the attack on his life. That's not right."

Sean closed his eyes. He'd been expecting this. The lawyer had told him any appeal would be pointless. They could scratch around to find grounds for challenging the whole-life sentence, but neither of Tommy's parents lived to old age. Cutting the sentence to twenty years meant him being inside until he was over seventy-five. Tommy would still be lucky to get out alive. Even with today's judiciary, any hope of less than a minimum sentence of twenty years was out of the question for torture and cold-blooded murder.

The pleasant Sunday lunch he had in mind was likely to

be off the menu. Sean poured himself a glass of Jameson's and wished Tommy was still a free man.

While Sean Walsh bemoaned the responsibilities of management, at Larcombe Manor, a replenished Rusty and Phoenix were hard at work in the orangery.

"How did the girls take the news we planned on working late tonight?" asked Phoenix.

"Artemis finishes at eight, so she's miffed at me not being there," said Rusty. "Athena reckoned you were too scared to tell her, so you got me to do it."

"You got off light, mate," said Phoenix. "I had to run the gauntlet of comical comments from Laurel and Hardy in the armoury."

"What was it this time?" asked Rusty.

"You know their level," said Phoenix, "when I handed in the road signs, they reckoned we could get done for false pretences. I said we weren't pretending to be working for the council or a firm of subcontractors. They said the Men At Work sign stretched credibility. We arrived home in daylight, having completed two missions. They said we couldn't call that a day's work."

"OK, next time, I'll go to the ice-house, and you can make the calls."

Phoenix gave Rusty a stare and tapped his left shoulder.

"Seniority, mate."

"Right, what's on the agenda?" asked Rusty, eager to get on. He wanted to be in bed before midnight tonight.

Phoenix placed three folders on the table.

"Take your pick, Rusty," he said. "These crimes are the work of gangs in Birmingham. So that's the next city on our list. We'll complete our provisional plans tonight and fine-tune them tomorrow. On Sunday, we'll be driving up the M5 to strike a significant blow in The Grid's midriff."

Rusty picked up the middle folder and read the first tragic story.

Awusi Debrah was born and grew up in Ghana's capital, Accra. Her family was poor, and she wanted to emigrate to Europe. Awusi hoped she could earn enough money to send a little home to help her mother feed her younger brother and sisters. She met a man who called himself Adam. He told her he had found her a good job in England. Adam helped her pay for her plane ticket and travelled with her to Birmingham Airport.

After she landed in October 2013, Adam took Awusi to a house. She soon realised it was a brothel. Awusi had sex with up to ten men each day. She received meagre amounts of food and drink and slept in a locked room with seven other girls. Every pound of the money the men handed over went to Adam. Unfortunately, he deceived Awusi, and she was trapped.

Awusi discovered she was pregnant. When Adam found out, he beat her so severely that she lost the baby. Because she was of no further use to him, Adam kicked her out. Awusi wandered the streets, bleeding, and a Salvation Army Envoy took her to the hospital. Unfortunately, Awusi had lost too much blood. She only lived long enough to tell the Envoy her story. Awusi Debrah died, aged nineteen, in December 2013.

"This guy Adam, do we know his nationality?" asked Rusty.

"He was born in Nigeria and has lived in the West Midlands since 2010," said Phoenix. "He works within the network of gangs based in the area and takes regular flights to West African countries. Adam travels out alone and returns with a companion. Her passport and other documents show she is a family member, a cousin, or a sister. The forgeries are excellent. Border Control officials would see no reason to query things. On the face of it, the girl is genuine, and what's more natural than a brother travelling with his younger sister?"

"More likely, they don't want to face accusations of racial prejudice," said Rusty

"It's not the first time I've avenged a victim of this despicable crime," said Phoenix. "Although it was before I worked for Olympus."

Phoenix told Rusty the story of Khalima Darbo, the seventeen-year-old Gambian teenager whose body had been discovered in a skip in Catford in 2010. Phoenix helped her relatives find and kill her trafficker back in Banjul. Meanwhile, in Lewisham, Usman Kamara Khan, who held Khalima captive from fifteen, had been shot in his Mercedes. That was while Phoenix cleaned the streets in his old persona, Colin Bailey.

"Erebus must have spotted you that summer, Phoenix," said Rusty. "You thought you were operating under the radar. Giles and the others picked up little clues, building a picture of what you did and why. I can see the reasons he 'headhunted' you. Your motives and methods were a good fit for the Olympus Project."

"Four years on, and although we've made progress, we've still got a long way to go," sighed Phoenix. "Human trafficking is the second most profitable crime in the world. In the UK, victims get exploited through forced labour, sexual exploitation, domestic slavery, and benefits fraud. Traffickers use force, coercion, fraudulent payments and promises of non-existent legitimate employment to entrap victims. It's a hidden crime. Unless the authorities identify more victims, secure more convictions and take long-term action to dismantle the organised crime groups, then the situation will continue to deteriorate."

"Awusi Debrah's death has gifted Olympus the opportunity to highlight the need for strengthening that process," said Rusty. "How do we make that happen?"

"We must get Giles Burke's help," said Phoenix. "His team can leak information to the media, so they spread the message for us. It can be a powerful tool when used for good. The sooner celebrity-obsessed journalism gets shown the door, the better."

Phoenix picked up one of the remaining folders.

"This details several instances of forced labour cases centred on the Midlands. The Polish Roma gangs are mainly responsible. Why don't you take this home with you for your bedtime reading? I'll study the other one."

"Terrific," said Rusty. "What time shall we get together in the morning?"

"Ten o'clock good for you?" asked Phoenix.

"It will have to be, I guess," said Rusty. "These cases won't go away."

Saturday, 3rd May 2014

After a night of broken sleep and unpleasant dreams, Rusty breakfasted with Artemis.

"My day off today looks like a major disappointment," said Artemis when Rusty informed her he was meeting Phoenix in an hour.

"Our weekend," Rusty corrected her, "we're off on the second mission in the morning."

"I might as well get the washing and ironing up together, then take a trip into Bath to go shopping," said Artemis.

"Hang on," said Rusty, catching sight of a familiar house on the television behind her. He turned up the volume. The reporter stood outside number 33, Ash Drive, where he and Phoenix had been yesterday: -

'A police spokesperson said they found four men bound and gagged inside this house. They haven't made official identification of them as yet. They are members of a gang that entered the country illegally from Jamaica a year ago. Homeowners in Ash Drive were unaware their quiet street harboured such a dark secret. The owner of number 35 told me, "I knew she rented it out, but I had no idea what went on in there. We never had any trouble with them or saw anything suspicious. They liked their music during the daytime, but at night, they were always out." Police discovered a drug factory here, in Westborough, after a tip-off from an anonymous member of the public. DCI Nick Yardley of Surrey police said they found thousands of ecstasy tablets packaged for sale. They seized equipment and raw materials that could have produced a further three thousand pills. They took away over one hundred grammes of pure cocaine. They discovered over twenty thousand pounds in cash under the floorboards of a first-floor bedroom and several dozen cannabis plants in the attic. The street value of the recovered drugs exceeded forty thousand pounds.'

"So that's where you went to yesterday," said Artemis. "Who tipped off the police, you?"

"Phoenix," replied Rusty.

The reporter handed back to the studio, and the newsreader read an item that had just landed on her desk: -

'The local councillor for the Westborough district of Guildford has just issued this statement. Circumstances surrounding this incident have yet to get confirmed, but it has raised serious questions about the safety of our streets. Questions too on the current policing and social strategies. Residents in Westborough are anxious about a growing drug and anti-social problem. They are demanding action, not vague expressions of concern. More thought on the social causes of such cases is urgent. Drug crime devastates lives. And now for the weather.'

Rusty muted the sound.

"Where else did you go yesterday," asked Artemis, "can you say?"

"We drove up to London from Guildford. It may have made the regional news up there, but we wouldn't get to hear it in the West Country. You might recognise our handiwork in a piece in a newspaper if you pick up a copy later when you go into Bath."

"I don't go into the city often," said Artemis, "the last time was with Athena before the wedding. I'm always looking over my shoulder for Phil Hounsell, Orion. I want to avoid bumping into him. He's bound to ask awkward questions."

"You never know, Phoenix and I might finish the preparation for Sunday early enough that I can come with you. That should ward off any unwanted advances."

Artemis kissed Rusty on the cheek.

"I love you," she said, "now, get ready for your meeting with Phoenix. I don't want you under my feet this morning if I'm going to be busy."

At ten o'clock, Rusty joined his friend in the orangery.

"Did you see the news item on Guildford this morning?" he asked.

Phoenix nodded.

"Abigail Gordon found Leroy's body when she got home yesterday afternoon. The team leader called me this morning. The Met police believe it to be a falling-out between rival drug gang members. They're not looking for anyone else for the killing. Deaths of that nature occur every few weeks up there. No reason to get excited."

"The Surrey police haven't connected the dots yet?" asked Rusty.

"What, between Abigail owning the house in Ash Drive and her brother getting shot in her home in Selhurst? No, not yet," said Phoenix.

"Did you sleep well last night?" Rusty asked.

"Hope's suffering from a cold, so we didn't get an unbroken night, no," said Phoenix, stifling a yawn.

"That folder you gave me was the stuff of nightmares, wasn't it?" said Rusty. "How people can do that to other human beings is beyond me."

"Let's make them see the error of their ways then, Rusty," said Phoenix.

They reviewed the trafficking case and planned the mission that promised to see them in Handsworth on Sunday.

The four victims had arrived by coach legally from Poland but were encouraged here under false pretences. They were promised well-paid jobs and a good life but lived in cramped, squalid conditions and worked long hours for little pay. The victims soon ended up in a desperate state. They were too scared to seek help. In some Birmingham areas, reports of groups of eastern European men coming and going from a property would be labelled anti-social behaviour. Neighbours were unaware trafficking was the cause, so they never alerted the authorities.

Properties used by gang masters are often death traps. There's no maintenance carried out, and they have dodgy electrics and no smoke alarms. It's only a matter of time before tragedy strikes.

In their mid to late twenties, four Polish men turned up at the soup kitchen in Birmingham city centre with no possessions. They spoke no English. With the aid of an interpreter, the men said they had come to Britain, been housed, and were put to work by Polish Roma.

Volunteers working at the street kitchen suspected human trafficking and called a homeless charity. The men told the charity staff that the coach trip had taken two days to arrive in Birmingham. They were collected by a Roma gang member and taken to a squat in Handsworth. The gang removed their documents and forced them to live together in filthy conditions. Every day, they were driven to Sparkbrook to work in a factory. The gang master who seized their documents forced the men to pay their wages to him. If they questioned the lack of cash, they got beaten. The four men escaped on the journey to work. They were travelling in the back of a van when it stopped for a long time at roadworks traffic lights. They kicked open the doors and scattered. Cold, hungry and homeless, they had found the soup kitchen.

"This is a familiar story," said Phoenix. "Men such as these are targeted by one of two main organised criminal gangs operating in the West Midlands. Criminals see this business as high-profit and low-risk. A trafficked man forced into labour can bring the gangs two to three thousand pounds per month."

The charity staff took one of the men to identify the

places where they lived. He pointed out the factory where they worked and recognised the street where they had been living in the squat. However, he couldn't be sure which house it had been. The homes in the Victorian terraced street looked the same. The men were found a bed for the night. When the charity staff returned in the morning to suggest they told their story to the police, they found the men had already left. Their whereabouts were still unknown.

"Do you think the Roma found them and set them back to work?" asked Rusty.

"It's crazy, isn't it?" said Phoenix. "You find yourself hoping that's the case, despite the terrible conditions. The alternative is that they killed them to set an example to others."

"I hope there aren't too many houses in this street," said Rusty, "these Roma need sorting."

"I've asked Giles to help us out. He's had drones flying over the street since early today. They will highlight the number of bodies in the properties with thermal imaging cameras. Most will hold less than four persons, so where they highlight a house with loads of bright white blobs inside, that will be our squat."

"The Roma gangmaster won't be living there, though, will he?" asked Rusty.

"No, but the drones will record traffic movements and relay those to local agents on the ground. We should soon find the main man and where he drives to after he's paid a visit to the soldiers who watch over the workers."

"I wouldn't want our agents' job," said Rusty, "it's a tough district."

"I reckon they can look after themselves, mate," said Phoenix, "don't fret."

Phoenix called Giles for an update. Rusty continued to work on the plans for the mission. It was two in the afternoon. Phoenix looked at the sheets of paper in front of him.

"I think that's it, Rusty. You get off and spend time with Artemis. I can put the finishing touches on these plans. We'll leave tomorrow at four o'clock to drive up to the Midlands."

"Why such an early start?" groaned Rusty.

"Four in the afternoon," laughed Phoenix. "When we get there, it will be Sunday evening, around seven o'clock, and nobody will be away working. We can release the maximum number of men then."

"Great, I'll meet you by the ice-house with the van at half-past three," said Rusty.

"See you tomorrow," said Phoenix. Rusty walked back to find Artemis. She had just left the apartment to drive into Bath.

"Finished already," she asked, "does that mean I've got a big strong man to carry my shopping bags?"

"I'm yours until tomorrow afternoon," Rusty replied.

"In that case, the shopping can wait," said Artemis, dragging him towards the door to their apartment.

Sunday, 4th May 2014

Phoenix was up bright and early. Hope was getting over her cold, and he and Athena managed eight hours of sleep. Then, for the first time in ages, he had time to sit and read the Sunday papers on the patio; the sun was bright and warm. Phoenix read it wouldn't last; showers were in the forecast for later.

One item on an inside page caught his attention. The

Met police had taken Abigail Gordon in for questioning. Their Surrey colleagues, at last, spotted the owner of number 33, Ash Drive, was renting it to the four gangsters they held in their cells. The Met was investigating whether there was a link between the murder of Lay-Z Leroy Gordon and the tip-off received by their suburban colleagues about the drug factory.

Abigail Gordon admitted to letting people use her premises to produce ecstasy. She claimed to be not guilty of producing either the ecstasy or the cannabis, nor was she guilty of possessing cocaine with intent to supply. It was turning out to be a terrible weekend round for the Gordon family.

Athena joined him outside, carrying Hope in her arms.

"Anything interesting in the newspaper?" she asked.

"The police are still playing catch-up," Phoenix replied, "and there's rain later."

"Did you get the go-ahead from Zeus for this second mission?"

"Ten minutes ago. We're leaving at four this afternoon. Could we do something together for the next four hours? Hope's feeling much better now. Why don't we take her to the pool? We can exercise, play with her, and pretend we're a normal family."

Athena smiled.

"It gets hectic. Will you complete your mission by tonight? Or do I have to lay awake tonight hoping to hear you and Rusty return?"

Phoenix folded his newspaper, stood up, and picked up his coffee mug.

"If everything goes to plan, we'll be home in the early hours. You get ready. I'll keep Hope occupied. Fifty lengths of that pool will sharpen my appetite for lunch."

Further up the corridor, while the Fox-Bailey family enjoyed the heated pool, Rusty and Artemis didn't surface until noon.

"A lazy morning, followed by a leisurely lunch, is the order of the day," sighed Artemis.

"I might need to nap after lunch," said Rusty.

"You're getting old," teased Artemis, "or out of practice."

"We have been on different work patterns for weeks," said Rusty. "When we snatch a few hours together, we're both knackered. Or so hyped-up over whatever job we're on that it's difficult to relax."

"We both knew it would be difficult," said Artemis. "I came into this relationship with my eyes open and had no regrets."

"Nor have I," said Rusty, slipping his arms around her waist as he stood behind her. He spotted Phoenix, Athena and Hope walking back from the old workers' cottages.

"It looks as if Phoenix has been swimming with the family," he said.

Artemis watched the trio as they walked across the lawn, unaware anyone was watching.

"Do you know what amazes me about Phoenix? He can put the stresses and strains to one side at the flick of a switch. Look how relaxed he appears. At just after twelve, he's carrying Hope on his shoulders and enjoying quality time with his wife. In four hours from now, he'll become the stone-cold killer I pursued across England with Orion."

Rusty watched the family as they reached the path. He, too, admired Phoenix and envied him.

"Have you ever considered us having a child?" Rusty asked.

"If we were both in normal jobs, then yes, in a heartbeat," replied Artemis, turning to face him. "But the situation is too volatile at present."

"Okay, fair comment," said Rusty, "but I'll ask again in six months or a year."

"We had better get lunch," said Artemis stretching up to kiss Rusty. "I've only got you to myself for another three hours."

Rusty collected the van from the transport section at three-thirty and drove past the stable block to the ice-house. There was no sign of Phoenix. Rusty descended in the lift to the armoury; Phoenix was talking with Bazza and Thommo.

"Ready in a minute, Rusty," said Phoenix, "but the Chuckle Brothers have news."

"We received notification from Athena this morning," said Bazza. "Zeus has two overseas veterans on their way to take our places in the dungeon. They arrive in two weeks. After that, we work alongside Kelly and Hayden with the training teams."

"Terrific news," said Rusty, "our recruits couldn't be in safer hands."

"Blimey, a compliment from the big man," said Thommo.

"If you'd let me finish," said Rusty. "I was about to say, provided you stick to the training manuals I wrote."

Phoenix handed Rusty half of the equipment required, and the two friends went towards the door leading out of the armoury. Rusty couldn't resist one last quip.

"Veterans taking over from you, did you say? So what does that say about you two comedians then, eh?"

Rusty and Phoenix were in the safety of the corridor leading to the lift as the verbal volley struck the door behind them.

Something Wicked Draws Near

On the surface, they loaded the van and started the journey to Birmingham. It was ten minutes to four as they drove along the sweeping driveway. Athena watched from the window of their first-floor apartment. Hope was asleep in the nursery.

"Come home safe, darling," whispered Athena.

Chapter Fourteen

The Sunday dinner was over in the Walsh family home in Kilburn, and the crockery was stacked away in the dishwasher. His wife and the two youngest children sat in the garden. Sean had told them to make themselves scarce while he discussed family business with his sister, Colleen. Dark storm clouds were gathering. It wouldn't be long before the rain would force his family back indoors.

"That was a fine dinner, Sean," said Colleen, "thank you for inviting me."

"Aye, it was better than what Tommy will get dished up, no doubt. Now, let's stop messing around and talk about this appeal. The lawyer says it's got no chance. You'll be throwing your money away — money you and the children will need. Tommy was the crew leader, but he wasn't in a scheme where they paid full wages for six months. Nor did he pay into any pension scheme. The boss doesn't give a toss now he's inside and not coming out. You need to prepare yourself for a drop in your standard of living."

"If you think I'm standing by to watch my Tommy rot

in jail, you've got another think coming," yelled Colleen. "Hannon is a jumped-up weasel who lord's it over the lot of you because he's good at sums. I'll sell the place in Marbella and keep my money abroad. They reckon the Caymans are the best place, don't they? His fancy motor can go too. I don't need to travel far, and when I do, I'll get one of the family to drive me or take a taxi."

"How will the kids manage?" asked Sean.

"They'll have to stand on their own two feet, the same as Tommy and I did when we moved in together. I'm not paying for them to lounge around in the sun."

"Are you still dead-set on launching this appeal?"

Colleen gave him a cold-eyed stare.

"Do you have any idea of my life with Tommy?" she asked. "I've known him since I was four years old. We were thrown together by our parents. There was no question about us getting married. I was head-over-heels in love with Tommy at fourteen. I was married to him at eighteen — two kids before I was twenty-one and treated like dirt every day since. I was at his beck and call every hour of the day. Yeah, I knew what he was when I married him, but I thought it would be a glamorous life. I was a gangster girl who climbed out of the gutters of those northwest London streets to live in a big house and have the cash to burn. Even inside Belmarsh, he's still got a long reach. How can I not launch an appeal? He's never coming out, but I'll end up on Hackney Marshes if I don't try."

Sean was stunned. He had always thought of Colleen as being happy. Sean wondered about his own family. Did they despise him because of who and what he was? Did they fear him too?

"We'll do what we can," said Sean. "But when you visit

Tommy, you must keep him thinking there's still hope. When did you go there this week?"

"He called me on Tuesday night, the day after he arrived. He told me to visit him on Wednesday afternoons. My first visit is this week."

"That means he's in house block one," said Sean. "Although, knowing where they're holding him doesn't make much difference. Nobody has ever escaped."

"Dad, it's chucking it with rain. Can we come indoors?"

It was Sean's daughter, Saiorse.

"Of course, sweetheart," said Colleen, "your father and I have finished talking for now. Will you give me a lift home, Sean? I'll get out from under your family's feet."

Sean and Colleen drove back to her home in virtual silence. As they pulled onto the drive, Colleen turned to her brother.

"I may have to tighten my belt for a while, Sean Walsh, but I'll not starve. Tommy never wanted me to be the woman I could have been. It didn't suit his style. I plan to play a part in your business. You wouldn't let your sister starve, so find me a job in the organisation. I've got more to offer than you might imagine. For one thing, I'm not frightened to stand up to that weedy punk Ardal Hannon. I thumped his head a few times in the playground. He was shit-scared of me then. I'll make him shit-scared of me now if he doesn't look after Tommy."

With that, she got out of the car and walked indoors. Sean sat and watched her go. Colleen didn't understand what a bastard the little weasel from the school playground had become. He may have been a weedy punk when he ws Ardal James Hannon, but Hugo Hanigan was pure evil. Dangerous waters lay ahead, and he was steering the ship straight for them. Families! He reversed the car off the drive and made his way home. A few hours remained before Hanigan flew back from Dublin. Sean was determined to savour every minute.

Phoenix and Rusty parked the van at Handsworth Park. It was seven pm. Phoenix made a call on his mobile. The local team were on the corner of the targeted street of Victorian terraced houses.

"How long will it take us to walk there?" asked Rusty.

"Ten minutes, according to the team leader," replied Phoenix.

The two agents took their weapons and ammunition from the van and started walking.

"It doesn't get dark until half-past eight," said Rusty. "Do we wait until then, or do you have an alternate strategy."

"I don't want to hang around on these streets, drawing attention. The sooner we can move on to Solihull, the better."

Rusty saw them before Phoenix. Two nineteen-year-old teenagers with swagger, the usual uniform, hoodies, jeans, trainers, and a reversed baseball cap. They had accessories, too, gold necklaces, various wrist bangles, and a hidden blade.

"Chumps at eleven o'clock," warned Rusty.

"Hand over your phone, old man," said the white one.

His coloured friend shaped to throw a punch at Phoenix.

"Big mistake," said Rusty. He grabbed the teenager by the wrist, and seconds later, he threw him into the nearby front garden. The lad was examining his fingers and howling.

"They'll straighten out at the hospital," said Rusty, "your mate will take you, won't you, son?"

"We don't want no trouble," squealed the white boy as he scuttled away to join his injured friend.

"We didn't need that," said Phoenix. "We're supposed to be keeping a low profile."

"You warned me these streets were dodgy," said Rusty.

Five minutes later, they joined the local crew on the street corner.

"Bring me up to speed," said Phoenix.

"It's number 19, up there on the left. Do you see the beat-up Ford van parked two doors further up the street? That's one of the transport vehicles for taking them to work in Sparkbrook."

"How many are inside the house?" asked Phoenix.

"Seven workers upstairs locked in the three bedrooms. Two armed Roma gang members on the ground floor."

"Is there a back way into the property?" asked Rusty.

"An alleyway runs the length of the street to the rear of the properties. There are lock-up garages, waste bins, and loads of rubbish. It's a favoured spot for fly-tippers."

"Do they have a bin at the rear of our target house with a number on it?" asked Phoenix.

"There is. It's black, but the numbers have faded so much it's all but illegible."

"Right, you know where this bin is," said Phoenix. "To save me stumbling in on an old dear watching Antiques Roadshow, kick the back door in when I ring. Rusty and I will eliminate the guards while you two get upstairs to free the workers."

The teams split up and moved into position.

"How do we get through the front door without the big red key?" asked Rusty.

"I thought you could knock for a change," said Phoenix. "A good shoulder hit should do it."

Phoenix made the phone call. Rusty thumped the door hard; it sprang open.

"Go, go, go," Phoenix shouted. There were no shouts of alarm inside the house. One guard was returning from the kitchen with two mugs of tea. The other watched a porno film with one hand on the TV remote and the other in his trouser pocket.

The team leader ran through the shattered back door and whacked the gangster with the butt of his gun. He fell to the floor, arriving on the tiles at the same time as the mugs of tea. Phoenix silenced the guard in the front room with two bullets to the chest.

"He had something in his hand," he muttered, "I couldn't be sure if that gun was loaded."

Seven frightened men were released from captivity upstairs. They were a mixture of nationalities, Czech, Polish, and Lithuanian. Rusty tried to calm them, to tell them they were in safe hands. Phoenix found the keys to the van on the table in the front room.

"What shall we do with the tea boy?" asked Rusty.

"No need," said the local team leader, "he must have had a thin skull. He's dead."

"Tough on him, but it saves us the hassle," said Phoenix.

Outside on the pavement, Phoenix threw the keys to the team leader.

"Drive into the centre, near the cathedral. You can drop these guys off near the soup kitchen; there's always a homeless charity on hand there, and they'll help them out. If we come across any documents that might belong to them at our next address, we'll make sure they find their way to them. Thanks for your help. Be seeing you."

Phoenix and Rusty set off to walk back to their van.

"No muggers in sight," said Rusty, "by the way, did you turn the TV off back there?"

"What, and try to prise the remote out of his hand? No, thanks." Phoenix shivered.

The journey to Solihull, one of the better suburbs in the West Midlands, took forty-five minutes. The house on the tree-lined avenue where the gang master lived was light years away from the dilapidated streets of Handsworth, which paid for it.

"Do we have a name for our target?" asked Rusty.

"Piotr Kowalczyk," replied Phoenix, "mid-fifties, from Krakow. He plays the hard man with the victims but always gets one of his soldiers to do the dirty work. He likes partying with young men at his house. Whether that's for his protection, or something else, we don't know. But, regardless of numbers, we have the right equipment in the van."

Rusty looked at his watch. It was ten minutes to nine, and it was dark. He turned around at the end of the avenue and parked two doors from the gang master's house. They were ready for a speedy getaway.

He and Phoenix got out of the van and, making as little noise as possible, opened the rear doors, collected their weapons, and dressed in their gear. In the distance, they could hear laughter and music.

"I guess we don't plan on taking prisoners tonight, Phoenix," said Rusty.

"This one is to send a big message to The Grid. Nobody is safe. We're putting a spoke in your money-making operations at every opportunity. Maybe this will bring Hanigan out into the open."

"If not?" asked Rusty.

"I've got plenty more targets we can hit," replied Phoenix.

Phoenix led the way. The closer they got to Kowalczyk's house, the louder the sounds became. The next moment, there were several massive explosions. Thousands of coloured stars illuminated the night sky.

"I wondered what the hell that was," whispered Rusty.

"Piotr spares no expense for his parties," whispered Phoenix. "He likes a mixture of mines and cakes for his fireworks displays. Our surveillance teams picked up on this Sunday ritual. Why do you think we're here?"

Phoenix caught Rusty's arm and pointed to the next-door neighbour's house. He led the way around the side pathway; there was no gate or proximity-triggered security lighting. Once inside the rear garden, they made their way across to the five-foot fence. The agents wore black SWAT-type night camouflage clothing. Their black balaclavas covering their faces enabled them to take cover unseen under the two ornamental trees at the bottom of the garden.

Next door, the party was in full swing. Light from the dining room bathed the patio. The patio doors were open wide, and they counted six men standing or seated watching the fireworks, drinking, and having a good time. These were the so-called soldiers, the men who travelled from Europe on the same route as the Polish victims but were now part of the Roma gang.

Their role was to keep the new victims in line, use the knowledge they had gained of language and culture, and convince the authorities that everything was 'cool'. They were the men escorting the victims to work each day, and if anyone asked, things were 'fine, no problem, we're being treated well.'

In the doorway stood Piotr Kowalczyk, a large man well over six feet tall and heavily built. His eyes were fixed on the skies, admiring the five minutes of sparkle he had added to his soldiers' lives. Piotr had his arm around the shoulder of a teenage boy who looked frightened and stared at the ground.

"Time to go," whispered Phoenix, "seven targets. You take the lead. I'll give covering fire if you need it and then join you."

A dark figure leapt over the fence as the next volley of explosions flashed twenty metres above the house. It took several seconds before anyone on the patio realised it wasn't the next-door neighbour's black cat scurrying over the fence, frightened by the bangs and screeches. Unfortunately, those several seconds were fatal.

Phoenix and Rusty carried FN F2000 assault rifles, capable of delivering eight hundred and fifty rounds per minute. Rusty landed with both feet on the grass, steadied himself, and fired six rapid bursts of five shells. Phoenix was on top of the fence, and his thirty-round volley followed.

Dead bodies littered the patio.

Piotr Kowalczyk slumped, dying in the doorway, while the scared young boy cowered by a water butt.

The last few fireworks fizzled above the garden, and the smoke thinned out and disappeared. Finally, the bottom of the garden lay empty.

The teenager saw his chance to escape. Whoever they were, those killers had saved him from Piotr and his friends. He had realised too late how the party was going to end. He would have been an integral part of the entertainment. As he collected his things from inside the house, he heard a vehicle revving up as it drove out of the avenue. He would have to walk home, but that was a blessing.

In the van, Rusty and Phoenix watched for signs the police had been alerted to the gunfire. Everything was quiet.

"The fireworks did their job," said Phoenix, satisfied another of his plans had proved successful.

"Bazza was right to suggest we used those F2000's on this job," said Rusty, "they are very effective at that range."

"Not so much killed as shredded." agreed Phoenix. "Looking at my watch, we'll be back at Larcombe before midnight. That should earn us brownie points with the girls."

Rusty drove in silence via the M42 to join the M5. They had been travelling for fifteen minutes. He told Phoenix about his conversation with Artemis about starting a family. After he finished, he expected a comment, even words of advice, but nothing was said.

Rusty looked across at his colleague in the passenger seat. Phoenix was fast asleep. It reminded Rusty of what Artemis had said earlier in the day. Less than forty minutes ago, they had eliminated seven men from a ruthless gang that played an essential role within The Grid.

Phoenix had tuned out the bloodshed and the mayhem and was relaxed enough to drop off to sleep in minutes.

Rusty was still 'wired'. He imagined how different things could have gone if the Roma on the patio had seen them coming; or if others inside the house had returned fire.

Rusty drove home. Alone with his thoughts. Every mile that brought them closer to Larcombe, he felt his tensions ease. He was as laid back as his friend when they drew up by the stable block to park for the night.

"Mission completed," said Phoenix, stirring as soon as the van came to a halt.

"A good week for Olympus," said Rusty. "A few questions asked of The Grid and its leader."

Phoenix nodded.

"Come out, come out, wherever you are," he said, and with a wave of his hand, he left Rusty and walked off across the lawn.

Rusty set off for the door leading to his apartment. It was not yet midnight. He wondered if Artemis was still awake. The steady, gentle snore which greeted him told him otherwise. The weekend was over. Another potential week of danger beckoned in the morning. Rusty hoped he could fall asleep as soon as his head touched the pillow.

Hugo Hanigan was still wide awake in his London penthouse apartment on the other side of the country. His private jet had landed at Heathrow Airport at ten-forty, as planned. A taxi delivered him to his building in the City in an hour. It was now midnight. The weekend in Dublin ended.

The trip had become an annual pilgrimage. Hugo hired a car at the airport when he landed in Dublin. He dropped his bags at the Merrion Hotel, then drove towards Dundrum and, from there, on to Glencairn Park. He stopped off at the shopping centre in Dundrum to buy flowers.

The Park had changed out of all recognition since they had visited on day trips with the church. He recalled the open spaces where he and the other street kids could run free. Those carefree days had gone. He parked the car and walked to the far side, to the spot, in the shade of a row of trees, where they found his murdered mother's body.

Hugo reverently placed the flowers where he imagined her heart had been. Sorcha Hannon, nee Hanigan of Bangor, died on May 3rd, 2010.

The loan shark who sent his thugs to punish her for the late payment of her debts was no longer trading. One of the first things Hugo did when he adopted his new persona was to arrange for the man's funeral. The total amount he offered for the contract included making him suffer before he died.

The loan shark's thugs died later that same year, too. Hugo paid someone to bludgeon them to death. He thought it appropriate.

Hugo stood for a while and gazed at the flowers. He had a few words to say to his mother, but this was not the time or place. He returned to the hire car and drove back to Dublin.

After spending the afternoon in his hotel room, Hugo made another sentimental journey. He could see the seven streets in his mind's eye. Hugo could name the families who lived in almost every home. Just as with the Park, there had been changes in the three decades since he lived on Thomas Street, Inchincore. The seven streets of the neighbourhood had a reputation back then. Hugo learned in his visits since his mother's death that nothing had improved.

Several council estates covered the area. Unemployment rates were high, and at night teenagers loitered on street corners. They awaited the incautious tourist they could mug or give a bloody nose. Hugo knew this was no place for him to walk the streets, day or night. He kept the car windows closed as he drove around his old patch. The locals could smell money; there was no point in alienating them.

The houses looked different, and the families had changed, yet he could recite his former neighbours' names when he drove past each door. His visit was brief, but as it ended, emotions ran high. These streets were where he grew up. A foot away from the gutter. Look at him now.

Hugo gave one last look at Thomas Street and drove back to the Merrion.

On Sunday morning, he went to St Patrick's Cathedral for the Choral Eucharist and Matins. His mother would have wanted him to attend. She had badgered him to confess his sins weekly, but although his parents raised him in the faith, Ardal James Hannon lapsed before he reached his twenties.

Hugo Hanigan had no time for religion, and there wasn't a confessional big enough to cater for his many sins. For the fourth year in succession, he stuck it out to the end of the service. In the afternoon, he had driven to Golden Bridge cemetery to visit his mother's final resting place.

The cemetery was an occasion for more flowers. They might have appeared bizarre at Glencairn, but in the garden cemetery, there was greenery and colour in profusion. The sun always seemed to shine here when Hugo visited.

It was the perfect setting for Sorcha Hanigan. No matter how weak of character she might have been, she didn't deserve for her life to end that way. The grave was neat and tidy, as always. Hugo didn't have to tidy away the remnants of the flowers he laid here last year. He paid a gardener from the city more than enough to ensure the grave received tender care. Hugo had stood back and studied the headstone and his flowers. Everything looked perfect; his mother would have approved. It was time to share those few words between a son and his mother in this serene spot.

"You always encouraged me, Mother. I longed to be like the other children on the estates. I was desperate to fit in. They always treated me differently because I was clever. You persuaded me that my talent for learning would allow me to turn out better than them. You were right. Since visiting you last May, I've expanded my network of organisations nationwide. Anyone who opposed me gets cast aside. The children that looked down on me when I was a child look up to me now. I hold their fortune and future in my hands; nothing can stop us. I shall count the days until I return. When everything goes to plan, my network will be in total control. No single financial transaction in the murky world I operate will exist unless I sanction it. The Grid will have a stranglehold on every city and town across the nation, and your son will have made it happen. I'll make you proud, Mother; you wait and see. Evil always finds a way."

Hugo kissed the tips of his fingers and laid them on top of his mother's headstone. His eyes were dry. He would shed no tears today. Other families would suffer in the year to come as he continued the battle for the control he craved. Hugo turned away from the grave and walked back to the car. It was time to return to the hotel, enjoy a superb evening meal, and then make his way to the airport for the flight home.

As he sat at home, alone with his thoughts, he was unaware that parts of his precious network had suffered deadly strikes. He would learn of those in the morning. But, for now, Hugo Hanigan looked out over the capital's skyline as it twinkled like a million stars and imagined he hadn't a care in the world. As he told his mother, nothing could stop them from achieving their goal.

Before he returned to visit Sorcha Hanigan's grave in the Golden Bridge cemetery, Hugo would come to know one opponent alone stood between him and success. The agents from the Olympus Project, led by the Phoenix, were not to be cast aside without a fight.

Next in The Phoenix series

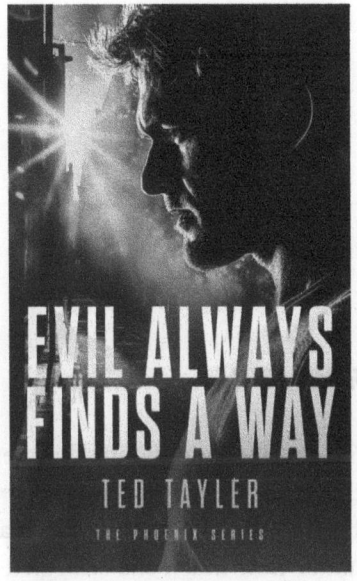

vinci-books.com/evil-finds-a-way

When terror reigns, only one team can save the nation from the brink of chaos.

The Grid's campaign of terror pushes the UK to the brink of collapse. As the Olympus team races to stop the plot, the stakes grow higher with each twist, leading to an explosive finale that promises an even more thrilling and unpredictable future.

Turn the page for a free preview…

Evil Always Finds A Way: Chapter One

Monday, 26th May 2014

The cellar walls were dark and damp. Her metal chair sat in the centre of the room, bolted to the concrete floor. They had strapped her feet to the legs of the chair with gaffer tape, and no matter how much she struggled against them, they didn't budge an inch.

They had secured her hands behind her, and the stress on her shoulders only eased when she passed out. Either from the nagging pain or the cocktail of drugs that they gave her. In a few minutes, she was lucid enough to assess her surroundings; she could not see a thing. Her underground prison was in total darkness.

If only she could get her hands free and cover her ears. As she sat there, hour after hour, alone in the pitch-black room, the sounds drove her mad. A constant drip from a pipe, somewhere high up on the wall behind her. The staccato movements of mice, or worse, when they skittered across the floor, heading for holes in the walls.

As much as those sounds preyed on her sanity, there was the ever-present fear of her captors' return.

The woman knew the exact moment her nightmare began.

She left her colleagues at five on Friday evening to drive the short distance home. After a busy week, she wanted a long soak in the bath, a pizza, and a cold beer. The others were going to a local bar before making a Tube journey to the capital's outskirts or a train trip back to the country.

Why didn't she listen to their cries as she headed to the underground car park?

"Aw, come on, don't be such a wuss," Brandi shouted.

"It'll be a laugh, babe. I'll get us Sex on the Beach," Selina offered, which brought squeals of laughter from the rest.

She had waved a hand in their direction, smiled a weak smile in reply, and carried on taking the stairs to the lower level.

Why did she prefer solitude to the heady social whirl of a raucous wine bar on a warm summer's evening? Memories of her past life shaped her present attitude; those places had been the building bricks of the lifestyle she led in her twenties. They had been the slippery slope into addiction and prostitution. These days she shunned every invitation that might tempt her back into her old ways.

Her drive home posed a few problems. Instead of making for Holland Park Avenue as she did nine times out of ten, she cut up Kensington High Street. Big mistake. Traffic was at a standstill. The roadworks she had forgotten to read about caused her to spend the next fifteen minutes in her hot little car, with no air-con, as hundreds of drivers negotiated the temporary traffic lights. Patience was at a premium. At last, she turned onto Abbotsbury Road. She endured a brief battle with pedestrians on Holland Park Avenue and reached a calmer spot where a red light stopped her progress near the Gate cinema.

Almost there now, she had thought; her flat lay just around the corner. The streets nearby were home to various stores, restaurants, and cafés, plus more specialist shops that dealt in rare records and antiques. It was the neighbourhood where she settled a year after leaving University.

The Gate, a Grade II listed building, had stood here since Edwardian times. She often visited the far more beautiful place on the inside than the façade through her windscreen might suggest. Several bars and clubs were dotted about, too, in the vicinity. Those weren't on her radar any longer. Despite their temptations, she was happy with her choice of where she lived and wouldn't change it regardless of her financial situation.

That thought drifted away in seconds as she experienced spasms of pain in her shoulders and lower back. On earlier occasions, she had screamed or cried for help. This time she laughed, and the more she thought how ridiculous this reaction was, given her current predicament, the more she laughed.

Why didn't the bastards come and dose her up again? She craved the release the needle would give. To be knocked out for hours, to not feel a thing, or to spend what felt like a day on a multi-coloured drug-fuelled trip was preferable to sitting here wide-awake, losing her grip on reality.

Nobody came.

Friday, at five pm, yes, that had been the start of this nightmare. Thirty-five minutes later, she reached her street. Then she parked the car and climbed the four steps to the front door of the Victorian terraced house she shared with five other flat owners. Her ground-floor flat was in the shade in the afternoons. She had opened a window and flopped onto the sofa. The stuffy atmosphere from the flat being shut up all day soon went. She relaxed in the fresh air, flicking through TV channel menus to find something to watch that evening.

Ten minutes later, with the pizza ordered, the bath filling, and a clean glass on the worktop by the fridge, she could relax. She entered the bathroom at six o'clock, just as the theme music for the news bulletin started. It struck her as strange that she could remember everything she had done during those sixty minutes.

How many hours had passed since then? How many days?

A cramp in her left calf replaced the aches and pains in her arms and back. But, no, if she concentrated hard, she could isolate five separate individual areas of pain. Her calf was now nine out of ten; her shoulders and back had subsided to eight apiece — the cramp in the toes of her right foot a mere six. The fifth remaining niggle came from her bladder.

As she leant over to turn off the taps back in her flat, however long ago, she had heard the doorbell. She cursed Domino's every stride she took away from the luxurious bath that awaited. At seven o'clock, she told the muppet on the phone; it wasn't a problem if they couldn't get there until a quarter-past, half-past seven even. But not before. She had wrapped her dressing gown tight around her and stood behind the door, with the chain on, as she opened it to give the delivery boy a volley of abuse.

The heavy wooden door hit her squarely in the face, cracking into her nose as it flew open. She had been stunned and fallen back onto the stripped wooden floor, unable to protect herself when the intruders burst into her flat. She tried to clear her head, to get back onto her feet. It was no use; she felt the point of a needle pierce the skin on her neck below her right ear.

That was when the passage of time got away from her. She drifted in and out of consciousness several times while her attackers prepared to leave. It was clear they were taking her with them; they placed a canvas hood over her head, and her hands and feet were bound. They collected items from her medicine cabinet and checked drawers and cupboards. Then she remembered nothing until she woke up here, in this room. Whatever they injected her with had taken effect, at last.

When she awoke, she had been seated where she sat now. The hood had gone, but it changed nothing. There was no light whatsoever — no amount of screaming, crying, or struggling made any difference to her situation. Her nose throbbed like crazy.

She felt vulnerable. She was naked under her flimsy dressing gown. Her early thoughts centred on why they broke into her flat. Was it a burglary gone wrong? Had she been kidnapped? Did they intend to rape her? Who were they? Where were they?

Her captor's first visit told her everything she needed to know.

A door opposite her chair opened, and lights in the corridor outside blinded her. She hung her head on her chest to shield her eyes from the glare. There were three voices. Guttural. East European accents, perhaps. Men in their thirties or forties, not kids. She had no clue how long she sat there, but her bladder betrayed the fear she felt. She wet herself.

The man closest to her grabbed her chin and lifted her head. Then he slapped her cheek with his open hand, cursing her in his native language. Was that Bulgarian? Hungarian? She must have peed on his shoes; it served the bastard right.

Another man now stood behind her. He pulled her hair away from her neck, and she felt another sharp prick. He whispered into her ear in English, this time, but heavily accented: -

"It would have been better for you to do as ordered," he said, "now we will use you as a guinea pig."

A chill had run down her spine. Dawn Prentice knew at that moment who had taken her and why.

These days she worked for a charity helping recovering addicts. Eight years had passed since she escaped her old life under the yoke of addiction. The wealth she inherited from her late parents went to good causes over the past year. Brandi, Selina, and the others she worked alongside battled daily in the fight to stop the spread of drugs. It was an evil that always found its way into every level of society. Their battle against that evil was relentless, but the forces they faced were brutal and almost overwhelming.

Dawn's past life was public knowledge. The press made great play of it soon after her parents died. The charity didn't shy away from her offer of financial help. They recognised there's no such thing as bad publicity. A former addict donating vast sums hoping she could help make a difference, gave the charity a boost.

The feel-good factor didn't last; her colleagues noticed a change in her attitude. Dawn became withdrawn and less engaged. There had been similar occasions to last Friday evening when Dawn rushed away rather than mix with them socially. Something troubled her or someone.

Dawn said nothing to her friends. Then, one Saturday morning, a man approached her in the street as she walked to the nearby deli to pick up something for lunch. He walked beside her, close enough to intimidate her but never laying a hand on her. She didn't recognise him, but he knew her name, where she lived and worked, and the car number of her little Fiat. He knew the things from her past she tried to keep hidden for eight long years.

The man mentioned a name. He said his boss wanted to get in touch. Dawn shuddered at the memories the name brought back. Adam Kovacs had been the last in a long line of dealers to have supplied her with the drugs she craved. Finally, they reached the door to the deli. Dawn waited for someone to exit the shop before entering. She realised no one was behind her when she pushed the door open. The man had disappeared.

Minutes later, with her sandwich, and smoothie in her oversized shoulder bag, Dawn stepped back onto the street, looking both ways. Dozens of faces streamed past, but she saw no sign of her old dealer's errand boy. Dawn thrust her hands into her coat pockets and hurried back to the flat. When she withdrew her house keys from her right-hand pocket, a piece of paper fluttered to the hallway floor.

Dawn grabbed it and ran inside, locking the door behind her. She emptied her purchases onto the kitchen table and threw her coat over the back of the sofa. Dawn imagined the slip of paper as a receipt or a shopping list of a few necessary items to buy several weeks ago. Dawn was on the point of screwing it up and throwing it in the bin when she saw the handwritten note.

'It's been too long, Dawn. Ring me in the next twenty-four hours if you want your little secret to stay hidden.'

The note was signed 'AK', and the mobile number scribbled underneath was unchanged from the old days. Adam Kovacs threatened to uncover her sordid secret.

Dawn had been desperate for a fix, flat-broke and too ashamed to ask her family for money. She turned to prostitution. Adam had been her first customer, and then he pimped her out to his colleagues. It had only been for six or eight weeks, but realising she had reached rock-bottom was the spur she needed to break free of Adam's clutches and try to get clean. If she continued, her outlook would have been bleak, and an overdose, accidental or otherwise, lay in wait.

For the rest of that Saturday, Dawn stared at the slip of paper and wrestled with her conscience. If she rang Adam, it could lead her back into the life she now donated tens of thousands of pounds to help conquer. If Dawn didn't call him, she would read of those horrid days in the media. It was bad enough that the world and his wife learned she was an ex-addict. Dawn dreaded the exposure of what she did to pay for those drugs at her lowest ebb.

It had been an awful weekend. On Sunday evening, Dawn rang the number she hadn't dialled for eight years. The mere sound of Adam's voice made her skin crawl. She asked him what he wanted her to do for him.

In return for his silence on her past, Adam told Dawn he imported designer drugs from Central Europe these days. Their potency meant small, easily transported packages could slip through customs. Dawn learned Adam wasn't working alone. He was part of a gang operating on both sides of the Channel.

Adam forced her to finance the import of those raw materials. His suppliers then manufactured and packaged the final product. Finally, when the drugs reached him, he and his fellow dealers got them to the consumer.

Dawn knew how damaging it could be to the charity if word got out that she financed the very trade against which she campaigned. That was why she distanced herself from her friends. It pained her to do it, but they must never discover the truth concerning her past, nor how she intended to protect it.

After a while, it became easier to cope. Adam gave her details of an anonymous-sounding bank account his fellow gang members had provided. She set up a monthly bank transfer, and thankfully, she heard nothing further from Kovacs while the money kept getting transferred. Neither did his errand boy happen to bump into her on the streets of Notting Hill Gate.

Dawn pushed thoughts of the matter deep into a dark corner of her mind. Something she had grown accustomed to doing with unwanted memories.

At the end of April, she arrived home one evening to discover a note shoved into her letterbox. It was from Adam Kovacs.

'We're having a party this weekend. You should come. I have friends who wish to meet you.'

Dawn hadn't called him on his mobile. She didn't want to hear his voice; she sent him a text.

'What's in the past stays in the past. You're getting the hush money, nothing more.'

She waited and waited for a response. After a day or two, Adam sent his reply: -

'OK. Sorry that you can't be available.'

Dawn heard nothing more. Although she continued to keep her distance from her colleagues, she hadn't anticipated the events of that Friday evening. As the days and weeks ticked by, she thought Adam was happy to take her money, which would be the extent of her involvement in the filthy trade.

She had learned of these new designer drugs through

her work with the charity. When she started using, she had taken the traditional route to the gutter; a little weed at parties, a few uppers and downers. Then a gradual but inevitable slide into heroin and cocaine.

In the days, or was it weeks, that they had strapped her to this chair, she came to know a new cocktail of products that hadn't been on the charity's radar when they kidnapped her. Her punishment for not attending Adam's party as a plaything for his foreign friends was to be a human lab rat.

The spasms in her shoulders were back. She tried to move her position slightly to ease the stress. The movement kicked off another bout of cramps in her toes. The urge to pee grew greater. That niggle fast became a necessity. After their first visit, her captors brought a metal bucket and placed it between her feet. With a few painful presses of her hips, she could get far enough forward to relieve the pressure on her bladder.

Dawn dragged herself back into the chair and tried to forget the aches and pains in her calves and toes. She fantasised about that hot bath she had run and how wonderful it would be to immerse her aching body in water. Her captors provided her with very few creature comforts.

The raid on her medicine cabinet allowed them to keep her on active birth-control pills so far, which was one less worry for her; also, it was one less problem for them to handle. When she needed to do more than pee, she held on until they brought her scraps of food and water. She imagined this was daily, in the mornings, but couldn't be sure. When she fell asleep through pain, exhaustion, or the effects of the designer drugs, she had no idea whether she slept for an hour or half a day.

The routine for the visits she received was simple. The

three men entered the room, and one released the bindings on her hands. She received a bowl of odd scraps of fruit, cold vegetables, and chicken to scoop into her mouth with her hand. A plastic cup of water helped her swallow her pill and whatever else they wanted to try out on her.

If she begged to squat over the bucket, they re-tied her hands and then released one leg from the chair. The first time, they laughed as she tried to sit, but the strength had gone from her legs, and she and the metal bucket toppled over.

Dawn received another open-handed slap that loosened a filling for that misdemeanour. She had needed the bucket only three times so far. Maybe that meant she had been here for between six and eight days? Who knew?

The last thing they did before they left each time was to wash her, which was further humiliation. One man drenched a sponge in cold water from the container they used to fill her plastic drinking cup. Then with her hands and feet securely tied once more, he wiped her face under her arms, and they took turns to stroke her breasts and between her legs.

The last two stages seemed to take forever. The conversation was limited. Each time Dawn thought they would rape her, but so far, they had gone no further.

When they were satisfied that she was clean or humiliated enough for one day, they laughed and prepared to leave. Her daily 'special' injection followed if a pill wasn't tested on her on that occasion. Then, after exchanging a few words in their native language, they left her alone in the dark.

Dawn knew what to expect after swallowing a pill or receiving an injection. Her only hope was she would get one dose of different synthetic drugs rather than successive hits of the same base synthetic. These new drugs could destroy life by triggering psychotic episodes of hallucinations, aggression, paranoia, suicidal thoughts and destructive tendencies.

Alone in her dark prison, Dawn had no way of controlling these symptoms. She twisted and turned on her chair, trying to break free, to run away from people she imagined were chasing her. She sweated profusely, saw flashes of colour, and experienced prolonged, dull headaches.

Almost everything they fed her produced a negative or negligible reaction. Her heart raced one minute and was normal the next. She was confused. One trip left her seeing Adam's face on all three men who next visited the room. She vomited as soon as the cold sponge brushed against her face. She was punched hard in the face. If her nose hadn't broken before, it did then.

Dawn assessed the pain in her nose at ten that morning. It registered only a six or seven now; she supposed it would need to be re-broken and set straight when she got out of here. If she ever got out. Dawn pushed that negative thought into the same dark corner as the bank transfer.

The wait for a visit seemed longer this time. Her bladder emptied maybe three hours ago. They didn't feed her much, but her hunger wasn't so great that she was desperate for food or water. Dawn wondered whether the next thing they tried on her would be a happy pill. She could suggest the men played with her a little longer in return for a real buzz that gave her several hours of grinning at the blackness surrounding her.

"I'm losing it," she said as the tears came unbidden and ran down her cheeks.

The door opened. One man stood silhouetted against the brightly lit corridor.

It was Adam Kovacs.

He walked across the room and stood in front of her.

Adam looked as if he had arrived from a company board meeting. He wore a well-tailored dark suit, a light blue shirt with a burgundy tie, and highly polished shoes. Dawn spotted the diamond stud in his left earlobe and remembered how it had felt against her inner thigh. The bile in her throat threatened to make her former drug dealer clean those smart leather shoes.

"We have a problem, Dawn," said Kovacs.

Dawn swallowed hard. Kovacs continued: -

"The bank transfer that should have arrived in our account this morning was stopped. We queried this matter. Your work colleagues were worried when you didn't visit the charity offices where you volunteered. Everyone knew of the money left to you by your parents. Two of your friends called your landlord and asked to be allowed access to your flat. They were concerned something may have happened to you. My boys forgot to tidy up after they collected you, and the landlord found the door unlocked. Inside, your friends found the number for your solicitor. You instructed him weeks ago to freeze your credit cards and bank accounts should you go missing."

"Your errand boy made me nervous," said Dawn. "I sat and fretted all weekend over that note you sent with him. I talked with my solicitor at once after I visited my bank to set up the transfer. I'd forgotten I'd done it. I'm sorry."

"Until you are seen in person by your solicitor to sign various documents, there will be no more money," said Kovacs. "This means, as helpful as you have been as a guinea pig over the past three weeks, I now have no further use for you."

Dawn struggled against her bonds; panic gripped her as

she realised what the drug dealer had said. Her kidnapping was not for ransom. There would never be any cosmetic surgery on her broken nose.

"Goodbye, Dawn. Sweet dreams," Kovacs said as he turned and strode out of the room.

Her three tormentors appeared in the doorway. Only one of them entered. The other two watched impassively as he approached her chair. He waited long enough for her to thrash around until she was exhausted. But, as always, it was to no effect, and the limp figure now slumped in front of him registered acceptance.

He gently lifted the hair from Dawn's neck, and the needle performed its final task.

Without a word, the three men left the room. Dawn was plunged into darkness once more.

Minutes passed, and she noted tiny flutters of her heart and subtle changes in her blood pressure. This euphoria was what she dreamed of, that intense excitement of well-being that nothing had given her in the past three weeks.

Dawn Prentice found she could relax despite her restraints. The pain levels dropped. Seven. Six. Five. Dawn understood what lay ahead and wanted it more than anything she had enjoyed in her life.

A few short breaths away stood oblivion.

Evil Always Finds A Way: Chapter Two

Wednesday, 28th May 2014

Colleen O'Riordan signed the forms the solicitor spread on the large oak desk in front of her. Apart from cards of celebration or condolence she scribbled on over the years, she hadn't done as much writing since she left school.

Tommy was the man of the house.

Colleen prepared and cooked his meals, poured his drinks, gave him what he wanted in the bedroom, and produced an heir and a spare. She had known it best to hold her tongue for the rest of the time. He required little else of her. She never needed to get involved with the household budget, school fees, or anything remotely financial.

In the gangland world Tommy inhabited, cash was still king. Colleen might have graduated to having a credit card in their domestic lives instead of a fistful of notes thrust into her hands if she asked for something. Still, she had no idea how much lay in the account she used to pay for her weekly shop or her few personal luxuries. It was none of her business.

Times had changed; Tommy was in Belmarsh nick. Colleen was visiting him this afternoon. They had things to discuss. First, he would want to know how Tyrone and Rosie were doing. Did they miss their Dad? Were they ashamed of him? When were they flying in from Marbella to visit?

Colleen hoped to keep him away from that subject for a few weeks. The ink was hardly dry on those forms she signed. She tried to recall the last time she held a proper fountain pen in her hand, with ink as blue as the Caribbean rather than a bloody black biro, but she couldn't recall it.

Maybe when they signed the register in the vestry on their wedding day?

Colleen wasn't one for looking over her shoulder at the past, not these days. She was determined to move forward. Colleen shook the limp, bony hand of the solicitor and stared at the top of his head. She thanked him for everything he had done and smiled as she turned away.

Colleen paid him enough to re-arrange the O'Riordan family affairs in double-quick time. She could afford to let him stare at her tits without reproach and dream.

Her brother Sean had his hands full with Hugo Hanigan and Grid's business. Seamus McConnell was being eased gently into a role as Sean's number two. A job for which he was unsuited as far as Colleen could tell. No matter, it meant she had a clear road to do what was required. It would be a done deal before Sean or Tommy realised and tried to put a spanner in the works.

As soon as Colleen noticed Sean was otherwise engaged, she started with the cars. Tommy didn't need one, and she was happy not to drive herself around town. Time to get rid. The cash could come in handy.

The Mercedes and the SUV went to auction. Colleen knew nothing about cars and cared less; it was a fire sale. Two lucky punters picked up decent motors for chump change. Colleen treated herself to a new dress and stashed the balance in the bedroom wall-safe.

As she had closed the door and spun the dials, she allowed herself another smug grin. Tommy thought himself so clever. He always forgot the combination. He wrote it on a playing card, the ace of spades, and tucked it into a drawer under piles of his socks and pants. Tommy didn't think she'd find it or realise what it meant.

When Colleen opened it for the first time, the day after the trial, she was stunned by what she had discovered. His gun and ammunition lay inside, which was no surprise. Instead, the rolls of notes, secured by elastic bands, made Colleen gasp and sit back on the bed with a bump.

"You bastard, Tommy," she muttered, "you had this much cash lying around. Yet you moaned every time I held my hand out for a few quid."

Colleen had spent an hour counting out the cash. Eighty-five thousand in English money and thirty-five thousand in euros. The sixteen and a half thousand she deposited from the car auction was peanuts, but it would find a home in time.

After her first trip to visit Tommy in Belmarsh on Wednesday, the seventh of May, Colleen called Tyrone. He and Rosie had lived the high life at their father's expense for long enough. She told him the apartment they shared must go on the market. Their nearly new open-top sports cars would return to the dealer. She'd try to salvage enough from the proceeds of the sale to give them the deposit on a modest place they could finance themselves.

Tyrone was apoplectic. Rosie, listening in the background, was in tears. Colleen had no sympathy for them. It was time for the spongers to stand on their own two feet. The bank of Mum and Dad had closed.

"What's this rubbish," stormed Tyrone, "where's the money going?"

"Where do you think?" snapped Colleen. "I visited your father yesterday, and he's hellbent on appealing. It doesn't matter that they had him bang to rights. Of course, it will be money down the drain, but there's no telling him. You know what he's like, Tyrone."

"What happened to the rest of his money, though, stuff that's not tied up in property and that?"

"While he ran the show, he had plenty of money," said Colleen, "but Uncle Sean is the big man now. Gang leaders don't keep the inmates of Belmarsh on the payroll, not when they're unlikely to work again for thirty years. Gangsters don't get benefits, Tyrone. It stands to reason. No, you two must stop messing around and get stuck into proper jobs. The private school education your Dad paid for has given you the tools. It's time you used them."

Colleen had ended the call. Tyrone and Rosie needed that reality check. Tommy never dreamt of questioning the way they wasted their money. Rosie was his princess; the Spanish sun shone out of her backside. Tyrone was intelligent and hard-working when it suited him. He knew damn well criminal operations were where the money came from and had been happy to take it, but he kept a million miles from the career path his father and grandfather had chosen.

The Marbella apartment should sell for seven hundred thousand euros. Colleen made up her mind on Wednesday afternoon as she sat in the taxi en route to Belmarsh prison. It went on the market within five days of the conversation with Tyrone. Tommy paid around three hundred thousand pounds for it, although he never told her exactly how much. They would make a decent profit.

The trip took her ninety minutes, there and back, on Wednesday afternoons. It wasn't for the stimulating conversation. Tommy expected her to visit him, week in and week out, on time, and look beautiful. Not for him; it was for appearance's sake. His status as one of London's leading gangsters demanded his wife keep up the standards expected. He couldn't have her turning up in jeans and a hoodie to let the warders and other inmates' wives think she'd let herself go.

Of course, it was rubbish, but Colleen dressed up for her prison visits to put on a show. She looked good when she made an effort. It didn't take long, and she knew what a mouthful she'd get if Tommy thought she disrespected him and his perceived importance. But, of course, her cleavage had to be covered, so Tommy and the warders didn't get excited. It was the little things you missed on the inside.

As the miles ticked by, she recapped what she had to tell him, what was safe to mention, and what subjects to avoid. The taxi driver dropped her outside the prison at two forty-five. He headed off towards Woolwich for a cup of tea. He was under orders to pick Colleen up at four twenty on the dot. As soon as visiting time ended, she wanted to be in the car and back home as quickly as possible.

Once Colleen booked in at the Visitors' Centre, she put everything not allowed in the Visit Room in a locker. She kept her visitor's ID badge, a small amount of cash and the locker key. She then went to the prison to go through the security process.

Tommy was a Category A prisoner, so, as well as a thorough search by a female warder, the hand geometry system recorded a 3D image of her hand on her first visit and stored it on a barcode recognition purposes against a photograph of her face. All this got checked as she went in and out of the visit.

Then after a short wait with the others in the waiting room, they were called through to the visit hall. Tommy sat at the table, waiting for her.

"Hello, darling," he said, "it's good to see you."

"Hello, Tommy," said Colleen, "how's life treating you?"

She listened as he gave her a blow-by-blow account of the past seven days. Prison life wasn't all people cracked it up to be. Boredom had become his worst enemy.

Tell me about it, thought Colleen, who listened to the same string of complaints last week. She heard something different today and concentrated on what Tommy said.

"Belmarsh maximum security is a jihadi training camp. The bloody extremists brainwash young prisoners and spread their terror message across the whole prison system."

"How can they do that, Tommy?" she asked.

"A group of jihadists who call themselves the Akhi have got the run of the place. The screws and the governor know what's happening but aren't doing a thing. The problem is Belmarsh is a holding prison and a home for blokes like me and young guys who get indoctrinated then move on in the prison system and create wider Akhi networks."

"The authorities are letting a whole heap of trouble pile up then," asked Colleen. "Has there been any violence here? Are you in any danger?"

Tommy shook his head.

"They don't bother me. I keep myself to myself. I try

to be positive and pray the appeal is successful. What's the latest on that, Colleen? When did you talk to the solicitor?"

Here comes the first hurdle, Colleen thought. I need to get my story straight. One slip from what I told him on my last visit, and he'll be sending a message to one of his mates on the outside to visit me.

"I dropped in to talk to him only this morning, Tommy. I wanted you to have the most up-to-date news. The old codger was keen to keep me abreast of his progress. Because they convicted you in the Crown Court, you must first apply for permission to appeal. A judge will examine your application and decide whether to permit you to appeal. There must be proper grounds for making an appeal and strict time limits within which we can get it done."

"Yeah, I get that," said Tommy impatiently, "so where are we then?"

"He sent off the form last Wednesday. Applications to appeal and leave to appeal against decisions made by the Crown Court are dealt with by the Court of Appeal Criminal Division. You got sentenced on the twenty-eighth of April, and you had to apply within twenty-eight days of the date you were convicted if you're appealing against your conviction. Or the same length of time from the date you got sentenced if you're appealing against the length of sentence."

Colleen could see Tommy struggling with the long words.

"It's complicated, isn't it?" asked Tommy. "Did he get the forms in on time?"

Colleen nodded.

"Think about it, Tommy. If the judge rejects your plea

to challenge the conviction, you might still get a shot at reducing the sentence."

"I want that solicitor to earn his bloody money, have the conviction quashed, and get me out of here. How long's this going to take, anyhow?"

"If we're successful, you'll get a letter before the hearing to tell you when and where it'll take place. Our case will go before the judges. Because you're appealing the conviction, representatives from the prosecution will present the case against you. The prosecution doesn't necessarily get a look-in if we use the sentence appeal path. Still, let's stay positive. First, get the go-ahead for the appeal; then, get the conviction overturned. Then, you'll be walking the streets of Kilburn a free man again."

"Have you heard from the kids?" asked Tommy.

"I had a quick chat with Tyrone shortly after you went to prison. He and Rosie were agitated. I should give them another ring to see whether they can take time off work."

"I haven't had a peep out of your Sean either for a while. I suppose he's too busy to spare an hour for his brother-in-law?"

"I assume so," said Colleen.

"What, you haven't talked to him either?"

"I expect Hugo Hanigan keeps him busy, and he must keep tabs on Seamus McConnell now he's his second-in-command."

"You are joking? That eejit couldn't tie his shoelaces until he was fifteen. Portmarnock's finest. What was Sean thinking, picking him as his right-hand man?"

"Maybe he hopes you will be back before long. Sean was always happier being your lieutenant; he's never a born leader. Seamus was probably the candidate who would be least pissed off with you taking back your natural role."

"You might have a point there, Colleen," said Tommy, "you're not just a pretty face, are you?"

No, thought Colleen, I'm not. A pity it's taken you twenty-odd years to notice. She glanced at the clock on the wall. What were they going to say to each other for the next half-hour?

"Fancy a few refreshments?" Colleen asked. Tommy nodded, and Colleen wandered over to the vending machines. Two cups of tea, a packet of biscuits, and two chocolate bars punched a sizeable hole in the loose cash she had in her pockets, but it helped pass the time.

Tommy blew on his cuppa.

"I can't believe they get away with calling this tea. We used to call this 'love by the river,' didn't we?"

Colleen laughed.

"Yeah, I remember. Love by the river is the cleaned-up version. So, there's no other gossip from the inside you've picked up, then?"

Tommy attacked his chocolate bar and stared at the ceiling, trying to remember if anything significant had surfaced in the past seven days.

"Oh," he said, sitting up straighter in his chair, "when I told you about the Akhi mob and prisoners moving on from Belmarsh. I forgot I heard a whisper concerning Durham. I can't see it happening because you only live twenty miles away. This bloke reckoned prisoners like me might get transferred to Durham. I can't see it. First, it inconveniences my family visiting; second, I'll be free as a bird when my appeal comes through. No point moving me three hundred miles, is it?"

Colleen had a sudden surge of hope. Despite Sean saying nobody ever escaped from Belmarsh, she insisted that if Tommy's appeal didn't materialise, they needed to make plans to help him escape.

"We can't let him rot in there, Sean," she told him. "Tommy will expect nothing less. Do you want to tell him we're abandoning him without at least trying?"

Colleen leant forward.

"If they did want to move you to Durham, Tommy, it might be our best chance of breaking you out."

Tommy's face lit up. In case the guards overheard, he didn't say a word, but he felt happier than when he took his place in the visiting room at a quarter past two.

"Let me know next week if something further surfaces on that rumour," said Colleen.

"Is it time to go already?" asked Tommy. Then he looked at the table. "Are you going to eat those biscuits?"

Colleen shoved the packet of custard creams across the table.

Visiting time was at an end.

Colleen and Tommy said their goodbyes. Tommy sat and watched his wife leave. Once she was outside, Colleen looked for her taxi. Her driver stood by the open passenger door, smoking his last fag on the first rank of the car park. Poised for a sharp exit. Excellent, with luck and only slightly manic traffic on the way back to the city, she should be home by six.

Her driver wasn't the talkative type. Colleen was glad. She had plenty to think over on the drive back to Kilburn.

She had convinced Tommy everything was on track with the appeals process. However, her solicitor had grave doubts they would grant an appeal against the conviction, which was why he delayed sending it until the last minute. He was happy to add the costs to his bill, but he preferred to advise his next potential client his firm just secured a good win, not be laughed out of court.

As for the sentence option, the wily old bird had a few cards to play. Colleen's solicitor thought they stood a chance of arguing thirty years excessive when weighed against other similar cases. There were enough cases in the media highlighting lenient sentencing by a limp-wristed judiciary.

Colleen hadn't told Tommy the solicitor warned her that often the judges re-affirmed the length of the sentence and ordered it to recommence from the date of the appeal hearing. So if it took a year to reach court, Tommy could be looking at thirty-one summers inside those high walls.

She had steered around the problem of talking about the kids and deflected attention on her, avoiding contact with Sean. Tommy wasn't mad keen on cars. They were just a convenient way of getting around town, so she wasn't surprised he never mentioned them.

Colleen O'Riordan's face wore a smile a mile wide the whole way back to the capital. The news her solicitor gave her this morning had been the icing on the cake. There was no way Tommy raised that subject during one of her visits.

'Have you checked our bank balance, sweetheart?' 'Will you find out how my stocks and shares are performing?' 'Did I ever tell you I have Cayman and Channel Islands accounts?'

No, Colleen thought, you always told me not to worry my pretty head about how much we had in the bank. If I plucked up the courage to ask outright, you always said, 'Enough.'

As for stocks and shares, or off-shore accounts, fair enough, she wouldn't have understood how they worked, but she could learn. Who said crime didn't pay?

It was just as well she was seated when the solicitor told

her this morning the overall sum Tommy salted away after laundering it through Hugo Hanigan's private bank. Her hand had still been shaking when she completed the paperwork. There wasn't a chance that Colleen would tell Tommy that access to all of his bank accounts was now in joint names. With him inside for the foreseeable future, she controlled the purse strings.

Her taxi driver glanced in his rear-view mirror. Mrs O'Riordan was a regular pickup for his firm. He wouldn't mind putting his name forward for being available every week. She would soon get lonely, and she was fit. He idly wondered whether he might get lucky today.

At that moment, Colleen pondered the inconvenience Tommy's move to Durham might cause. If Sean and the other gang members managed to disrupt the transfer and get Tommy away to a place of safety, she needed to act quickly to protect her newly acquired fortune. The steely look in her eye the driver saw when she caught his eye made his blood run cold. Ah, well, it might be best to share the job with the rest of the lads. He kept his eyes on the road and the heavy commuter traffic for the last few miles.

It was ten past six when Colleen walked into the house she, Tommy, and the kids had shared for so long. There were happy memories amongst the fiery arguments and bruises. It was a toss-up which had a higher number. Colleen would be glad to see the back of it. What use did she have for a four-bedroomed detached house in a desirable district, kicking around in it alone?

Colleen prepared herself a meal and then relaxed for the evening. None of her favourite soaps was on TV, so she searched for a new place. Tyrone and Rosie had been well into computers for their work and playing games. They taught her the basics when they still lived at home. Tommy never trusted technology unless it involved weapons and ammunition. There was a laptop in the spare bedroom. Tyrone had left her idiot notes to help her find her way around before he moved out to Spain.

She decided to search online to gauge what price she might get for the house, then browse the local estate agents for something suitable for a single woman of means. How difficult could it be?

After the odd false start, Colleen found the information she wanted. Once again, her eyes lit up when she saw prices asked for similar houses. She was smart enough to appreciate London prices were off the scale compared to other parts of the country. Yet, the news that these prices applied to the area they lived in came as a surprise.

When she and Tommy first got together, they lived with Orla, Tommy's mother. Tommy Senior spent more time in prison than he did at home, and Orla needed the company; and his contribution to the housekeeping. Tommy had bought this property on the edge of the borough of Kilburn for eighty-five thousand pounds.

It was close enough to his roots on the South Kilburn estate to keep tight control of the business but far enough away that he didn't have to smell the poverty when he sat on the patio with a beer.

Colleen got up, wandered around upstairs, and then went downstairs to her lounge diner and kitchen. Tommy made sure they had a downstairs cloakroom and a utility room when they moved out of Orla's terraced house. It was a huge step up from the living accommodation on the seven streets back in Dublin that their parents rented. Tommy wanted the wider community to know he had moved up in the world, no matter that he had blood on his hands in getting there.

She retraced her steps and sat back at the table with the laptop.

"One point one million quid," she grinned, "bring it on."

The following site she browsed was the estate agency whose 'For Sale' signs littered the capital. Something she had noticed, but not considered important until now, was how soon the 'Sold; subject to contract' sign appeared. The quicker she could get the sale agreed upon and move to her new bolt-hole, the happier she would be.

There were plenty of apartments from which to choose. But, for a simple Irish girl, the idea of a one-bedroomed penthouse to come home to after a hard day's work sounded too good to be true. Yet she could afford two of the damn things with a fighting fund from the Marbella apartment, the family home, the cars, and the cash Tommy had stashed in the wall-safe.

It gave her such a great buzz she ran downstairs and poured herself a large glass of Prosecco before carrying on with the pursuit of her dream pad. As night fell, she looked out of her first-floor window at the garden beneath. Tommy was no gardener. Everything was low-maintenance beds or grass and paving slabs.

Over the fence, the panorama showed other gardens and houses whose owners had much the same outlook on life. They sweated their guts for their wages during the week, played hard at the weekend, and then did it all again.

Once, or maybe twice a year, if they were lucky, they flew off to the sun to escape the rat race and the little boxes they called home.

Colleen cursed, not bringing the bottle upstairs with her.

She looked back at the screen: -

'Residents enjoy the services of a twenty-four-hour concierge. In addition, they benefit from secure underground parking, and each property has stunning views over the City.'

'London's financial hub and its cosmopolitan surroundings are on your doorstep. You will live in an area that has become a sought-after London address. The eclectic mix of chic restaurants, stylish bars, cosy cafés and cool clubs across your near-neighbourhood accentuates the apartment building's fashionable reputation.'

Colleen drained her glass and resisted the urge to pinch herself.

"Perfect," she purred, checking the distance between her choice and other prominent sites in and around The City.

Colleen closed the laptop and returned to the kitchen for a top-up of her glass. She sat on her sofa, leaned her head back, and gazed at the ceiling. Colleen had marked today's date on the calendar by the fridge when coming past. She mentally ticked off the days she thought it might take to be savouring a glass of wine in her fashionable new apartment.

A place that didn't have views over gardens and little boxes but of the historical financial centre of the capital. An apartment only a hundred yards, as the crow flies, from the one occupied by Hugo Hanigan.

"Let the Games begin," said Colleen.

Grab your copy...
vinci-books.com/evil-finds-a-way

About the Author

Ted Tayler is the international best-selling indie author of the Freeman Files and Phoenix series. Ted lives in the English West country, where his stories are based. He was born in 1945 and has been married to Lynne since 1971. They have three children and four grandchildren.

His thought-provoking mysteries appeal to readers of Sally Rigby, Joy Ellis, Pauline Rowson, and Faith Martin. His action-packed thrillers are a must for fans of Mark Dawson and J C Ryan.

Gus Freeman's cold case investigations are carried out with reasoned deduction rather than bursts of frantic action. In each of the 24 books, unsolved murders are accompanied by romance, humour, and country life. The core message in the 12 Phoenix novels is that criminals should pay for their crimes. Unfortunately, the current system fails to deliver the correct punishment, so Phoenix helps redress the balance.

Acknowledgments

The love and support of my family; without them, this would have been impossible.